A BLACK ORCHID CHRONICLE

BEWARE
THE
SPIDER

DAVID L. HAASE

BEWARE
THE
SPIDER

DAVID L. HAASE

BEWARE THE SPIDER

Things are rarely as they seem.

David L. Haase learned that lesson during his career in investigative and political journalism. Probe deeply enough, he found, and all sorts of strange things come to light.

Haase has now turned his reporter's eye and inquiring mind on the world to produce supernatural suspense and sci-fi stories.

An amateur photographer and dirty-thumb gardener, he loves prowling through greenery, taking close-up shots of macro nature and discovering new life. His explorations provide the backdrops for reality-laden supernatural adventures into jungle and desert, suburban flower gardens and vacant city lots.

Beware the Spider is the second book of the **Black Orchid Chronicles,** featuring nature photographer Sebastian Arnett. It follows **The Mark of the Spider.**

An earlier book, **HOTEL CONSTELLATION: Notes from America's Secret War in Laos**, recounts his experiences as a young reporter during the Viet Nam war.

www.DavidLHaase.com

ALSO BY DAVID L. HAASE

The Mark of the Spider
A Black Orchid Chronicle

HOTEL CONSTELLATION
Notes from America's Secret War in Laos

Books may be purchased by contacting the publisher and author at

www.DavidLHaase.com/Contact/

Trade Paperback ISBN: 978-0-9994847-5-3
eBook ISBN: 978-0-9994847-4-6

Library of Congress Control Number 2019935666

Cover design: Damon Freeman, Damonza.com
Interior Design: Damonza.com
Editor: Donna Verdier

For my son, Richard
A demanding taskmaster and enthusiastic supporter

EMPAYA IBA SPEAKS

Empaya Iba, they call me,
My enemies and slaves.
To the people, I am Abah.
What say you?
I am Empaya Iba, spirit of the Black Orchid People,
Guardian of the Mother Soil, giver of the Long Sleep,
Seer of the Many Eyes, mage of the Many Legs.
Hear my words and know me.

The people of the midnight flower are my children;
Their land is mine own.
He who bears my mark serves me and mine.
Attend all who would harm me,
You winged creatures of the fire and light.
I am not what you see,
And my servant bears my power.

Come to me, you who would do me harm.
Seek me in my land.
Take the gift of the ebon blossom, and
Accept its eternal sleep.
My minion bears the mark of my home;
He will accept your oblation
And make your sacrifice.
Fear the one who bears my mark.

So say I—who am Abah and Empaya Iba.

CHAPTER 1
HEADS-UP

I KNEW IT WAS a mistake to pick up the buzzing phone.

Amanda breathed quietly beside me, her naked back against my chest, my arm resting lightly on her hip.

The cell phone vibrated on the side table. Zzzt. Only one person called at this time of night, and I didn't want to hear whatever bad news he had to convey. But, even more, I didn't want him to waken Amanda. Zzzt. I disentangled myself as hastily as I could without rousing her. Zzzt.

I thumbed the face of my cell.

"Sebastian—"

With just one croak, the caller confirmed my suspicions. U.S. Marine Corps General Mike Owens was calling. And, yes, at this hour that could only mean bad news.

"Hold on," I whispered in a voice husky with sleep.

I slipped from under the gray satin sheets, grabbed the running shorts lying on the floor, and sneaked out of the bedroom to my study next door. The first golden rays of dawn filtered through the windows.

"Your secret's out!" my cell phone shouted.

I put the device to my face.

"What?"

"Your secret's out," Mike said, his voice gravelly from an injury I'd caused. "I have a team on the way. We're establishing on-site protection, effective immediately."

"Good morning to you, too, Mike."

I slouched into my swivel chair and shivered as my bare back hit cool leather.

"Okay, Mike, what's going on? You realize it's not even dawn here Denver."

"It's still early here in DC, too, but I suspect you've been lying awake for hours trying to figure out your latest nightmare."

I grunted my acknowledgment of another night of bad dreams featuring Empaya Iba, the spider demon. Iba intersects my life from time to time and gives me the power to kill people with my thoughts. For the last several weeks, the demon had played the same confusing nightmare in my head over and over. I didn't know whether it was a warning or a prediction or just some part of my psychological makeup that reacts poorly to beans and rice, a favorite dish of mine.

Vines curl around my feet and legs, and creepers grab at my arms and torso. Above me, some kind of dreamlike, winged beast circles, its claws sharp and grasping. One blood-red eye meets mine.

I call out to the spider demon: "Iba. Empaya Iba!"

Above, the shadow glides closer in tighter and tighter circles, that red eye locked on me.

"Why, Iba?"

I search my memory, frantically trying to recall how I landed in this mess. The photo assignment from the sheikh, of course. The old Dyak woman offering me the rarest of rare flowers, the black orchid. The native's dart. Three heads strung along a pole.

Is this all because of an orchid? A black orchid no Westerner has seen and lived to talk about. Except me.

Overhead, the creature shaves the treetops. Maybe the trees will slow it long enough for me to find a weapon to fight back.

"Sebastian Arnett."

I feel the sound more than I hear it. Like sand tumbling onto a taut drumhead.

"Be still, Sebastian Arnett. Disappear as I do."

A dark shadow flashes past my eyes. The creature. The voice distracted me, and I'd forgotten. It found a path through the trees. It's going to attack before I can find Empaya Iba, I just know it.

"It sees only you, Sebastian Arnett. Empaya Iba is pleased."

Grasping claws reach for my face—and my scream wakens me. Every time.

"Hello. Sebastian, are you there? Hello?"

"Yeah, I'm here."

"As I was saying, this is critical. Have you heard from your buddy from Down Under?"

"Not recently," I said, conjuring an image of Australian intelligence operative Jimmy Beam. "Why?"

"He tipped us a few hours ago."

Mike coughed and cleared his throat, trying to expand his damaged vocal chords.

"The Chinese know all about you and have a search team combing through Borneo for connections to you. Given your profile there, it won't take any time to track you to Denver. I thought maybe he would have alerted you first."

"No," I said, paying more attention. "No. I'll have to have a chat with him. He thinks some Chinese are about to storm my door?"

"No. They're in Borneo, but they could come knocking at any time. I'm not waiting until they do. I'm putting my people at Amanda's house, and I don't want any argument."

I was in that strange space between being awake and being alert, when dream and reality merge and clarity comes slowly.

"Is it the Chinese government, or some mob-related group?"

"Since when are business and government different things?"

"Not my area of expertise. I guess it's not all that surprising,"

I said, my brain gaining traction the longer I was awake. "This all started in their backyard, and they have a large presence in Borneo, mining, logging and everything else. That's one reason the Australians keep such a close eye on things there."

"I don't care whose yard it is. It's my football, and I don't feel like playing," Mike said.

"You are aware that I'm not a football and my life isn't a game, right?" I said, more briskly than I'd intended. "You may think I'm just a piece in some game you're playing and that you can order me around, but that's not how it works."

"Come on, Sebastian. Are you still asleep? You know our concerns about you—and that damned demon. It's much better for everyone if we discourage threats against you or Amanda, or even T, I guess."

Somewhere in the Pentagon, Mike exhaled his frustration, his voice growing even more hoarse. He spoke again, his voice lowered but firm: "We can't let someone like you fall into hostile hands."

"Someone like me?"

"Geez, you're a pain in the ass. You want me to spell it out for you? Fine. You have the power to kill with your thoughts; distance doesn't matter; and your body count in the last year is—What? A dozen or more. And most of them were my men!"

He paused.

"You have to be… I was going to say watched, but maybe chaperoned is a better word. The United States Government cannot even consider the possibility, however remote, that you would be used against our interests. I've done my best to stay out of your hair, but this is a real threat, and I'm—"

"I don't want a security team in the house or on the property," I said. "I can't control what you do on the street and service alley. Amanda and I are trying to live normal lives here."

The front doorbell hummed softly. I tapped the laptop in front of me, and our home security dashboard lit up. A camera aimed at the front door popped open. Two men in desert camouflage stood on alert, their fingers resting beside the triggers of the assault weapons they carried.

"I assume these are your people at my door," I said.

"If they rang the doorbell, they're mine," Mike said.

"Okay. Guess I gotta go."

I punched the call to an end.

"Who was that?"

Amanda's voice startled me. She leaned against the door, her curved figure wrapped in a long-sleeved, floor length maroon silk gown, her auburn hair sleep-tousled and her arms crossed over her chest.

"Hi. Sorry about that," I said. "It was Mike. Why don't you go back to bed? It's still early."

"There are two military vehicles in the circle out front," she said. "Is that Mike's doing?"

"Yeah. He wants to beef up security for a few days. No big deal."

"Liar."

"All right. Mike's in full panic mode. He wants to station a team here. I told him no."

"He must be very worried even to suggest that, much less do it without consulting us in advance."

She padded barefoot across to my chair and settled onto my lap. I wrapped my arms around her.

"Are you worried?" she asked. "The ExecSecure people are at the front gate. Can't they handle it?"

"If it were just me, I'd say they could. But Mike pointed out that the Chinese might not play by civilized rules," I said.

"The Chinese?"

"Yep. All 1.4 billion are out looking for me, or so Mike says. Actually, Jimmy Beam says it from Australia; Mike just agrees and apparently has the troops to spare."

We heard T answer the door, cursing a blue streak, demanding to know what was going on, piling question on top of question and giving the soldiers no time to respond. For an instant, I felt sorry for the soldiers.

"Do you want me to call Mike?" she asked.

"It's your home, babe. Your call."

"Hmm. Deferring to me. That sounds ominous. You always leave me when you do that. Are you thinking of leaving?"

She kissed me on the head. Her robe slid open, exposing two perfect mounds of soft flesh.

"Not immediately, no. I've got some time if you do."

"If you promise to talk later, I think I can free my schedule."

She stood and pulled me by the hand back to her bed. I could—and would—worry about Mike and the Chinese and Empaya Iba later.

CHAPTER 2
AMANDA

I GOT HOLD OF Jimmy Beam—my "buddy from Down Under"—later that morning. He filled me in on the Chinese threat and urged me to take it seriously. Then he stunned me.

"One more thing, Sebastian," he said. "Someone out here wants to meet you to discuss 'spirits' and your experiences, things like that."

"Who?" I asked.

"I'd rather not go into details, but—and I don't envy you the long flight—I think it might be worth your while. They may be able to explain some things about Empaya Iba."

Empaya Iba. Always the spider demon. Iba latched onto me in Borneo and killed three of Jimmy's colleagues. Cut off their heads with a machete. In my recurring nightmare, I saw their heads dangling from a pole. Empaya Iba's surrogate, a Dyak native with a spiderweb tattoo covering half his face, shot me with a dart. I woke up with my face on fire, sporting an identical spiderweb tattoo—and the power to kill people without touching them.

Yes, I would take a seventeen-hour flight halfway around the world for information about Empaya Iba. In fact, I would do anything, literally anything, including kill myself, to be rid of the demon.

"What else can you tell me?" I asked.

"That's about it for now, mate. Telephone security and all that."

I stared into space.

"Sebastian? Mate?"

"Okay, Jimmy. I'm in. Set it up. Let me know where I have to be, and when. I'll be there."

It all sounded vague because it was.

Jimmy is not really my buddy, although saving my life, not once but twice, probably qualified him as more than a passing acquaintance.

He works for the Australian Intelligence Service, the Down Under equivalent of our CIA and Defense Intelligence Agency put together. Officially, he is an ethnologist specializing in the native customs of the southwest Pacific islands. His encyclopedic brain holds minutiae on hundreds, if not thousands, of island subcultures.

A Popeye-sized figure of Scottish extraction, his red hair and fair skin burn to the roots at the slightest exposure to sun. But no amount of physical discomfort keeps him locked in a university library or classroom or secret office. He's a field operator with considerable sway inside his organization.

I just thought of him as a friendly guy who happened to be a spy who had helped me out and never asked for payback—a situation that I knew could not last forever. I had to trust someone sometime, and I struggled with Mike Owens because of his threat to take me out if it was the only way to prevent me from endangering the U.S. So Jimmy would have to do for now, and I could afford a quick trip to Sydney.

But I wouldn't go any farther, I promised myself. I would not hop over to Borneo, Empaya Iba's homeland. Twice I had ventured there, and twice I had narrowly escaped with my life.

∾

I put off telling Amanda my plans until that evening. I had a lot to think about, and I really wasn't crazy about discussing Jimmy's invitation. Not because I was afraid she'd throw a tantrum or anything like that; she wasn't like that.

Amanda Cox Campion was the whole package as a life partner, as far as I was concerned. Wicked smart, fun to be with, caring. Yeah, she was a silver heiress, a commodities expert, and wealthy several times over, but all that mattered less than I ever would have imagined. I did pretty well as a nature photographer, especially after my last assignment, but I was nowhere near her league financially. I cared because she was good people, good to me and for me, and she deserved good things to happen to her. If she thought I was one of them, all the better for me.

For now, I wanted to figure out how to keep her safe (and happy) in her eight-bedroom mansion while I jetted across the globe to see a spy about a spirit.

I caught up with her in the living room, its floor to ceiling wall of glass looking out over an acre of sculpted gardens. On the horizon rose the snow-covered Front Range of the Rocky Mountains. It was just before dinner. She was sipping a Manhattan and studying the fine print of the day's *Wall Street Journal*. She looked up, smiled, and patted the sofa cushion next to her.

"Let me get a drink," I said, "and I'll spend all night with you."

She laughed and ran her red tongue around the edge of her glass. I wanted to grab her right then and there.

But there were too many people around. Maria, her long-time gofer, cook, and friend; T, her ex-husband's illegitimate son, who was a story unto himself; and God knows how many of Mike's protective soldiers, or marines, or whatever they were, now ensconced in the basement, along with the wine cellar, billiard room, movie theater, and miscellaneous storage facilities.

I mixed my usual from the drinks cart—half Tanqueray gin, half diet tonic and a quarter wedge of fresh lime— and settled in beside her.

I related my conversation with Jimmy and told her I wanted to go.

"Is this trip really necessary?" she asked. Her poker face revealed nothing of the emotions she might be feeling. "You've got this threat about the Chinese in Borneo. Wouldn't it be better to stay here, at least until we know more?"

I sipped my Tanq and tonic.

"Jimmy thinks it's important. He's never asked me to come before. That tells me it's out of the ordinary and worth doing.

"I know you're worried about Borneo; I would be, too, if I were going there. But I'm not. Sydney has to be three or four thousand miles away. That's as close as I plan to get," I said. "And I'll be with Jimmy. On his turf. So, I figure that's pretty safe."

She took my hand in hers and sighed.

"I like you, you know. We've been through a lot in a short time, and I'd hate for you not to be around anymore."

I experienced an aw-shucks moment. To find love twice in a lifetime seemed to defy the odds, and I felt unworthy.

"I'll be careful," I said and leaned over to kiss her lips. She kissed back.

"What about your dreams?" she asked.

"Other than the dream, which I can't figure out, Empaya Iba seems to be quiet," I said. "I haven't had any crazy desire to off some-one since we came back from Montana, and that's been months. I guess I'll have the dreams wherever I sleep. Maybe Jimmy will have some ideas. You know I'll ask him."

She nodded.

"Will you do something for me?" she said.

"Anything I can. You know that."

"I want you to take T with you."

Just like that, I regretted my promise.

"Why? What am I going to do with him? I mean, he's just a kid.

He can't be around when Jimmy and I are talking. Jimmy may not even want anyone else to know that he exists. He's a spy, after all."

"You're inventing excuses."

"All right. How about this?" I said, sitting up and placing my drink on the glass table in front of us. "I don't like T, and he doesn't like me. I don't understand why he has to keep living with us. He's recovered and more than able to live on his own, if he would just get a job or even look for work. The only thing T and I have in common is you, and he has only known you a couple months."

"Whereas you have known me, what, almost a year?"

"That's hitting below the belt, Amanda."

"I know. I meant to," Amanda said. "T is my ex-husband's son born when we were still married. I get it."

Tears rimmed her eyes.

"Sebastian, he should have been my son."

She covered her face, and I hated her ex-husband enough to want him dead. I checked myself immediately. Empaya Iba responds to my anger, often immediately, with lethal effect. I calmed myself. I cannot be responsible for that death, I told myself.

I put my hands on Amanda's and pulled them away from her tear-stained cheeks.

"I'm sorry for all the pain he caused you."

"It's not your fault," she said.

"No, but I hate to see you hurt. And I don't have to make it worse. I'll take the kid with me, even if we end up killing each other. Have you talked to T about this?"

"No, I haven't, but I'm sure he'll go if I ask him. It would make it easier if I could tell him you wanted him to come along."

"Amanda, he may be a slacker but he's not an idiot. He knows I'm not going to ask him to come along."

She smiled a weary smile, knowing she would get her way with both of us.

"I think it will be good for both of you. You could use the company. You take far too many trips alone."

"Taking photos out in nature is a solitary business. Besides, I'm okay being alone, knowing I have a place to come back to. And I've always got Iba."

She didn't smile at my wisecrack.

"Yes, I know. That's what worries me."

"Don't worry. Before I go, I may slip down to the cabin and see if Joe is around. See what he thinks of all this."

"You mean Pony That Sees Far?"

Amanda was a stickler for names; she never forgot one. I, on the other hand, remember faces, like flowers. I can look at a blossom and know for certain whether I've ever photographed it. Remember a name? Not so much.

I did know Joe's Indian name; I just couldn't pronounce it. I made it sound like I was chewing my tongue. He translated it for me as "Pony That Sees Far," a good name, I thought, for an Indian who can see spirits. But Pony That Sees Far is a mouthful, too. He felt sorry for me—he pities all white men—and told me to call him Joe. I am happy to oblige.

"Yes, that's the guy. Joe, the old Ute medicine man who hangs out around your family's cabin," I said.

"That's a good idea. He knows things. Maybe he can help you with the dream."

"That's what I was thinking. Have a good sweat and see what he says. He's bound to have an idea since he's the only one who's ever seen Iba."

"Do one more thing for me?" Amanda asked.

Despite my earlier regret, I agreed immediately.

"Ask him to use his sight to kill Empaya Iba."

CHAPTER 3
SPIRIT SEER

JOE APPEARED OUT of nowhere, as he always did, around sunset. I was sitting on the porch of Amanda's ancestral cabin in the remote southwestern corner of Colorado, not far from the Four Corners. The porch faced west toward the mountains and the setting sun. The old Indian and I liked to watch the evening light show sitting on the porch step with an iced drink in hand.

"Why do you call me, Sebastian?" he asked, kicking up dust with his boots.

"Fix yourself a drink first, old man," I said. "Then we can talk."

I have no idea how old Joe is. Seventy-five for certain; maybe eighty-five or even ninety. Or a hundred and ten, for that matter. I had only known him a year, but it felt like forever. I thought of him like I thought of our friendship, timeless and enduring and a total mystery.

"Your Hendricks is on the table," I said. "Limes are cut; ice is in the cooler."

"That is good, Sebastian. Before this night is done, I think I will need many drinks," he said. "The news you bring, I do not like it."

I watched him shuffle off. He stood maybe five-one or five-two, board-thin but tough as oak. His long gray hair, parted in the middle, hung down to his shoulders. His attire never changed: Baggy faded jeans, red checkered shirt, black leather vest, and dusty cowboy boots, topped off with a sweat-stained cowboy hat and a dirty brown duster. He looked like any homeless drunk stuck on a remote Indian reservation. Joe was anything but that, and I wondered if the truly powerful all wear disguises.

We settled into a comfortable silence that carried us to darkness. Without speaking, we both rose and stepped into the cabin. I struck a stick match on the doorframe and lit the antique kerosene lantern. Joe knelt to build a fire against the oncoming desert cold. I fixed us another round, then settled on the floor, leaning against the bedstead.

"I'm going to Australia," I said. "Visit Jimmy Beam. He says there are Chinese types in Borneo trying to track me down. Also, there's someone who wants to talk to me about spirits."

"Amanda, she don't like this plan," Joe said.

"How did you guess?"

"No guess. That Maria tells me," Joe said.

"Might have figured."

Maria Reina, a middle-aged Mexican woman who traced her lineage back to Aztec shamans, runs Amanda's household in Denver. And, somehow, she and Joe can communicate telepathically. Joe insists it's all about dreams—he's a big believer in dreams. I was counting on that.

"What this Jimmy Beam know?" he asked.

"I don't know. I don't even know who it is or what they do."

"You don't know but you still go all that long way? Risky, I am thinking."

"Not really. Thanks to the sheikh, I can afford the trip. I'm not working right now. And the demon is quiet, too."

"If it so quiet, why you go so near his home? Maybe you wake him up. Make him want to go back to his people."

I shifted against the bed stand to get the blood flowing into my butt, which wasn't used to sitting on hard floors.

"It won't be that close to Borneo. It's more than 3,000 miles," I said.

"More, farther, you stay here."

"You think I shouldn't go? Did you have a dream or see Empaya Iba?"

"I don't have a dream. You have a dream. Maybe you even tell Joe about it."

"Yeah, you're right. It's giving me nightmares. Or one nightmare, over and over. Like it's playing with me, taunting. Scaring me and putting me in my place at the same time. I can't figure it out, and I'm not getting much sleep. Neither is Amanda."

Joe watched me without a trace of emotion.

"You told me once to talk to the demon," I said. "I never did. I knew it gave me the power. I can kill people who make me angry. I don't even have to touch them. I don't even have to be anywhere near them. I think of them dead, they die, and I don't remember much about it."

I rubbed the tattoo engraved on my right cheek; it felt cool, normal, not how it burns when I've killed. I took a long pull on my drink; ice clinked against my lips. I lowered the empty glass.

"The demon is trying to tell me something. But what? Am I going to go on a killing spree like last time? I just don't know."

I turned to face Joe.

"That's why I'm willing to go to Australia. I'll do anything I can to try to get rid of this thing. Do you think I can find out about this demon inside me?"

"I cannot say the future, Sebastian. The spirit is real. Sometimes it is maybe a demon, like you think. Sometimes maybe not. Maybe it protects people there, in that forest. Who knows? It is your spirit. Many people have spirits. You are not the only one."

"But you say you don't have a spirit; you just see them. Who else has a spirit inside them?"

"Catholics say everyone."

"Other than the Catholics."

"Maria. I have told you this. She has the mother bear spirit. Very powerful. Maybe not like your spider spirit."

"So why did my spirit mark me? Maria doesn't have any marks that I can see."

"Who knows why spirits do what they do? They do it. You must accept it."

"I can't accept it. It turned me into a murderer!"

I slammed the glass onto the floor and it shattered into pieces.

Joe turned to me and handed me his glass.

"We need new drinks."

I rose and kicked the broken pieces of glass under the bed. I had neither broom nor dustpan. And my supply of glasses—Mason jars, really—had just diminished by 25 percent. Joe talked while I poured drinks.

"Spirits are like people, Sebastian. Not all bad, not all good."

"Not even Iba?" I said.

"I think no. Your spider, it was not always so, Sebastian; it was maybe not always hungry for blood, for people's heads."

"Well, what about my dream, Joe? I can't move, like I'm stuck in a spiderweb, Iba's spiderweb. A big creature, like some kind of bird, only maybe not, tries to eat me. Joe, I feel like I'm bait. Iba's just hiding, watching. What does that dream tell you?"

"Some spiders do that, Sebastian. They make decoys that look like themselves. Keeps them alive. Not magic."

"How do I get rid of this thing? I don't want to be a killer. Joe, what do I do?"

"I never heard of anyone getting rid of a spirit if they have one. Sometimes, maybe, spirit and man just learn to live together."

"Joe, how do I learn to live with something that makes me—you know—what I am?"

"You take that spirit home, back to its forest. Then you talk to the spirit," Joe said. "Maybe it will tell you."

CHAPTER 4
JIMMY BEAM

"JIMMY, THIS BETTER be important. We're a long way from Denver."

I wrung the Australian's hand as my fellow deplaning passengers flowed around us toward the baggage claim area at Sydney Airport.

Jimmy Beam, overt ethnologist and covert intelligence operative, crushed my hand in his grip.

"It's important," he said.

If he was surprised or upset at seeing T with me, he didn't show it.

"Who's this?" he asked. "I know he must be with you. He's more dinged up than you are."

T scowled. I stifled a grin. T and I had gotten along on the flight, and I didn't want to spoil things now, just when we had reached our destination.

"Jimmy, meet Tom Kingston, also known as T. T, this is Jimmy Beam. We discussed his occupation on the plane."

I left out any mention of T's background. Jimmy would find out on his own soon enough. He could do that sort of thing.

"Hello, mate. Looks like you've been watching too many pirate movies," Jimmy said.

T's face turned red, making the black patch over his right eyehole all the more obvious. Jimmy was testing T; I had no idea why or whether T would pass.

I confess, T and I both stood out in a crowd and attracted unwelcome attention.

A dark tattoo, embossed in scar tissue, covered the right side of my face from hairline to jaw. The tattoo was unmistakably a spiderweb, the mark of the demon Empaya Iba.

In addition to the eyepatch, T also wore a still-fresh red scar that ran from his eye to his right ear. And yes, people stared—that's what people do.

I hated the way the demon's tattoo attracted attention, and T was struggling, too. On the flight down to Australia, he insisted on taking the window seat next to me and kept his head low most of the time.

One day down the road, I thought, *he would see himself as a dashing daredevil. For now, however, I knew he considered himself damaged goods, a one-eyed man with a cut-up face and a load of guilt over his girlfriend's death.*

T scowled at Jimmy.

"Spider-Man here warned me that hanging out with him could be dangerous; I thought I'd better look like I can take care of myself," he said.

"Good plan, mate. Very good plan. By the way, no offense about the wisecrack," Jimmy said, offering his hand. "It was really aimed at Sebastian, whose ass I have saved innumerable times. I've heard your story, and I'm sorry for your loss."

"None taken," T said. "This loser brings out the worst in everyone."

"He does rather make a hash of things, doesn't he?" Jimmy said, glancing my way. "You should have seen him trying to drown that bug of his. For a man who can't swim, he has a hard time drowning, too."

They chuckled; I smiled. T had passed. I didn't mind being the butt of their jokes if it kept the peace.

"Come along, mates. We have a train to catch in a few," Jimmy said.

"What about Mike Owens's people?" T asked. "The ones from the plane."

Jimmy winked.

"I promised General Owens that we would take care of you. He doesn't like it—and I'm sure he'll try to circumvent it, if he can—but we can't have them tromping around interfering with my people here. We are more than capable of protecting visitors."

T shrugged.

"So, where are we going?" he asked. "We just got here."

T was good with the questions. Sometimes it drove me crazy. This time, it didn't.

"To see an aboriginal about a spirit," Jimmy said.

✍

Four hours after landing in Australia and a quick trip to buy T some hot-weather clothing, we pulled up in front of the Sydney Central Station.

"What's here?" T asked.

"Trains," Jimmy said. "Let's get aboard. Ours will pull out soon, and this line only runs twice a week. The next one's not until Saturday."

We followed Jimmy down the platform toward the front of the train to a car marked Platinum and hauled our luggage aboard.

Along the way, Jimmy paid close attention to our fellow passengers, most of whom were Asian. I recognized Japanese and Indians, Malays and Indonesians, Vietnamese and Thais. He eyeballed the Chinese closest of all and cautioned us about any who looked Chinese.

"I don't mean to sound racist," he said, "but I've got solid intel that we should be wary of about one-fifth of the earth's population right now. They're all Chinese," he said.

"Can't we fly?" T asked.

"Not easily."

"If you're so worried about running into Chinese on the train, why not just drive to wherever we're going?" T said.

Jimmy put his hand on T's shoulder.

"Ah, young one, always looking for the adventure," he said.

Surveying the plush accommodations—our Platinum Class compartments contained a double bed and a bathroom with shower—he continued.

"This here is a big country. Even traveling in luxury—and believe me, the Indian Pacific is the height of traveling in style—the trip will be long enough; driving would take forever, even on national highways. We're heading through some pretty desolate territory.

"Besides," he added, "I don't know exactly where we're going."

"What!"

T and I spoke in unison.

"How do we—where do we—" I couldn't find the words.

"I think Sebastian is trying to ask how will we know we have reached our destination if we don't know where it is?" T said.

"I have a very eager young man, not unlike yourself, narrowing that down right now. He'll let us know. In the meantime, let's make ourselves comfortable—and keep an eye on our surroundings."

He nodded down the narrow aisle toward the end of the car. A thin middle-aged Chinese man escorted a woman half his age into a compartment. He wore a black suit, white shirt and a black and white paisley necktie. *Pretty formal for Australia*, I thought. She had on the female equivalent in silk with a very, very short skirt.

If that skirt were any shorter, I thought, *my imagination could take a vacation.*

The woman—girl, almost—gave one of us a come-hither look; I assumed she was eying T, and I was jealous.

Sorry, Amanda, I thought, *but wow.*

We were standing in the aisle at the doors to T and Jimmy's compartments. Jimmy pulled us into his and closed the door.

"You think the Chinese who are curious about me know we're here?" I asked. "I mean, we didn't know we were coming till two days ago."

"We don't know what they know. We are just being cautious," Jimmy said.

Wow, again, I thought. *Being tracked by unknown bad guys. Déjà vu all over again.*

CHAPTER 5
INDIAN PACIFIC

J IMMY MADE HIS dramatic announcement sotto voce.

"Stop using the Internet," he said, looking from T to me. "Both of you."

We sat in cream-colored, padded leather bench seats across a chrome cocktail table in a corner of the club car, an Edwardian dream of polished wood and plush seating.

Several pleasant hours out of Sydney, the Indian Pacific clacked westward along the south coast of Australia toward Adelaide.

Ever ready to challenge an order, T asked, "Why? What's up?"

Jimmy sipped a seventeen-year old Balvenie DoubleWood Scotch whisky straight up. He looked admiringly at the rich golden hue and leaned casually across the table.

"We're monitoring every communication that enters or leaves this train. It's one reason for taking it. We might get an angle on who is taking an interest in you," he said.

"Is that really necessary?" I asked. "I mean, as I said earlier, how could anyone know we would be on this train? T and I didn't even know it when we arrived at the station. And almost no one knows we were planning this trip."

Jimmy leaned back into his leather seat, turning to put a knee on the seat, the better to prevent anyone asking to join us.

"As you can see," he said, waving his whisky glass at the surroundings, "the Indian Pacific is not your ordinary go from Point A to Point B train. Each of your fares cost more than $4,000 US."

"Whoa," T said.

"I didn't know you liked me that well," I said.

"There's this couple—a middle-aged man and a young woman—ring any bells? This couple booked passage just before we arrived at the train station. Not long after that, a party of four made arrangements to join the train in Adelaide. All six are Chinese. Needless to say, most bookings for the Indian Pacific are made well in advance, not on the spur of the moment."

He eyed his glass again, looking beyond it to the crowd behind T and me.

"We don't know how they might know of your movements, and that, of course, worries us. Internal security and all that. So, yes, I think it's necessary. If I'm wrong, no harm done. If I'm right, I want to give as little information about us as possible. So, please, stay off the Internet; no email. The practice will get you ready for what comes next."

"What's that?" T asked.

"Waiting for the right aboriginal to stumble upon us in the outback," Jimmy said and knocked back the rest of his drink.

Around us, passengers' voices rose as second, third, and fourth rounds of Australian beverages were served. The dining car maître d'—yes, the Indian Pacific has one—announced the first seating for the three-course dinner for Platinum Class members.

As couples filed over to the next car, Jimmy raised a hand and waved it in a circle, another round for our table— Jimmy's Balvenie neat, my usual Tanqueray and tonic on the rocks, and a chilled but not iced James Squire Nine Tails Amber Ale for T.

I was feeling a bit hungry and could have easily enjoyed eating, but I suspected Jimmy had his reasons for staying put. I wondered where that Chinese couple might be. I hadn't seen them in the club car, which now sported more empty tables than not.

With another tumbler of scotch in hand, Jimmy got down to business.

"How much does he know?" he said to me while looking at T, "and how are we to treat him?"

"He's all in," I said. "He made a dumb mistake getting involved with Amanda and me, but he never backed out and never backed down. I'm alive—more importantly, Amanda is alive—because of him. As you can see, he's paid his dues. In terms of Empaya Iba, I would say he has moved on from denial to disbelief to confusion."

"So, he's about like the rest of us," Jimmy said.

"Pretty much."

"All right, mate. Just wanted to know. We'll be vacuuming up all your secrets, the ones we don't already know," he said to T. "Bottom line, we're interested in my mate here because of his unique ability to, ah, inconvenience adversaries."

"Kill people," T said.

"That."

I felt like a little kid.

"You two do know I'm sitting here, right?" I said.

"Yes, mate, we do."

T returned to the matter at hand.

"What do you want from Sebastian?" he asked.

"First, we want to know where he is at all times, just like your own government. General Owens is cooperating with us on that."

Jimmy held up a hand and grabbed two fingers.

"Second, we want to make sure he does not fall under the influence of our adversaries, particularly the Chinese, but not just them. That means we also want the people who know him and love him to be safe. For the moment, you fall into that category. Third, we want to know more about how he got this little power of his and, quite frankly, whether we might get some of it ourselves."

"Does this mean you don't want to use him?" T asked.

"Of course, we want to use him," Jimmy said. "We would do that in a heartbeat, but he has resisted the notion rather strenuously. We respect that. We want to make sure others respect that as well."

"And if they don't?" T asked.

"We are prepared to give them sufficient reason to go along with the program."

"Sounds like making them an offer they can't refuse," T said.

"Something like that, yes," he said, drained his drink, rose and wandered off back toward our compartments.

"No Internet," T said in Jimmy's wake. "Good thing I already did my research."

∽

After our drinks Wednesday evening, Jimmy disappeared and stayed disappeared, not unusual in my experience. I assumed he spent most of his time in his compartment, listening in on phone conversations and reading other people's email.

I spent a lot of time daydreaming and people-watching in the lounge, especially admiring the young and extremely well-dressed Chinese woman traveling with the older man. The longer I looked at him, the older he seemed. Every time we passed one another, we nodded as train passengers do, but I always got an uneasy feeling. I chalked it up to the obvious age difference between him and his escort; old guys who date women barely out of their teens creep me out. I should have been more like T and asked questions.

The Indian Pacific clacked through switches in the rail yards outside Adelaide on the southern coast Thursday afternoon, and T suddenly got talkative.

"Did you know that we'll pass within about fifty miles of a big British nuclear testing ground tomorrow?" he asked.

"No," I said, coming down from the clouds. "I didn't know they did nuclear testing here. Does that raise any alarms for you?"

"Some," T said. "I'm interested in where we're heading. I've been looking over the maps and the research I pulled off the Web before Jimmy shut us down. The scenery is about to get seriously bleak when we get to the Nullarbor Plain tomorrow."

"Well, I've seen bleak Australia before," I said, recalling my hospitalization after the first trip to Borneo. "What's this plain like?" I asked.

"Apparently nothing. As in nothing. Nullarbor means "no trees" in Latin. Some of the travel accounts I've read claim that Australians call it Nullar-boring," T said.

I chuckled, enjoying our personal ceasefire.

"You mean like this train trip so far? If it weren't for that pretty Chinese girl who pops up now and again, I think I would have died of boredom already, and it's only been a day."

"You think Amanda is okay with you staring at other women, especially ones less than half your age?"

T's voice had a protective edge to it.

"Amanda doesn't care if I look. Besides, this is a scrawny little kid. She barely looks like she's out of high school. Skinny as a board. She's nothing like Amanda."

"Don't be fooled. That's a woman, and those skinny arms have muscle," T said. "She probably knows martial arts and could throw you through the wall."

"Well, I'm glad you're noticing women again."

It was the wrong thing to say, and I regretted it immediately. Jenny was dead and buried less than six months. I knew that pain, still did years later. I quickly changed the subject.

"So, we're heading into a desert? I thought that was farther north, more in the heart of the country."

"You're close. The Nullarbor's dry, but not officially classified as a desert, whatever that means. It's squashed somewhere between the ocean to the south and the Great Victoria Desert on the north. The only two things that have ever happened there involved an old spaceship, something called Skylab—you know it?—that crashed there in the late 1970s, and a hoax involving a half-naked woman living among the kangaroos."

"Not much to go on then."

"No," T said, "but given the summer temperatures, somewhere around 120 degrees, it makes sense that she would go topless. I, uh, guess I'll need those shorts you made me buy."

"Well, it's only December, which is the start of summer here. Let's assume it won't get quite that hot," I said, sipping my iced gin to push the thought of all that heat to the back of my mind.

"One other thing about Nullarbor," T said.

"What's that?"

"Aborigines, or aboriginals, as the Australians call them. Lot of different aborigines around."

T typed on his tablet, waited an instant and started reading.

"I'm going to butcher some of these names, but we'll be right in the middle of about five or six tribes. The Wirangu, the Kokatha, the Mirning, farther west a bigger group that is described in parentheses as the Spinifex People. Doesn't sound very aboriginal, does it?"

"More like science fiction," I said.

"The group that intrigues me is this one," he said, pointing at the words "Maralinga Tjarutja/Ngalea."

Neither of us tried to pronounce those names.

"Why that group?" I asked.

"Maralinga," T said, using the only word either of us might have mastered alone. "It's where the British did their nuclear testing. There's a big military area around it that's still off limits."

"You think that's where we're headed?"

"It might have been where they kept you when you were healing," T said.

"I wonder what all those nuclear tests did to the aboriginals,"

I said. "They take the land seriously, or so my reading informs me. Having the land glow in the dark must have made some kind of impact on them."

"Hey, Jimmy's your pal. Why don't you ask him?"

Jimmy chose that moment to join us.

"Mates. Having fun, are we?"

"Loads," I said. "We can look out the windows, or we can look out the windows. So many options to choose from."

"This is Adelaide," he said as the train jerked to a halt. "Let's get off here. Not exactly the garden spot of Australia, but for the next three hours, we can stretch our legs without swaying like a drunken sailor."

"And maybe you can explain where we're headed," T said.

"Soon," Jimmy said. "And be careful what you ask for."

As we followed him off the train, I wondered what the hell that meant.

EMPAYA IBA SPEAKS

Children of the Midnight Flower,
Empaya Iba, your Abah, speaks.
I pass through a land of nothing
To our home in green mountains.
Of trees embracing one another,
There are none where I abide.

Empaya Iba hears his children.
Abah, father, they call.
Return to us, they cry,
Take the gifts of the black flower.
Bring to us,
The one who bears the mark of your home.
Let him receive our offerings
And return our father.

I am Empaya Iba, spirit of the Black Orchid People,
Guardian of the Mother Soil, giver of the Long Sleep,
Seer of the Many Eyes, mage of the Many Legs.
I hear the cries of my children, and I come.

CHAPTER 6

DEPARTURE

I SLEEP WELL ON trains, what with the gentle swaying and the rounds of cocktails. After dinner in Adelaide with Jimmy and T, I returned to my compartment aboard the Indian-Pacific, intending to clean up before joining the guys in the lounge. I was curious to see whether four new Chinese had joined the train while we were out.

I lay down on my rocking bed for a moment and dropped into a deep sleep. Empaya Iba invaded my rest and taunted me awake around four o'clock the next morning. I rolled over, momentarily confused about where I was, where Amanda had gone, and why I still wore the previous day's clothing.

I peered out my window, and a soft glow of light from the lounge several cars back kept pace with us. Otherwise it was dark as only rural places can be. I thought about Amanda, wondering what she would be doing twelve hours away and wishing she were here. *That would be silly*, I thought. *If she were here, she would still be asleep. But she would be by my side.*

Realizing I would never get back to sleep, I decided to shave and shower and head to the lounge to watch the sun rise. I was surprised to find several parties still in progress, one group of European tourists and another of Asians who had yet to call it a day. The Chinese girl was with that group, and I thought at least one of the men was new to our journey. She smiled when our eyes met. Apparently, she wasn't put off by the spiderweb tattoo, or was too intoxicated to notice it. Her escort was, as usual, attached to her side. My hackles rose as I passed their table.

I sat down as far from the partiers as I could and ordered a Virgin Mary and coffee, black. I was settling in to a suspense novel when a movement caught my eye. It was Jimmy, heading my way, looking all business.

"Thirty minutes," he said. "T's up. Make up an overnight bag. Leave everything else in your compartment. Lock the door and leave the key with the porter. My people will pick up your gear in Perth."

With that, he turned and was gone.

I waited for my glorified tomato juice and caffeine infusion, then headed after Jimmy. On work trips—and I considered this a work trip—I carry a survival bag, something I can grab and run with if the need arises. This small backpack contains a change of clothes, first aid kid, some power bars and a water bladder, and my antique but fully functional .455 caliber Webley revolver. While I was far from a gun nut, I did know how to hit what I aimed at, and the events of the past year had more than justified keeping the Webley at hand. (Mike Owens had happily provided the paperwork that allowed me to carry it, really, everywhere.)

The Webley, a six-shooter of exactly the same model that T.E. Lawrence carried during World War I, was a kind of security blanket. It had almost no moving parts so even I could operate it. At close range—say 20 feet—its slug could stop a charging camel dead in its tracks. I didn't expect to encounter any camels, but I had learned to my initial dismay that I was able to point and fire the weapon at another human being. Not everyone could do that, but then not everyone is possessed by a demon.

T was not as experienced a traveler as I, but Jimmy had taken that into consideration and bought him a sling bag before we boarded the train. T carried his cell phone and tablet without thinking; Jimmy had him throw in an extra pair of walking shorts and a T-shirt.

T and I opened our compartment doors at the same moment. I wore my tan boonie hat. Not exactly fashionable, but it keeps the sun out of my eyes, and I can flip the brim up and bring my eye close to my camera's viewfinder.

T had bought an Australian bush hat, the kind that buttons the brim up on one side. Along with his eye patch, it made him look devastatingly roguish. I felt a tinge of jealousy for his youth and appearance, at least until I noticed his knobby white knees. The guy was definitely a geek. I looked down on my knees, tanned and scarred from years of close-up nature photography, and concluded I would take my legs over his.

"Good morning," I said.

He grunted.

Jimmy popped out of his compartment, a dirty-brown camouflage backpack draped across one shoulder. He looked like he had done this many times before.

"Mates," he said. "Ready?"

"Are we going to wait for the train to stop or are we just going to jump?"

I barely got the words out when the train's speed slowed.

T and I followed Jimmy back to the lounge. We surrendered our keys to the bartender, who gave a knowing nod to Jimmy.

I had to pass the creepy Chinese guy, but his young girlfriend was nowhere in sight. He stood and grabbed my arm, a drunken smile plastered over his face.

"Hey, where you going? Can we come along?"

I removed his hand and walked on, even as he tugged at my backpack.

"Gotta go," I said without looking back.

A moment later, Jimmy, T and I were standing by the side of

the tracks watching the red tail lights of the train disappear into the darkness.

"What kept you?" Jimmy asked.

"Oh, God. That Chinese guy grabbed me. He's drunk as a skunk and wouldn't let me go," I said.

"Did he touch you or your bag?"

"He grabbed my arm, then tugged on my pack as I passed him. Why?"

"Let me see your bag."

I handed my pack to him. He pulled a Maglite from his pocket and shone it all over the bag.

"Was this pocket open when you finished packing?" he asked.

"Hard to say; probably not. I make sure everything on my camera bags are closed up tight, so I probably do the same for any bag I pack. What's up?"

Jimmy fingered every pocket on the backpack.

"Hello. What's this? Well, well, well."

"What is it?" T asked.

Jimmy held up a disk about the size of a quarter.

"That, mates, is a GPS tracker."

"That S.O.B.," I said.

"Indeed. That pretty much ends any doubts we had about whether you were being followed. And we can put faces on them. I've already sent photos of all our fellow passengers back to HQ; the boys back home will see if they can identify them.

"Meanwhile, we'll see if we can distract them, but from here on out, just assume they know where to find you."

I took a breath.

"Right."

I trusted Jimmy, but I didn't like being alone in the middle of nowhere in the dark, apparently about to rendezvous with an Australian aboriginal who might, or might not, know about spirits like Empaya Iba. And now the Chinese had found me. What next?

CHAPTER 7
NULLARBOR TAXI

I sat on the hard ground beside the railroad tracks in near total darkness with a zillion stars blazing overhead.

"All right, Jimmy," I said, "Now what?"

"We wait, mate."

"How long?"

"As long as it takes," Jimmy said.

"And how does this help me with the demon?"

"Simple. After your last visit, I put out word among our aboriginals about you and the spiderweb tattoo. We got a hit. An old Maralinga expressed interest in seeing it," Jimmy said.

I shot a glance at T, but in the darkness couldn't see his face. I imagine he raised an eyebrow or two.

"This old gent said he'd seen something like that when he was a boy. He apparently didn't like it then but would like to be in its presence again."

"Be in its presence?" I said.

"He's blind," Jimmy said, "at least according to my informant."

"And that's what brought me umpteen-thousand miles? An old blind aboriginal wants to relive a bit of his youth?"

"Don't underestimate the power of curiosity, especially among the old. They know the stories and legends and myths. Symbols are real out here, just as in a lot of less-developed cultures. Be patient. Give it a chance."

"This old guy knows where we are?" T asked.

"He knows where we'll be. Everyone in the area knows. Word will get around. I expect he'll show up."

"So, what do we do? Just pitch camp here and wave at the Indian Pacific the next time it passes in a few days?" I asked.

"We could do that, but I was thinking of catching a ride. And unless my ears deceive me, I believe that's it."

I couldn't see anything—could really only tell where Jimmy and T were by the sounds they made—but I definitely heard a motor from the north side of the railroad track.

"Your blind aboriginal drives?" I said.

"Not that I'm aware of, but then, I've not met the man yet either. The Australian Army drives, and this will be a G-Wagon coming to pick us up."

"G-Wagon. Is that like a Humvee?" T asked.

"Our version, yes," Jimmy said.

"How did it know we were coming and where to meet us?" I asked.

"Nothing mysterious, mate. I've been in constant contact with an Interior Defense Force unit since before we left Sydney."

"So, we're going into the old British nuclear test area at Maralinga," T said.

"Good research, lad," Jimmy said. "Yes. That's exactly where we're going. More specifically, Tietkens Well near a little community called Five Ways."

"I thought Cook was the only inhabited community in the Nullarbor Plain," T said, revealing more of his research.

"It is," Jimmy said, "all four permanent residents. Five Ways is not inhabited, at least not that I'm aware. Just ruins now, after the tests."

I inserted myself into the conversation.

"Is that safe? What about radioactive waste?"

"Not to worry, Sebastian. We won't be there that long," Jimmy said.

"The aboriginals are waiting for us there?"

"I doubt it. But there's a well, and everyone and everything seeks out water in these parts."

"What if the water is contaminated?" I asked.

"Oh, I don't plan to drink it. I've got some clean water packets in my bag, and our ride will have more. Not to worry."

Jimmy shone his Maglite at the approaching G-Wagon. What I saw of it reminded me of the boxy old-fashioned Land Rovers in 1950s movies about Africa. Four doors, big pipe grille in front and a rack on top. A bug-eyed monster—our driver wearing night vision goggles—wrapped in a checkered shemagh drove. He stopped; we threw our packs into the back and climbed in. Jimmy rode shotgun. No one said anything, and the driver pulled a U-turn and headed back into the darkness he came from. The driver didn't turn on the headlights, which explained the goggles.

"Hey, Jimmy," I said. "Why no lights?"

"Not necessary, and unexplained lights in the desert tend to start stories about UFOs. We don't want pesky journalists crawling all over here."

We lapsed into silence. Jimmy and T seemed to doze. I stared out my window. As the day grew lighter, I started to make out scenery that reminded me of the American Southwest, tan dirt, rocks ranging from gravel to football-sized, some kind of whitish-gray brush. Not a single tree or hill in sight.

After about an hour of slow rumbling, the driver peeled off his goggles and unwrapped his shemagh. Jimmy and T didn't stir; the driver plowed on. Low sand dunes appeared off to our right, casting long shadows as the sun peeked over the horizon.

Tourist brochures don't advertise this part of Australia, I thought.

This is not the populated coastal Australia—the southeast coast of Brisbane, Sydney, Canberra and Melbourne, or the southwest coast of Perth or the northern coast of Darwin. It is not even the remoteness of Alice Springs and Ayers Rock. This is just emptiness.

As scary as the jungle can be, I found this more disturbing, and shivered at the thought of what kind of creatures might be able to survive here. I wondered how Empaya Iba would do in this climate. He seemed impervious to environment.

T stirred and turned in his seat to dig his sling pack out of the rear of the G-Wagon. He pulled his tablet out of the bag and flipped it open. He tapped at his keyboard. Colored light filled the back seat as a map appeared on the screen.

"Any idea where we are?" I asked him.

"Yeah. This should be Maralinga. Back that way," he said, nodding over his shoulder, "beyond the dunes is Choolalie Lake. Five Ways is about 15 miles north. Am I right, driver, or aren't you allowed to talk to civilians?"

The driver responded in a thick Australian accent that made Jimmy's seem positively Midwestern: "Beautiful downtown Five Ways about a half hour ahead. Road gets better from here," or so I interpreted.

Jimmy stirred.

"You interrogating my driver?"

"Nope," I said. "Just confirming our location."

"Scotty, the old one is Sebastian Arnett, otherwise known as the Look of Death," Jimmy said. "The young one is Tom Kingston, known as T. Sebastian, T, meet Sergeant Scott Brown of the Australian Army. No need to get too friendly. As soon as he drops us off, Scotty will disappear, as he does so well."

"So, Jimmy, are you sure your aboriginals are out there? I'm not seeing much that could sustain life," I said.

"They're here, and they've managed for millennia. You and I would die out here in days, but I wouldn't worry too much about them."

"What did the nuclear tests do to them?" T joined the conversation.

"Unfortunately, reduced their population, and that is a state secret, mates, so no more about that," Jimmy said.

"Well, are they okay with whites now?" T was a dog with a bone.

"Depends. Government's trying to make sure they get included, provide them a modern education, economic opportunities, give them more control over their future. Not sure how well that's working out for them. But the ones out here, they realize we've got some powers they can't match. They tolerate individuals, but mostly avoid us. In return, we try to give them their space."

"Except when you want to blow it all to hell," T said.

"Yeah, except then."

"So, did the nuke tests change their—I don't know—their ideologies, cultures, belief systems?"

"Bloody hell, he don't give up, does he?" Jimmy addressed that to me.

"Not so much, no."

"Well, T." Jimmy's accent turned to a long slow drawl. "I should know, but I don't. Can we leave it at that?"

"Okay."

"All right then. When we get to where we're going, we will hunker down, find or make some shade and try to move as little as possible. It's not the worst heat in the world, at least not yet, but it can sneak up on you," Jimmy said.

"And how do we get out of here?" I asked.

"Oh, Scotty's taxi service is always available."

"And where do you live, Scotty?" I asked.

"Here and there," he said. "Here and there."

True to his timetable, we entered Five Ways just under thirty minutes later.

It was light enough to see roads, or where roads used to be. I counted only four.

"Why is it called Five Ways?" I said. "I only see four tracks."

"This isn't Five Ways. That's just a little farther ahead. Over here is the well," Jimmy said. "Let's unload and have a rest."

The sun was rising, and I could already feel the heat. Now all we needed were the aboriginals who had summoned me to chat about spirits.

CHAPTER 8
WANDERERS

WE DID NOT have long to wait.

About an hour after Scotty's G-Wagon disappeared behind a low sand dune, a man who could have been 40 or 100 walked from behind the lean-to Jimmy had set up to provide us with shade. His skin was a deep black, his bushy hair and untrimmed beard a mottled black and white. He wore a loincloth and carried a walking stick that was as thick as my wrist and about a foot taller than he was. All I could think was, where in God's name had he found such a stick in this barren wilderness?

He stared at us. We looked back. He eyed my tattoo, took a few short steps forward and inspected it harder. Then he turned and simply walked away.

"Shouldn't we have said something, told him what we wanted?" I asked Jimmy.

"As soon as he saw your tattoo," Jimmy said, "he knew what we wanted. We'll just wait. I believe I will take a nap."

He dug into a supply pack Scotty had left us and pulled out what looked like an ultrathin yoga mat.

"There's one for each of us," he said, anticipating our questions. "Inflates in no time."

He arranged the sleeping pad in the shade and settled down. He pulled the brim of his hat over his eyes, leaving his mouth and nose uncovered. He started to snore softly almost immediately. T and I exchanged glances; T followed Jimmy's lead.

I lay back, but couldn't make myself comfortable. One of the marble-sized pebbles that littered the area always seemed to find a way to poke through the pad at a critical point of my body. I tried lying on one side, then the other, aiming to find the right princess-and-the-pea spot. I ended on my back, my boonie cap rolled under my neck for a pillow, but sleep eluded me. I kept thinking of Empaya Iba's nightmare, which had followed me halfway across the globe, and wondering what Iba was making of all this.

✍

I awoke in an oven, despite the shade our lean-to provided. Jimmy passed out six-ounce plastic packets of water and told us to sip slowly. The water was warm but tasted good.

T propped himself on an elbow and pointed. In the shimmering distance, two men who looked pretty much like our first contact approached from the shimmering distance. I thought it odd then, and even more so now, that neither we nor they showed any caution or wariness.

They stopped about five feet from us and squatted. We nodded our greetings; they nodded back. I turned my right cheek to them to give them a good look at the tattoo. They squinted from the sun, but showed no evidence of caring.

After a few minutes of this, Jimmy dipped into his pack of goodies and pulled out two clear pouches of water and handed them to the men. I thought we were about to do a peace pipe kind of ceremony, each one of us taking a sip from the same packet. I was wrong. They tucked the water pouches into their loin clothes, rose and walked away.

"Jimmy, aren't you going to try to talk to these people?" I said.

"How do we get a conversation going if you don't even say hello? You must know a few words of some sort of aboriginal language."

"I said hello, mate. Also asked them if it was all right if we camped out here on their land. They said we were welcome."

"I must be going deaf then, because I didn't hear anything like that. In fact, I haven't heard any noise that I didn't make since getting here."

"It is peaceful, isn't it?"

"No. It's eerie. So how did you say all that?"

"We sat together. Didn't pull any weapons. You showed them your tattoo. They accepted our water. Nonverbal communication, mate. You should try it sometime. Or you should try something other than your peevishness."

"I'm not peevish," I said.

"Yes, you are," T said.

I shot him a look, proving his point.

"See? Hostile nonverbal communication. You look like you're ready to wring T's neck, or have someone do it for you," Jimmy said.

I steamed, literally. Then a change came over me.

"Ach. I'm out of my depth out here."

"Patience, mate. We're making progress. The word is spreading. Sooner or later, someone will want to talk. Then we'll just hope we can find a dialect everyone speaks."

I flopped onto my back and closed my eyes. I seemed to join the dead. No dreams came to me that day. No nightmares either.

I could have stayed in my death state forever, I guess, if T hadn't shaken my foot. I could tell from the shadows that the sun was setting but I couldn't see it. Jimmy had rearranged our tarp again and it completely blocked my view of the west.

"What's up?" I mumbled. "Time for more water?"

"You have visitors," T said.

I rolled onto my right side and looked around. Half a dozen

aboriginals squatted just outside our lean-to facing Jimmy, who sat cross-legged facing them.

"Good morning, sleeping beauty," he said. "Nice rest?"

"No. Yes. I mean I don't know. It's like something has sucked all the energy out of me. Did you and T sleep too?"

"No, we've just been getting to know one another, watching the visitors come and go."

"Oh, yeah. How many?"

"With this lot," he said, surveying a half-dozen black men with frizzled white hair and bushy beards, "it's fourteen. We think they want to talk."

"Great," I said, levering myself into a sitting position and twisting around to face the aboriginals.

One man, at the end of the line of natives, pointed at me and spoke.

Jimmy answered.

The man shook his head ever so slightly and said something else.

Jimmy shook his head and said something.

I did not get the sense that they understood one another. T and I exchanged glances. He shrugged.

Finally, the spokesman launched into a speech, pointing again at me.

Jimmy said something brief and turned to me.

"I thought they were Ing-gal-ee-ah or Spinifex, but they're not," he said. "They're Yang-koon-chat-chara. Way outside of where I would expect them to be."

"What did they say?"

"They want to know where you got the tattoo. They did not say so, but I got the sense they do not approve."

"Well, tell them for me, I don't approve either."

Jimmy launched into a long speech, pointing at me, then them.

The aboriginal spokesman responded, becoming insistent at one point, raising his voice and stabbing an index finger in my direction.

Finally, the conversation stopped. Our visitors stared alternately at Jimmy and me. It was as though T did not exist. Jimmy scratched his sweaty forehead with the back of his thumb.

"Well. Long and short of it is these fellows are Yang-koon-chat-chara from way northeast of here. They're just on a walk-about, visiting neighbors, collecting gossip, seeing new things. They've been at it for months and expect that they will take a year or more to get back home. They were west of here when they met the scout, the first fellow we met. He's been spreading the word about you, Sebastian. He tells of one man with the spider mark, not the three of us. T and I don't exist. They don't like your tattoo. They want to know how you got it. You don't fit in their creation myth, and they don't understand why someone would wear such a tattoo.

"They see you are not openly hostile, but you give off a very bad aura. They want to know what you plan to do, where you plan to go, because they don't want to share the same desert as you."

"Are they afraid of me?" I asked. "They don't seem afraid."

"They're tense. Aboriginals usually don't point. It's not polite. It would be like waving a spear at you. Like they're warning the spider that they will stand up and fight if it comes to that. But they don't want it to come to that. They say if you are heading toward their territory, over to the northeast, they want a head start so they can warn their tribe to disperse."

I looked around at the dimming emptiness around us.

"How can they disperse more than they already are?"

"That's beside the point. The point is they don't want to be where you are. Sit up straight and pat the ground; make like you're going to stay here forever."

I did as Jimmy requested. He and the spokesman exchanged a few brief sentences. The six aboriginals stood and headed off to the northeast, not back toward the west where they had come from.

"I guess they don't believe me," I said. Neither Jimmy nor T said anything.

❧

We got no more visitors that day, but two groups squatted near our lean-to when we awoke the following morning. It was eerie how they could approach without our notice and just hunker down and wait.

They came from different tribes, ones Jimmy said lived in the neighborhood, the Spinifex People and the Ing-gal-ee-ah. Despite their differences, they brought the same message: A wise man was on his way but would not arrive for a day or two. They asked if we would stay to meet him. Jimmy said we would. That was Friday.

More visitors, all men, in ones and twos, arrived, stopped, observed, and moved on. It amazed me that so many people could live in an area so empty and barren.

Less than two days after leaving the civilization of the Indian Pacific, I noted a sense of isolation settling over each of us. I didn't know if it was the heat, the boredom of waiting, or if it was something more. T and I had our issues, but we'd made progress and this seemed neither the time nor the place for further discussion. It was too hot to explore, and there was precious little to see. We saw not one single creature—not a lizard, snake, or insect—except for our wandering aboriginal visitors. It was like being in solitary confinement, imprisoned by the hostile environment and our dubious mission.

So we just sat, or lay, in the shade of our shelter. We read, occasionally chatted, but mostly kept to ourselves. Every three or four hours, we changed the tarp's orientation as the sun burned across a white sky. We drank warm water and ate body-temperature packaged meals.

As Jimmy had predicted, I missed the comfort of the Indian Pacific and cocktail hour. Heat enveloped us, shimmering waves lapping against our skin, welling up beads of sweat that left tracks on our exposed dusty faces, arms, and legs.

Empaya Iba hated this dry heat as much as I did. I know, because he came to me in daydreams and told me so. Go back, he said. Go back home.

But which home? His, or mine?

CHAPTER 9
STRANGERS

On Saturday, our fourth day in Australia, our third here on the Nullarbor, Scotty delivered a new pack of water and food and bundled up our trash. During the transfer, Jimmy grabbed two extra magazines of ammunition from the G-Wagon's supplies. I raised an eyebrow; Jimmy ignored it.

The next day, two strange images appeared in the east with the dawn. All our visitors had walked from the west and, except for the Yang-koon-chat-chara, had retraced their steps. These two differed in other ways as well. One was short, the other shorter still. They moved slowly, erratically, in a stop and start cadence. With the sun rising behind them, we could make out nothing more.

For the first time, we saw wildlife. Lizards in several shapes, sizes, and coloring dug themselves out of camouflaged burrows and from under rocks and fled west.

"That's odd," T said, pointing as a trio of horned reptiles skittered toward the western shadows. "Have you ever seen that before, Jimmy?"

He watched the creatures disappear into the darkness.

"No," he said.

I stood up, suddenly antsy to move my limbs after days of lying around. I shaded my eyes with my hand, but still could make out no details of the approaching duo.

T pulled his cell phone out of a baggy pocket in his cargo shorts, opened the camera app and zoomed in on the two, using it like binoculars.

"One of them looks like a kid," he said. "He's not wearing any clothes and—I can't make out the other one. Jimmy, do you have binoculars?"

"No. We'll know more soon enough."

The three of us stood side by side, peering into the red light.

Unable to distinguish anything more, I started pacing outside the shelter, raising dust and kicking at small stones we had cleared from the ground over the past four days.

Minutes ticked by, and the pair grew larger as they stopped and started their way toward us. The shorter one did appear to be a boy of six or seven. He walked slowly, head down, matching his pace to the ancient creature he led with a stick. The old man, wearing a loincloth, wobbled along, each step a deliberate decision. Start, stop. Start, stop. His young guide was endlessly patient.

His back and shoulders bent, the ancient's head topped the boy's by a few inches, no more. Curly white hair and a bushy untrimmed beard stood out on his wrinkled oblong head. A broad flat nose occupied most of his face.

T aimed his tablet camera again.

"His eyes look red, like a bad snapshot," he said.

"Blind," Jimmy said. "This should be our man, but it doesn't feel right."

"What's not right, Jimmy? Look at him," I said. "He's barely as big as the kid. He's not much more than skin and bones. He almost looks like a sick crane, all legs. Where's the harm? I mean, every other aboriginal we've seen looked bigger, healthier, more—I don't know—more formidable."

"Looks can be deceiving," Jimmy said without taking his eyes from the duo. "Just look at you."

"Jimmy, can you make out what's on his chest?" T asked. "Some kind of markings. White paint or chalk. Chalk, I guess, given the lack of water out here. It's, ah—"

T zoomed and focused, rezoomed and refocused.

"Um, there's a circle on top," he said. "Then three lines."

"Vertical or horizontal?" Jimmy asked.

"Horizontal. They go from one side of his chest to the other. Then two vertical lines connected to the bottom horizontal like. Maybe like legs. It could be an image of a man."

"Anything coming out of the circle?"

"I can't tell. It's not great art work," T said.

"Probably put on by a blind man or a six-year-old kid," Jimmy said. "Can I take a look? That sun is blinding me, and I just can't focus for long."

T passed him the cell phone. Jimmy turned his back on the rising sun and hovered over the tiny screen. T picked up his tablet and started making a video of the pair. Trying to find an angle that would not blind him, he sidestepped a dozen paces.

History in the making, or something like that, I thought.

I kept my eyes on the old man. He was less than a hundred feet away, but the closer he came, the slower he walked. If that was possible. At the rate they were coming, I figured he and the kid might have spent the night just a few football fields away.

The old creature sniffed the air, jerked his head from side to side, stared with blood-filled eyes. He really did remind me of a crane or heron, especially one on alert for danger. For some reason, that made me jittery. I twitched and resumed pacing, never taking my eyes off the old man.

Jimmy looked up from the phone.

"T, can you make out any detail on your tablet? I think there's a mark coming off the left side of that circle."

T wobbled the computer and fiddled with the keyboard.

"Okay. Yeah. It's messy, but it looks like a nose or a cigar or something."

"A nose? Like a beak?" Jimmy tensed.

"Could be, yeah. I'm not much on abstract art," T said.

"This isn't good," Jimmy said, staring hard right into the sun. "Sebastian, go. Bugger off. Get down the road and keep going."

Jimmy was emphatic. I wondered if I should grab the Webley out of my backpack.

"Go, will you?"

He shoved me toward the track we had come in on.

"We'll pick you up. Go. And keep going. Don't stop for anything."

He spoke to me but his eyes never left the old man, who seemed to be twitching now, like the start of an epileptic fit.

"Why? What's going on?" I said. "Something's wrong with the old man. We should try to help him. Especially if this is the guy I'm supposed to talk to about Empaya Iba."

Jimmy turned his back on the old man and pushed me south toward the desert track.

"Sebastian, go. He's marked with Bunjil, the creator spirit. Bunjil and his family and shamans are represented by birds; he destroys bugs, including spiders. Go, go, go!"

CHAPTER 10
DEATH

I HAVE READ ABOUT near-death experiences, how people feel themselves rise out of their bodies and watch themselves doing things without actually participating—like a fly on the wall.

That's what this was like, mixed up with my recurring Empaya Iba nightmare. And, I swear, this was no dream. It really happened.

The flying creature soared past me, all chalky white and ragged around the edges.

"My God, that was close," I said to no one.

I tried to swivel so I could face the creature as it circled for another pass. My feet stuck like they were glued to the ground.

I called out.

"Empaya Iba, let go of my feet. Let go of me, or we both die."

Bunjil—was that what Jimmy called it?—twisted and spun, diving back at me. At the last instant, I fell forward onto all fours—no, six; no, eight limbs.

"What the—?"

My antagonist spun around again, arcing lower, straight at my head. I scuttled right.

I can't move like that, I thought.

Bunjil screeched and clutched at my head with stick-figure claws.

I swatted with my arm—an incredibly long, thick, hairy arm with neither hand nor fingers at the end. The creature swerved, unhappy to face an enemy that would at least fight back.

I lowered my body—this round thing as big as an exercise ball—and shuffled quickly backward, left, then right, back again. Always moving. Never looking. Never needing to look. Waving an extra limb now and then, holding Bunjil at bay.

The predator twisted away, climbing straight into the desert sun. My eyes—two, four, six, eight—followed it. Bunjil twisted away from the yellow orb, and I took the brunt of the sun's rays. I ducked, but white light burned everywhere I looked.

I felt the creature diving at my head and thrust two limbs up. Pain streaked through my left arm, my leg, my entire left side. I scuttled right, then back. I felt part of me rip and tear loose.

My head twisted, mouth spitting and hissing. My limbs, all eight, alternately lashed the air overhead, stabbing, puncturing, piercing, flaying.

Bunjil screamed a harsh cry and flew off into the sun.

Blood pooled beneath me. Mine, his, mingling on the ground around my heaving body. I twitched once, twice. Then moved no more.

⁂

The battle lasted a heartbeat, then I dreamed.

I saw a girl. Neither white like me nor dark like an Australian aboriginal. Not a child but not a full-grown woman either. She resembled someone I had seen before, but I couldn't place her and my memory would not give up a name. She held out her hands, cupping something dark. A flower. An orchid. A type I'd never seen before. Or had I? It was so confusing.

My brain raced through an inventory of the hundreds and

thousands of orchid species I'd photographed. Yet here was an orchid, a black orchid, I thought, that I had never seen.

The girl, who was pretty in her own way, offered the flower to me. I felt ambivalent. I love orchids and thrilled at the idea of seeing and touching a new species. But part of me held back. *It was not my orchid; it belonged to someone else,* I thought. *Isn't that interesting? Thinking a flower belongs to just one person?*

The girl never spoke. She just stood there, proffering the black orchid while I pondered what to do.

"That is not yours," I heard a voice say.

I looked around and saw a handsome young Asian man with tattoos up and down his arms and a spiderweb spread across half his face. The web was more than a tattoo, more like a scar.

"The black orchid is not for you," the man said.

"I wondered," I said. "Is it yours?"

"No, I have taken my orchid," he said, pointing at his tattooed cheek. "That is the mark of the orchid's spider."

"The orchid has its own spider? Like a symbiote? Some plants are like that. I don't see it," I said. "It must be tiny."

"No, not small. It is as big as the land. It protects the land. It is the land. Without the spider, the land cannot be; and without the land, the people cannot be; without the people, the spider cannot be."

"Why is she offering the orchid to me if it is not for me?"

"The one who should take it has not come. It is for him. Not for you."

"What will happen if I take it? She wants me to have it."

"If you take what is not yours, you will have to die, just like I did."

"What if I took it and I lived?"

That seemed to perplex the man.

"Do you have a name?" I asked.

"Of course, I am named. The people call me Oololoo."

"Oololoo, what would happen if I took the black orchid and I did not die?"

He looked stricken.

"You must die. If you don't, the spider will die. And the people will die. And the land. You must not take the midnight flower."

The handsome man and the young girl disappeared. Not in a poof kind of way. Just, I saw them and then I didn't see them.

⁊

"Sebastian. It's T. Come on, man. Wake up."

"T?"

"Yeah, it's me. Wake up."

I opened my eyes. T's face hovered over mine.

"Where are we? It's not hot."

"You're in a hospital. How do you feel?"

"Fine, I guess. I had a really interesting dream," I said, trying to remember it. That's the way with dreams. On one level, they are so vivid they seem real. And when you wake up, you can't even remember what they were about.

"Why am I in a hospital? Where's Jimmy? What happened?"

T gave me a strange look.

"Jimmy's in Kalgoorlie, fixing things up."

"What's he fixing up?" I asked.

"Not important," T said. "Are you sure you feel okay?"

"Yes. Why do you keep asking?"

"Sebastian, you died."

CHAPTER 11
CHANGE OF PLANS

M Y MOUTH OPENED, but no words came out. I reached out and touched T's arm. It was solid. I looked side to side. A white sheet covered me from chest to toes. Tubes ran from a bag of translucent liquid hanging over my shoulder to my right arm.

The walls bore institutional pastels. The room had both more, and less, lighting than needed. Aside from my bed and a rolling stand, the room contained one easy chair.

T stood at my left side, his hands resting on a bed rail. His face wore a quizzical expression.

"I'm not dreaming. I'm here, and I'm fine," I said, continuing to take in the hospital room.

T shook his head.

"You and that old aboriginal got into some kind of—I don't know what. The little kid died. You and the old man collapsed. Jimmy had to call in the cavalry. You've been out almost two days. And before the Australian medics arrived, you stopped breathing. For more than a half hour. Jimmy and I kept working on you, but— you were dead."

I didn't know what to say. I couldn't remember being dead. I wouldn't know what that felt like. I dreamt, I know, but... But what? This was kind of how Empaya Iba worked, too. When he attacked— when I used his power to attack—I never remembered the details.

"I'm really sorry about the boy," I said.

"It wasn't your fault. Well, not totally, I guess."

"What about the old man?" I asked.

"He's in Kalgoorlie; that's the complication Jimmy is working on."

"Good," I said. "I mean, I'm glad about him being all right."

≪

T fetched doctors and nurses. They looked me over top to bottom: took blood, X-rays, CAT scans; asked me a million questions—none of which I could answer to anyone's satisfaction, including mine— and marveled at my recovered condition.

T and I did not get to talk privately again until the evening. It was Monday, two and a half days since we watched the blind old man and the boy approach our camp.

He fired up his tablet, and I watched the deadly battle unfold between Empaya Iba and Bunjil. That's how I thought of it. Not me and the old man, but Iba and Bunjil.

The old man did his stop-step until he got to within about ten feet of me. Then all hell broke loose. The boy toppled. The old aboriginal and I twitched, trembled, and shook. We dropped to the ground, convulsed and rolled. We made incomprehensible sounds, little more than grunts and growls. T's computer camera caught us writhing and thrashing in the dirt, raising a mini dust storm.

It lasted one terrifying minute. Our bodies slowed their wild gyrations to the occasional twitch, like a dying gasp, and lay still. I saw Jimmy bend over me; he listened to my chest and felt my neck for a pulse. He started pushing my chest in a fast, deliberate rhythm.

No wonder T wanted to know how my chest felt, if they had kept that up for thirty minutes.

"T, get over here," Jimmy called in the video.

The camera level dropped to the ground, and T appeared in the video shot and took over from Jimmy. The Aussie went to check the boy, then the old man. He rushed out of the picture. We could hear him rummaging in his pack and then shouting, talking to Scotty, calling him to us urgently.

The recording rolled on, but I stopped watching.

T told me a helicopter arrived in about 20 minutes; medics bundled up the old man, the boy, and me and flew off to Kalgoorlie. After a while, Scotty arrived with a bush plane and flew Jimmy and T to Kalgoorlie as well. Jimmy was still there; he arranged for T and me to fly via air ambulance to Perth, which has a bigger hospital, better health care, and is far from the Nullarbor, the wandering aboriginals, and the old man.

∽

That evening in my room, T and I tried to make sense of things. I had walked up and down the halls a few times and felt fine. The doctors were stumped. All symptoms pointed to a heart attack or seizure, but tests revealed no heart or brain damage. Absent other evidence, the docs were inclined to diagnose severe heatstroke. Neither T nor I chose to enlighten them about other alternatives.

In private, however, we focused mightily on a different kind of reality.

"Jimmy said it was a battle royal between your demon and that bird spirit the old man had marked on his chest," T said. "Bunjil, the aboriginal creator spirit, is represented by an eagle. Apparently, birds eat spiders, and aboriginal mythology has nothing good to say about spiders."

"So, since I died—and I use that term loosely—that must mean the eagle spirit beat the heck out of Iba," I said. "Maybe they killed each other."

"Possible." T ruminated. "The old man went down, that's for sure, but he never stopped breathing. Now, he's gone."

"He died?"

"No. Jimmy called a couple hours ago to check on you. He said the old guy just walked out of the hospital overnight. The hospital and government authorities overseeing treatment of aboriginals are very upset. They don't like the idea of a blind old aboriginal just disappearing like that from the hospital the same day a dead aboriginal boy is brought in from a restricted part of the bush. They are apparently asking questions about the nuke aspect. Jimmy's afraid it's going to hit the press."

"How did the old guy just disappear? He was blind."

T shrugged.

"I think we've established that the normal laws of nature don't apply around you, so maybe they don't apply to him either," T said. "And I can't believe I just said that."

I watched the skinny young man—still a kid to my mind. He slouched in the easy chair, one leg hanging over the arm, musing on how his life had changed since meeting Amanda and me.

"Well, at least Amanda's not here to see all this," I said.

T shifted on his seat.

"Well, Sebastian," he said.

"You didn't tell her?" I said.

"She made me swear to keep an eye on you and to let her know if anything happened to you. You died. That seemed important enough to tell her, although I just told her you had collapsed and we had taken you to the hospital," T said. "She's on her way here, or will be as soon as she can get out of Denver. Blizzard there. No planes out yesterday. I don't know about today. She's supposed to text me when she leaves, and I haven't gotten anything from her."

Not good, I thought.

"When is Jimmy coming?"

"He doesn't know. He's got a real mess on his hands where he is. Could be several days."

"What about Mike's people? Are they around?"

T shrugged.

"I didn't tell them. That's Jimmy's deal."

"Does he have anyone watching us?"

"No one I've been introduced to. The docs know you're something special, but there are no guards around. You're in a normal room in the cardiac unit," T said.

"Good. That's good," I said. "Let's get out of here. See what you can do about getting us over to Kota Kinabalu in Borneo. ASAP."

"Borneo? Why do you want to go there?"

"Empaya Iba may be dead. I don't know. I figure if he's still around, that's where he'd be, licking his wounds, or whatever spider demons do after getting their furry butts handed to them on a platter."

"This is not a good idea, Sebastian. We really should wait for Jimmy. Maybe Amanda, too. Let's talk about this a little more."

"No. I don't want Amanda anywhere near Borneo. And we have no idea how long Jimmy will be. This eagle creator spirit, Bunjil, seems to have knocked the crap out of Iba. If Iba is dead, I may be free of the curse. I want to get to Borneo and find the black orchid woman.

"She'll know whether Iba is dead or alive."

EMPAYA IBA SPEAKS

Children of the midnight flower,
Abba, your father, speaks.
Our enemies have struck,
Those who would steal the protection of the midnight flower.
In the land of nothingness,
With no sight of green trees
No plants, no flowers, no blooms, no shade,
We saw them come, as if in devotion.

A blind and aged spirit bereft of wisdom,
Led by a babe, an innocent,
They came in vile deception
Afoot on parched ground.
Then struck as lightning
Splits open the storm-tossed sky.
Fools they be,
Me, they could not see.

My servant, he who bears my mark,
They struck him down.
I know. I watched. I saw.
But I was harmed not at all.
Wise as our land is old,
I am Empaya Iba, spirit of the Black Orchid People,
Guardian of the Mother Soil, giver of the Long Sleep,
Seer of the Many Eyes, mage of the Many Legs.

CHAPTER 12
TENOM PLOT

OUR ESCAPE FROM Perth to the old Dyak woman in upcountry Borneo demanded that we take the reddest of red-eye flights. Our initial destination, Kota Kinabalu on the northern coast of Borneo, lay 2,600 miles, and six hours, due north across the Indian Ocean from Australia. Only one airline, Malaysian Air, made the flight, and then only three days a week. The flight departed a half hour after midnight and arrived in Kota Kinabalu with the dawn.

In Kota, we trudged up the airline ramp into a heat oppressively humid. *This is what it feels like being hugged by a sumo wrestler after a long match*, I thought. *Welcome home.*

If Australia's dry heat parched throats, Borneo's humidity drowned lungs. I was breathing heavily by the time we reached the end of the ramp and the airport air conditioning cut through the wet air.

A few steps ahead of me, T did a double take.

"What's up?" I said, happy to stop in the a/c.

"Did you see that Chinese guy?"

I looked around.

"You'll have to be more specific. Lots of Chinese in here," I said.

"Over by the coffee kiosk. It was the guy from the train, the one with the babe. The guy who planted the bug. He was just over there with a couple of other Chinese. Big guys. Looking our way. Almost like they expected to see us."

"That's not possible," I said, swiveling in a 360, searching for that familiar face. If T had spotted him, he'd disappeared in an instant.

I stepped slowly out of the way of other deplaning passengers

"What do we do?" T asked.

I inspected every face around us.

"Did you see the girl?"

"No, just the guy."

"Hmm."

"I wonder if maybe we should have let General Owens know we were coming here," T said.

"Too late for that. Besides, I hate being hounded by those babysitters. Better they stay in the U.S. and focus on Amanda," I said.

"I'm glad they're looking after Amanda, but I wouldn't mind some backup here."

"Trust me. They would be absolutely no use against Empaya Iba, and that's who we have to worry about."

"What about the Chinese?"

I exhaled slowly.

"They seem intent on following us, or at least me. If that's all they want—I'm not sure how to stop them. I'm guessing they lost us in Australia and figured this was our next logical destination."

Aside from planting the tracker on my backpack, they'd demonstrated no hostility toward me. As long as Amanda was all right, I was okay with that. But I really wished I knew what they wanted.

❧

We made it through immigration and customs quickly without catching sight of the Chinese trio and taxied over to Tanjung Aru

Railroad Station with moments to spare before our train departed at 7:45 a.m.

T and I were heading to Tenom, a sleepy town in the interior, the end of the rail line and the beginning of the Dyak wilderness. Our route from Tanjung Aru Station in Kota to Tenom measured just less than eighty-four miles, but the trip consumed more than seven hours, pretty fast by Bornean standards.

At Beaufort, the unofficial midpoint between the civilization of Kota Kinabalu and the sparseness of Tenom, the train weaned us further from civilization. We stepped out of the modern air-conditioned rail cars and into a rust bucket on rails equipped only with rotating fans embedded in the ceiling. Its unscreened windows opened to the world, the humid heat, and the insects.

I was introducing T to the wilderness as gradually as possible while still making time. He was a Utah boy, and despite his twenty-three years, he had not traveled much outside the state. In the last week, I had taken him nine time zones away to Australia. This next leg would take us back decades in time before we truly plunged into a wilderness unchanged in thousands of years.

The big attraction of Tenom—actually the only attraction—is the Sabah Agriculture Park, with its collection of more than 3,000 species of orchids. I had spent months there documenting the more glorious varieties for my patron, an enormously wealthy Middle Eastern sheikh.

We checked in at Tenom's best hotel, the Perkasa, a decaying seven-story version of Motel 6 with dirty tubs, unscreened windows that don't close, and phones that work on a schedule I had never figured out. It was so much nicer than what we would face when we headed into the forest.

The best thing about the Perkasa, other than the funny, helpful staff who remembered me and asked where my camera gear was, was the view. Perkasa sits on a hill overlooking the town of Tenom and the entire Tenom Valley. It provides magnificent views, and I ponied up an extra three bucks a night so that T and I could both have valley views. Even with the view fee, our nightly charge was less than $95 for "suite" rooms, the best in the house. I felt like living large since I would soon be using a tree as a toilet.

Having survived the encounter with Bunjil, I felt desperate to find out whether Iba had truly lost its power and what that meant for me. The only place I could think to find out was Iba's home turf, deep in the interior of Borneo, a place so remote that the border between Malaysia and Indonesia—the two countries that claimed the largest chunks of Borneo—could not be demarcated reliably. Even Google Maps turned blurry in those dense forests.

Borneo is a forest-covered lump of mountainous rock plopped at the eastern end of the Indonesian archipelago. Getting away from the coast, where the bulk of the population lives, and into the interior presents several unpleasant travel options. Roads don't carry you far before they turn into mud tracks that eat up even the old Land Rovers. If you have the money, you can stuff yourself into a tiny, single-engine bush plane and hope the motor doesn't die and that you don't hit a wild boar while trying to land on a grass runway.

Most people simply travel by boat, pushing upstream toward the mountains in chocolate waters alive with crocodiles, water snakes, and submerged debris. My fear of drowning, however, born of too many near-death experiences with water, demanded that I be desperate before using that mode of transportation. In fact, only large overdoses of strong tranquilizers allowed me to travel any distance by boat.

I'd done the trip twice before, each time with a horrible ending. This time, I hoped that the proper preparations would facilitate a better result. *Yeah*, I thought, *wishful thinking*.

Nonetheless, I bought a local-area cell phone at one of the Indian general merchandise stores that you find all over Asia and called my old assistant, Firash Taufik. Officially, Firash worked for Sabah Park, but he spent a lot of time freelancing for whoever would pay him. And he knew everyone, and everyone knew him, including a band of timber rustlers I'd had a run-in with. Just knowing Firash had kept me alive.

And he was just the man to arrange for a large boat, two guides, an interpreter, camping equipment, and a load of food and pure water. While Firash and I consulted back and forth on the arrangements, I suggested that T take a walk down the hill into town. He happily obliged.

Less than a half hour later, however, the hotel room phone jangled to life. I figured it was Firash. I was wrong. Oh, so wrong.

≪

"Sebastian."

It was the only word T got out before the phone went silent.

"T, are you there? T?"

"Mr. Arnett. You don't know me," a voice said. "We have your friend, Mr. Kingston. We wish him no harm. We wish you no harm. But we do need to talk."

Ice spread through my veins.

T had told me about seeing the Chinese, and I had done nothing. I recalled Mike Owens's specific warning of the threat not just to me but to the people closest to me, and I had resisted the increased security and belittled the threat.

What had I gotten us into?

CHAPTER 13

UNINVITED

THE VOICE ON the other end of the telephone line was cultured, British English with a Chinese underlay. I could picture the man, boarding the Pacific Indian just minutes before its departure; nodding silent greetings in passageways; drinking in the club car; calling out to join us as Jimmy led us off the train—and always with the beautiful young Chinese woman in tow.

He'd seen T with me countless times, I thought, both of us on our best behavior. He knew a connection existed, if not its origins, details, or the glue that mattered.

If he'd actually snatched T, that meant he'd followed him from the hotel, which meant they had followed us from the train station and probably on the plane as well. Someone had tailed us almost 3,000 miles. This was serious, and I was... on my own. Jimmy was still somewhere in Australia, and Mike Owens had called off his watchdogs, assuming that Jimmy would keep me safe. At least I'd seen no evidence of them since departing Denver a week earlier. What a mess.

"Listen," I spoke calmly into the hotel phone—more calmly than I felt. "Why don't you let T—Mr. Kingston—go, and we can talk right now? You bring him back to the hotel, and we can chat in the bar."

"I fear that will not be satisfactory. You are making arrangements to leave here. We do not intend to lose track of you."

"You won't lose track of me if we talk right now."

"I think you misunderstand," the voice said reasonably. "We intend to accompany you on your trek. We have an interest in your talents."

So, Mike and Jimmy were right. The voice, and whoever was with him, knew about Iba. Did they know that Iba, defeated by Bunjil, might no longer have any powers?

"If you know so much about what you call my talents, then you must know that you might be in danger yourself."

Only I knew how desperately I was bluffing.

"We totally understand. One of my associates has already attached a small explosive device to Mr. Kingston. The only thing that prevents its detonation is my associate's thumb on a pressure trigger. If he should suddenly experience breathing difficulty, for instance, his thumb could unfortunately release the trigger. But, please understand, that is not our desire. We do not wish to harm either you or Mr. Kingston. We are businessmen, and we have a business proposition that should satisfy all of us. What could be more reasonable than to sit down and discuss it?"

"And then have you hound me wherever I go for as long as you want? That does not sound reasonable to me," I said.

"Mr. Arnett, since learning of your unique talent, we have made a study of you. You interest us a very great deal. You may raise all of your questions and… concerns. Over dinner tonight. I know you enjoy the Indian restaurant across from the Orchid Hotel downtown."

I bristled at the thought of how much he knew about me. Jimmy had warned us that they were making inquiries here. I wondered if they had gotten to Firash. No, no need to suspect Firash. I'd made a splash once or twice here in Borneo; quite a few people knew about me. They didn't need Firash.

"Mr. Arnett?"

"Okay. Dinner tonight. Six o'clock. Let me talk to T."

"Of course."

"Hey, man, they jumped me. I never saw it coming. I'm sorry, Sebastian," T said, all in a rush.

"No big deal," I said. "You okay?"

"Yeah. They don't seem to want to mess me up too much, but they sure aren't going to let me go. They have guns. It would be okay with me to do an Iba on them."

"Did they wire explosives to you?"

"They put a cloth shoulder bag on me. Taped it to my side. It's not that heavy."

I heard a shuffle, and T was gone.

⨏

I sat on the bed, wondering what to do next. I dialed Firash, but got his voicemail.

"It's Sebastian. Call me when you get this. Something has come up."

I disconnected and placed a second call. Jimmy answered on the second ring.

"Jimmy, it's me, Sebastian."

"Speak of the devil," he said. "I was just emailing with someone over at the Indigenous Affairs Group in the Prime Minister's office about you. It's probably better that you're out of Australia just now, but you could have warned me or said good-by."

"Sorry about that. I didn't know how you'd feel about me leaving."

"Worked out for the best. I've contacted Mike Owens. He is not happy. In fact, he distinctly mentioned putting an ankle bracelet… around your neck."

"I'll have to worry about that later, Jimmy," I said. "Hey, listen.

I've got a problem. Somebody grabbed T. They have him and insist that I meet with them. They know all about Iba and want to accompany me into the forest."

"Bloody hell." Jimmy never cursed. "Chinese, I assume."

"Yes," I said meekly.

"All right. That trumps what I'm working on. What do they want you to do?"

"I'm meeting them at a restaurant in Tenom at six local time. They've wired T with some kind of bomb with a pressure trigger. If I try to use Iba, it all blows up and T with it."

"My nearest assets are in Kota Kinabalu. They can be there in time for your dinner. I'll have them stay dark. Don't be looking around for them. We don't want to alarm these people. Anyone we know?"

"T saw the man from the train with two others at the airport in Kota. I assume it's him. He spoke English, but I'm pretty sure he's Chinese."

"Interesting. Not amateurs and very well connected and financed," Jimmy said. "You should take this seriously."

"As seriously as that old man in the Nullarbor?"

"Yes."

We formulated a plan. The only thing we had going for us was that the kidnappers did not seem to know that we were not sure whether Empaya Iba was still active.

CHAPTER 14

WEBLEY

BEFORE ARRIVING IN Australia with T, I would have been conflicted, but confident, that with Iba in my pocket my loved ones and I could not easily be harmed. My run-in with the old Australian aboriginal and Bunjil had demolished that confidence. Now I was just conflicted, disturbed with myself that I wanted to be able to use a fearsome power that already exerted too much influence over me. Only now, I wasn't sure the power was available to me.

Well before dinner, I idled my way down into Tenom's business district to scope things out. Over my shoulder I wore a cloth bag I'd bought in the hotel gift shop. It sported Dyak tattoo patterns embroidered into the fabric, and in it I placed my tablet, a water bottle, and the Webley six-shooter, fully loaded. Extreme threats seemed to justify extreme precautions. I was a good enough shot, but I did my best shooting with a camera.

I strolled up and down the short main street of Tenom, reacquainting myself with the layout of town, its shops, streets, and alleys. I stopped often, hoping to catch anyone who might be following me, but I didn't notice anyone more suspicious than myself.

A few minutes before six, I stepped under the awning that

covered the entire front of the Indian restaurant. I sat down at one of the half dozen outdoor tables with my back against the wall of the building. To my right was a huge planter separating the restaurant from a Chinese tailor shop next door. I leaned my bag against the planter.

As I extracted my tablet, I cocked the Webley and pointed it roughly in the direction of the seat across from me. Call me crazy, inexperienced in weaponry or just seriously ticked off. My Mark IV .455 caliber monster had a six-inch barrel but no safety. Having it cocked and aimed made it extremely dangerous for anyone near the muzzle end of the weapon. I would have to be careful not to bang the table.

A skinny Malay waiter in a white shirt, black slacks, and sandals took my order for a Kingfisher beer and disappeared. Having eaten at the restaurant dozens of times, I thought I knew all of the cousins who served as waiters, but neither the owner nor the regulars were in sight. I assumed they were in back, leaving the new hire to his job.

Out on the street, a familiar well-dressed, lean Chinese business type stepped out of the rear seat of a black SUV with tinted glass. He closed the car door, and the vehicle drove off down the street. Clearly, the pretty Chinese girl's escort from the train in Australia was not concerned about *his* safety.

"Mr. Arnett, how nice to meet you formally," he said. "We never did have a chance to speak on the Indian Pacific. You were always accompanied by someone."

"You, too. How's your daughter? And more to the point, where is T?"

"He is safe, I assure you. May I sit?"

"Do I have a choice?" I asked.

"Of course. I can walk away and dispose of Mr. Kingston. But that would create a certain difficulty with Mrs. Campion, wouldn't it?" he said, pulling back the chair across from me.

"I don't know who you are or what you want," I said between

clenched teeth, "but I will tell you once and only once, if you so much as refer to Amanda Campion again, I will jump across this table and strangle you, and T can go to hell."

I startled him, but he recovered his business face quickly.

"American straight talk. Very well. Let me reciprocate," he said. "My name is Lee. I represent an international import-export business. I do not know how much you understand about business, but trading is extremely competitive. Cutthroat, one might say. We all seek any advantage we can gain over our competitors. We believe you can assist us in gaining such an advantage."

The waiter returned with my beer, and Lee—I didn't know whether it was his first name or last name—ordered hot tea for himself.

"What advantage would that be?" I asked after the waiter departed.

"The ability to affect the health of key personnel at critical junctures, of course," he said.

"And what makes you think I can do that?"

"Please, Mr. Arnett. We both know that something happened to you here in Borneo about one year ago. Four men went off into the interior; only one returned, and his face was badly scarred, almost as if he had been tortured.

"A Middle Eastern entity—it is difficult to separate personalities from business and government in that region, don't you think?—rushed in, bought up thousands of acres of land in the remotest part of the country. This entity paid a small fortune to clear-cut a narrow slice of the new holdings. Then activity stopped, but the story does not end there; it just begins," Lee said.

"Shortly after this, the sole survivor of this unfortunate expedition returned to Tenom. He hired guides and a boat to take him upriver. Once again, he ended up very briefly in what passes for a hospital here. He was waterlogged. And the scars on his face had resolved themselves into a tattoo. A tattoo of a spiderweb. One exactly like yours."

He paused. I sipped my beer, shrugged.

"What does this have to do with your kidnapping my traveling companion? I should have you picked up by the police. The Malays have a troubled history with the Chinese, you know."

"All in the past. And Malay police are as underpaid and susceptible to financial blandishments as police anywhere. They will not be impressed with any story you might tell them. It will just cost my firm a little more every month."

Cornered again, and my mind was blank. I sighed.

"How do I get T back?"

"You know, Mr. Arnett. You are the man who entered the forest and emerged scarred. Something happened to you. You are associated with five deaths in a matter of months, deaths that have no logical explanation that we can discover. We want to know how you came by this talent of yours, and, of course, we want to acquire one like it for ourselves. Failing that, we want to borrow your skills from time to time, with an appropriately high level of remuneration."

Stalling for time, I waved at the waiter and ordered another Kingfisher.

"Is that all? Why didn't you just say so? It's very simple. I was hit by some type of blow dart. When I awoke from whatever poison was in the dart, I had this tattoo. I think—I can't prove it—I was stung by a spider of some kind that lives in black orchids. If you like, I would be happy to shoot you in the face with a blow gun."

"You, of all people, must know there is no such thing as a black orchid," he said.

"You're right. And what you suggest of me is also impossible. So, there we are."

While he thought, the waiter returned with my beer.

"You *can* kill without touching people?" It was the first sign of doubt he had shown.

"Shall I demonstrate?" I said.

"That won't be necessary. Why are you here in Borneo again?"

"Same reason as last time. I'm trying to get rid of what you want to acquire. If I knew of a way to make it happen, I'd give it to you right now, free."

He watched me pour beer into my glass and came to some kind of decision.

"Our proposition is quite simple," he said. "We accompany you into the interior. You introduce us to everyone you know or meet. You make no attempts to do us harm. For our part, we will pay all expenses. We will protect you from any hazards we encounter. We will not interfere in any way with your business. When we return safely here to Tenom, we will release Mr. Kingston and we will provide you with financial compensation for your time at the premium rates you charge your most significant client."

He definitely knew about my patron, Sheikh Ibrahim bin Abdullah bin Rashad Al Ain, one of Abu Dhabi's power brokers.

"Well, what if just having you along interferes with my business?" I said.

I was trading now. I thought Amanda would be proud of me.

"We don't see it that way."

"What if I do?"

"We have Mr. Kingston. He is quite comfortable now. It does not have to continue that way," Lee said. "And, of course, we know where Mrs. Campion lives."

That was all it took. He wasn't expecting what happened next; neither was I.

I reached across the table, knocking my beer to the floor, and grabbed Mr. Lee by the shirt. With my right hand I snatched the Webley from my bag. I don't think I intended for it to go off. I just wanted him to know that I had it and was prepared to use it.

The explosion shocked us both. I released Lee's shirt and he plopped back onto his chair, then toppled to the ground, holding his knee and screaming in pain. Blood flowed freely between his fingers. I slipped the Webley back into the shoulder bag.

The waiter raced out of the shop, a semiautomatic pistol in his hand. He surveyed the scene. Lee was writhing in pain, holding what remained of his left knee, blood pulsing out with every heartbeat; I was standing over him, a shocked look on my face.

"What did you do?" he said, leveling the gun at me.

CHAPTER 15
POKER

ARROGANCE MAKES PEOPLE careless.

Lee bet correctly that he could temporarily disable my use of Empaya Iba, the spider demon, by grabbing T and rigging it so that any attempt to use Iba's lethal power to free him would kill T as well as the kidnappers. But he did not factor in my irrationality over Amanda.

I had lost my wife, Sarah, to cancer. After a long period of loneliness, too frequently drowned in alcohol, I had met Amanda and then briefly lost her as well. I would not tolerate even the slightest threat against her. I had warned him; now it was too late.

The waiter and I looked around, spotting one witness after another on the street. A taxi, one of a handful in Tenom, screeched up to the restaurant. The driver jumped out, carrying a pistol as well. Apparently, there was more of the Wild West in Tenom than I had thought.

I reached for the Webley again.

The waiter grabbed my left hand and pulled me toward him.

"Jimmy sent us. We have to get him out of here," he said, glancing down at Lee.

He said something in Malay to the taxi driver, who flung open the rear door of his car.

The waiter disappeared for half an instant and returned clutching a handful of white towels. He wrapped one around Mr. Lee's bleeding leg and together with the driver bundled him into the back seat of the taxi. Lee screamed in pain.

The driver yelled "In!" as he raced around the car.

I didn't need a second invitation. My leg was still on the pavement as the car started to move.

"What happened back there?" the waiter said as he wrapped more towels around Lee's leg.

"He made one too many threats," I said.

The driver piloted the car through what traffic Tenom presented, quickly but without drama, giving no hint we were fleeing the scene of a crime.

"Where are we going?" I said.

"Doctor," the driver responded.

"Will he report us to the police?"

"No," the driver said, "she's one of ours."

"Go a little faster," the waiter said from the back seat. "He's losing a lot of blood. You really did a number on him."

"I don't care if he dies," I said savagely. "I just want a couple pieces of information from him."

"First we stop the bleeding. Then you can interrogate him all you want."

That gave me an idea.

"No," I said. "Lee, can you hear me?"

Lee turned his head toward me as I hung over the back of my seat. "Lee. Answer me."

"You shot me." His voice was weak, the smooth poker player's voice suddenly gone.

"And I'm going to shoot you again if you don't answer one question," I said, reaching for the shoulder bag that held the Webley.

The driver shot me a glance.

"You can't do that," the waiter said.

I ignored them both.

"Lee, you know my reputation. You said it yourself. Five guys. I've killed five guys. It's not a novelty any more. I've come to grips with it. You answer me, or I swear I'll blow your other knee off. And if you still don't answer me, I'll shoot you in the groin. That might kill you, but it might not. You think about it real quick, Lee. One question."

I saw suspicion and fear in his eyes and knew that I would win this hand. I played it out any way. I slowly cocked the Webley and used it to nudge the waiter back away from Lee. As he released the pressure on the towels, they reddened more quickly.

"One question, Lee. One chance. Do you understand?" I said.

His eyes were wild with panic; he nodded.

"Where is T?"

He could not talk fast enough. The waiter had to slow him down to catch all the details.

I turned in my seat and faced the front of the taxi.

The driver whispered at me.

"Nice bluff."

I uncocked the Webley and slowly turned toward him.

"I don't play poker," I said. "No poker face. I don't know how to bluff."

⌀

We arrived at the doctor's home a few moments later. Lee was quiet, and his bladder had emptied. Jimmy's team would have to find a new taxi.

The driver parked in the rear of a small, three-story building surrounded by seven-foot-high walls lined with broken glass, a typical Asian compound. He rushed through a gate in the back wall and returned in a moment with a handsome Indian woman in her forties carrying a medical bag. She looked over the waiter's shoulder as he held bloody towels against Lee's leg, then she ran to the other side, opened her bag and pulled out a tourniquet and syringe. She lashed the tourniquet around the shattered leg at midthigh. She pulled it so tight I thought it would slice through his leg. That was all right with me; I was just surprised the doc felt the same way I did. Then she jabbed the syringe into his neck and backed out of the taxi. Lee relaxed completely, either dead or knocked out by some fast-acting painkiller.

The waiter opened his door and stepped out. He looked like the victim of a massacre, bloody from head to foot. The doctor and driver, also stained with Lee's blood, joined him and spoke softly and quickly in Malay. Their plan of action decided, the doctor entered the compound.

"We have to get rid of this blood before we can do anything else," the waiter said. "Doctor Shakti is bringing a blanket that we can use to carry him into her house. We'll leave him here for now. She doesn't know if he'll make it. Too much blood loss, and she doesn't have access to more, not without taking him to the hospital."

"All right," I said. "We need to grab his cell phone, wallet, and passport. Anything that might have information about who he works for."

"You don't know?" the driver said.

"Know what?"

"Who he works for. He's the head guy for XiZi Limited, one of the largest Chinese conglomerates in Singapore. He ran the forest clearcutting for your sheikh. We assumed you knew that."

"No," I said. "No, I didn't know that. That explains a lot. But it doesn't matter. We need to get T before they figure out Mr. Lee is not coming back."

CHAPTER 16
BLUFF

OVER THE PHONE, Jimmy didn't sound nearly as upset as I had expected. Apparently, the Australians didn't like Lee any more than I did, but they had had no reason to shoot him.

"Why'd you do it?" Jimmy asked me after the waiter briefed him.

"He threatened Amanda," I said.

"Foolish man. How could they have known so much about you and understood so little?"

"I know how we're going to get T out," I said, focusing on the task at hand.

"How?"

"I'll tell you about it when I see you next. When will that be?"

"Soon. We'll come tonight. I'll arrange a military flight into Brunei. We'll drive from there."

"We who?"

Jimmy hesitated.

"Amanda will be with me. She arrived in Perth a few hours ago."

"Can't you leave her in Australia?"

"You want to tell her not to come."

"No, but Borneo forest is no place for her, especially after all that's happened in the last few days," I said. "So, are your guys with me on this?"

"Yes. Try not to get them killed. The paperwork would be enormous. I'm still filling out forms from Johnnie's death, and that's been a year," Jimmy said.

"I'll do my best, but I'm taking the Webley."

᪥

We drove past the kidnapper's place in another of Tenom's diminishing supply of taxicabs. It was a compound like Dr. Shakti's and only two blocks from the Perkasa Hotel. If I had taken a side street into town, I'd have walked right past it. They had been either incredibly brazen or stupid in snatching T and bringing him back to this place.

The cab driver, whose name I learned was Adi Putra, parked on the opposite side of street and up a few houses. Ujang, the waiter, skittered around the back.

They were an ironic pair, an Asian Mutt and Jeff. Adi Putra, a Malay whose name meant "first son," was in fact the only son and youngest child in a family of nine. His older sisters had fed him into stockiness. Ujang, a Malay with an Indian mother, was called "the bachelor;" he had just celebrated his fifth wedding anniversary and the birth of his fifth child.

Irony aside, they seemed to know what they were doing and were comfortable doing it.

My plan was simple: I was going to walk up to the front door and demand that they return T.

Lights from the neighboring compounds guided my steps from the car to the locked metal gate embedded in the cinder block wall of their compound. I was careful to step over the open sewer that ran in front of the place. I pounded on the gate.

"Open up," I yelled. "It's Sebastian Arnett."

The lights in the house went out. I was relieved. That meant Lee had told the truth and T was probably inside. I might die in the next few minutes but it would not be from the embarrassment of assaulting some innocent Malay's peaceful home.

"Come on. Open up," I yelled again.

I heard a door in the house open and close. Gravel plinked against the wall.

"What do you want?" A disembodied voice spoke with a Chinese accent from the opposite side of the gate.

"I want my friend. I have your boss, Lee. We're going to do a trade. Now open up."

The voice considered its options.

"You wait."

In a few moments, the bar locking the gate slid open. A beefy hand reached through the opening, grabbed my shirt and pulled me inside. I felt metal against the side of my head and assumed it was a gun. So far, so good. I was inside.

A second set of hands grabbed the back of my shirt. They marched me across the gravel drive and up wooden steps to a veranda. They shoved me through an open door, and lights blazed on. I was blinded as someone pulled the bag off my shoulder and dropped it on the floor. The Webley clunked loudly. Someone kicked the bag away.

As my eyes began to focus, I could make out two Chinese men, somewhere in their thirties or forties. One, a weaselly looking guy, aimed a semiautomatic pistol at my chest; the other, as thin as Ujang and wearing wire-rimmed glasses, stood staring at me, some type of device taped to his hand. I assumed this was the bomb trigger. Behind me, I felt someone as big as a house leaning into me and breathing nasty fish odors. I didn't see T in the main room, but the house had plenty of other places where he could be held.

"Who's in charge?" I said, carrying on my bluff.

"What are you doing here?" It was the bomb trigger speaking.

An international crew with a lot of English speakers, I thought. These guys are—well, fluent in English, if nothing else.

"Are you in charge?"

"Tell me why you are here," he said again.

"I'm here to get my friend. You have him, and I want him."

These guys lacked the aplomb their boss had. They knew who I was and were openly shocked. They might be too stupid to deal, and that worried me. I had not considered that possibility.

"Well?" I said.

The triggerman turned and headed down a hallway toward the rear of the house. The rest of us stood quite still.

Wow, I thought. This might actually work.

CHAPTER 17
NEGOTIATIONS

A MINUTE PASSED, THEN another. Five minutes. Ten minutes.

"Anybody got the time?" I asked. "I have friends I have to meet."

I shifted from one leg to another, and the Chinese wall holding me up by my shirt tightened his grip and the arms of my shirt dug into my flesh. I began to hope that Adi Putra and Ujang had worked up a secret backup plan with Jimmy.

The floor suddenly vibrated, and all three of us jumped. The man pointing the gun put it against my forehead, and the big guy behind me pulled my shirt so tight I thought the buttons would pop.

The floor rattled again.

I waved a hand at my shoulder bag on the floor.

"My bag," I said. "The phone in my bag."

The man with the gun eased over to the bag, his eyes never leaving mine. He squatted, pulled at the fringe on the bottom of the bag and turned the whole thing upside down. Lee's cell phone and my Webley clattered to the floor.

The gunman looked at the Webley, then up at me. He kicked it aside. The cell phone vibrated a third time.

"Answer it," I said.

He picked it up, thumbed it on and held it to his ear and spoke.

"Ni hao."

Hello.

A squawk screeched on the other end; a door at the rear of the house flew open. I thought Ujang would burst in blazing away. Instead, a lovely young Chinese woman in a figure-hugging blue pantsuit stormed into the room. It was the girl from the Indian Pacific. The thin man with the wire-rimmed glasses followed her.

She addressed the gunman in Chinese, and he handed over the cell phone like it was on fire. She played with the phone for a moment, then looked up at me.

I had recovered enough from the panic of the last few minutes to go on the offensive again.

"Are you in charge here?"

She took in her three male companions.

"I am," she said.

"My name is Sebastian Arnett, but you probably know that. You kidnapped my friend. I want him back, and I want him now."

She considered me a moment.

"Mr. Lee?" she said.

"He's with a doctor."

"Why is he with a doctor?"

"I shot him," I said.

She smirked.

"You have some proof?"

"That's his cell phone," I said.

"He could have misplaced it."

"Not likely," I said. "Check the photo gallery."

She gave me a look, then tapped at the phone with her long fingernails. When she gasped, I knew she had seen the first photo, one I had taken of Lee's bloody face before Dr. Shakti cleaned him up. She kept clicking so I knew she was seeing the full-body photo of Lee, his knee swathed in bloody towels.

Her concentration on the photos allowed me to focus on her. She had an enigmatic quality about her, like a chameleon, seeming to be a schoolgirl one moment and a—I don't know what, but older, smarter, not at all innocent and quite likely not friendly.

"Ming"—she made him sound like a tiny yap dog, not a thug—"says you did this to Mr. Lee."

"He made a threat he shouldn't have," I said.

"What do you propose?"

"You give me T. He and I walk out of here and never see you again. Pretty simple."

"And Mr. Lee?"

"He's not going to walk anywhere for a very long time, if ever. I'll deliver him to the hospital."

"You expect us to trust you."

"Here's how I see it. Lee screwed up. His career with XiZi is over. That gives you a chance to make a real big career move. You clean up the mess here without a lot more fuss and you probably get a bonus and a promotion. You screw up like Lee, and your career is toast. These three don't matter. Who else are you going to trust? Remember, you started this."

"You seem to think you have leverage. I could call the local police and have you arrested. You have already admitted shooting Mr. Lee, and you have provided the evidence."

She smirked, which did not fit the schoolgirl persona.

I get so irrational so quickly. It's why I could never be in business. I take the game personally.

"Look, kiddo. Did Lee tell you anything at all about me? About why he wanted me?"

She needs to work on her poker face. She's good, but not as good as Lee. She knew about Empaya Iba and understood what it could do.

"How about we have a race, okay? You call the corrupt cops

you have in your pocket. I call my friend in here," I said, thumping my chest, "and I destroy every living creature in this house. Don't threaten me. That's how your boss ended up a cripple."

"I am sure we won't let you get away with this," she said, backing down.

"Your boss–I assume he's not your uncle–gave me the name of a couple members of the XiZi management committee. That's all I need to kill them. Just their names. I don't need to know them, to see their faces, to see them in person. I can kill them all with little more than a thought," I said.

For a guy who never makes bets, I was placing one helluva bet with nothing in my hand.

"We will not be met with more shooting?" She meant it as a statement, but it came out a question.

"I only have one gun, and Ming has it," I said, nodding at the triggerman. "I'm not sticking around here. I get T. You do what you want. You come after me, I kill you. Period."

"You take your friend. You figure out how to disconnect the explosives."

The woman, the human wall and Ming stormed out the back door, leaving me with Ming and his bomb trigger finger.

I did not think for a moment that this was the last I would see of her and her companions. From now on, I would just assume they were watching me. I could make it harder by heading upriver, but I knew I couldn't ditch them.

The guy with the wire-rims led me to another room where T was taped to a chair, a strip of gray duct tape across his mouth and a Dyak shoulder bag, apparently containing explosives, hanging around his neck.

For a few tense moments, Mr. Eyeglasses unwrapped the tape holding his thumb to the trigger. Then I slowly slid his thumb away and replaced it with mine. As soon as he was free of the device, he hotfooted it out the back door.

With the last of the kidnappers gone, Ujang and Adi Putra slipped into the room.

"Are they gone?" I asked.

"Yeah. Did you want us to follow them?"

"No, let's cut T loose and get out of here," I said.

"What about these?" Ujang said, toeing the explosives.

"Do you know how to disconnect the trigger?" I asked.

"Not really, no."

The four of us stood and looked at one another, my thumb still pressing the trigger.

"Adi, can you take T over to Dr. Shakti's for a quick check-up and bring Lee back?"

"Sure. T, nice to meet you all in one piece. I'm Adi Putra."

They shook hands. T turned to me.

"Thanks," he said. "You know, I never doubted that you would get me out of this, but this isn't quite the way I expected."

"Yeah, me either. Go. Ujang and I have to figure out how to disconnect me from this contraption."

Eventually, and in retrospect this seems really stupid, Ujang and I decided to tape the trigger down and leave the shoulder bag with Lee. We left the unconscious Lee lying on the floor near the bag and scurried up the hill to the Perkasa Hotel.

Ujang reported to Jimmy, who contacted the Tenom police. Not long afterward, Ujang and I heard a siren—unusual in all my months working here—and peered out the hotel window with the other bar patrons wondering what was going on. After a while, when nothing blew up, we packed up and left to pick up T at Dr. Shakti's.

It seemed we were out of the woods, at least for now. Then Mike Owens's security people caught up with us.

CHAPTER 18
MIKE'S PEOPLE

THE KNOCK ON the door was soft, hesitant. I figured Ujang or Adi Putra was trying not to waken any other guests.

T started to get up from my bed, where he'd been watching me pack, but I waved him down.

"I'll get it. It's probably one of the guys come to pick us up."

I turned the knob, and the door flew open, shoving me hard against the wall. A gun pressed against my forehead nailed me to the wall.

A tall, sunburned, and deadly serious Anglo held the weapon, his stare gluing T to the bed. T slowly raised his arms, and the intruder swung the door shut with his foot.

The good news: He clearly wasn't Chinese. The bad news: All the rest of it was bad. He had a gun and appeared to know how to use it. He had gotten past Ujang and Adi Putra. We were in more hot water, just a different pot.

"Mr. Arnett?" he said.

I nodded.

"Jeez, you are such a pain in the ass," he said. "Don't you know better than to open a door without knowing who's on the other side?"

"I thought I knew."

"Don't think. Know."

He dug into a pants pocket, pulled out a laminated photo that looked more than a little like my passport. He held it to my face.

"Sir, my name is Lieutenant Dylan Wilson. General Owens sends his regards and says if you ever try that crap again, I am to shoot you dead."

Lieutenant Wilson did not crack a smile as he spoke.

"Hi to Mike next time you talk to him, lieutenant," I said.

A second knock sounded at the door.

I looked at the lieutenant for permission to answer the knock. He nodded.

"It's okay. He's with me."

I opened the door, and Amanda flew into my arms, planting one long kiss on my lips.

"Thank God you're safe! I am so angry with you," she said.

"Hi. I missed you, too."

"You know exactly what I mean. You tried to avoid me."

"I didn't want you to get involved in anything bad that might happen," I said.

"Like this?"

"Um, yeah, pretty much."

"May we come in?"

Jimmy followed Amanda inside, leading a parade into my hotel room: Ujang and Adi Putra, and another American, also holding a black pistol.

"I think we are all here," Jimmy said. "Lieutenant, can we dispense with the firearms? We are on the same side."

"So long as Mr. Arnett agrees not to try to evade us, we will be friendly," he said. "But my orders stand, sir."

He addressed his remarks to me.

I took in the crowd and thought, *This is exactly what I wanted to avoid.*

"Any more out in the hall?" I asked.

"I think we're going to keep that kind of information to ourselves," the lieutenant said.

I shrugged.

"Jimmy, can we accommodate two more?" I asked.

"I don't believe we have a choice."

❧

At 5:30 the next morning, we were motoring upriver in two boats, heading for what could be a showdown between an old Dyak woman and me.

Despite not getting any sleep, everyone was determined to head off any possible encounter with the police or T's Chinese kidnappers. Neither Jimmy nor I thought the XiZi people would complain, given the givens, but we were taking no chances. Mike Owens' people—Lieutenant Wilson and Sergeant Mick Alexander—were content to follow the Aussie's lead as long as one of them could stay within arm's length of me. They didn't ask how I felt about it.

Jimmy figured we would head straight for the new village, now more than a year old, where an old Dyak woman had given me the black orchid. He wanted us to rest there overnight and plan our next steps.

Amanda sagged against me. She looked great as always, decked out in pressed khaki slacks and a safari jacket—chic by any standards but dressed down from her usual high style. Her exhaustion showed through the glamour.

T had been jumpy since the duel in the desert, but after his kidnapping he displayed his nerves even more. The skin around his mouth and along his jawbones glowed red like a sunburn, a reaction to having several layers of duct tape ripped off his face. He kept rubbing it, which only made it redder.

I didn't know what the overweight Adi Putra and underweight Ujang had been doing before I met them, but they had not stopped working all night and now I caught them yawning.

I was in a drug-induced la-la land, the only state in which I could get anywhere near water without panicking.

Only Jimmy and Mike's people showed any energy.

Adi Putra, Sergeant Alexander, Jimmy, and a female interpreter who joined us on the riverbank in Tenom led the way in the first boat. Ujang, who apparently knew his way around motors and boats, piloted the second boat carrying Amanda, T, and me. And, of course, Lieutenant Wilson.

As we motored against the current flowing down from the mountains ahead of us, I noticed a steady stream of boat traffic. A year earlier, Jimmy's spy colleague Johnnie Walker and I had begun our explorations of the interior; we saw fewer than five other boats during a long day on the river. This trip, we saw that many in the first hour. Civilization was spreading its tentacles farther and farther inland. I could guess how the Dyaks felt about that.

With my eyes glued on the horizon, the better to ignore the water all around me, my mind wandered. Glimpses of the Chinese party on the Indian Pacific floated to the surface, and I tried to count the partiers. I mourned that nameless young aboriginal boy who got caught in the battle between Empaya Iba and Bunjil. I imagined that blind old aboriginal just wandering out of the hospital in Kalgoorlie and down some thoroughfare that would take him back to the desert, stopping every now and then to sniff his surroundings.

I half hoped that Lee had died; if he hadn't, I hoped his leg would hurt him forever. I wondered at my anger with Lee, a man whom I had to admit had not really harmed me. Amanda shifted against me, and I remembered why I had gotten so angry. But what was I doing, allowing her to come into a tropical forest that housed poisonous snakes and spiders, insects, and worms that find their way inside a human body, and a dangerous old Dyak woman who hands out black orchids cursed with death?

EMPAYA IBA SPEAKS

Children of the midnight flower,
Your Abah comes.
Joyous is he
In the thought of his return.

Swifter would I run to you,
But for the servant who bears my mark.
This way he goes, and that,
Forgetful of his master.

Patience is my name,
But I long too much
To be among again
The people of the Black Orchid.

Soon, soon you will see your Abah.
So say I, Empaya Iba, spirit of the Black Orchid People,
Guardian of the Mother Soil, giver of the Long Sleep,
Seer of the Many Eyes, mage of the Many Legs.

CHAPTER 19
NEW VILLAGE

WE PLOWED OUR inflatable Zodiacs into the mud banks at what we called the New Village in midafternoon. Two other boats already lay against the river bank, their occupants dickering with the villagers over some trade that likely involved dead monkeys, a favorite source of protein in these parts.

The village had grown to eight small houses. Corrugated tin roofs had replaced thatch on all but one. This tribe of Ma'anyan Dyak lived in individual family dwellings, not in a single longhouse like most Dyaks. I immediately noticed that two paths on the inland side of the village led into the interior. The first time I had visited this place, I had searched in vain for a way in and out of the village by land.

The headman extracted himself from some trade negotiation and stepped to the river to greet Jimmy like an old friend. They gabbed while the rest of us climbed out of the boats and stretched stiff backs and legs. As I helped Amanda up the incline of the riverbank, my fingers tingled just holding her hand. Our eyes met, and she smiled.

"Don't worry about me, Sebastian," she said. "I'm just tired. I'll be my old pushy self after a good night's rest."

I grinned like a schoolboy. She was warm, wonderful, and a mind reader. How had I lucked out?

"Where will we sleep? I think I could turn in right now," she said.

"The guys will set up a tent and mosquito net for you. Sleep in your clothes, just in case," I said.

"In case of what?" she asked.

"Just in case. You don't want to rush out of your tent in all your glory."

"I'll bet you wouldn't mind that," she said.

"Actually, I would. I don't like to share."

That seemed to please her, and I sidled off to find Adi Putra and get a tent going.

Amanda turned in as the shadows deepened around us. Sergeant Alexander settled outside her tent. The rest of us gathered around several fires to exchange some of our canned goods with the villagers and share their monkey meat and rice. The other boats were long gone. Jimmy and the interpreter had pried what little information they could from their owners. It wasn't that they were reluctant to talk; they just didn't know much.

Over our shared meal, the headman and several others filled in some details. A group of Dyaks from downriver had settled about a half-day farther up river, probably about midway between this village and the clearing where Johnnie Walker and I had been ambushed. After a few months, however, the village had died out, and the forest was quickly reclaiming the clearing.

"Why did they give up on the place?" I asked, yawning.

"People got sick and died," the headman said.

"All of them?" I asked.

"No. About half of them. The young and the very old, they lived and went away."

"What did the others die of?"

"Who knows?" he said, with the look of someone who knows but does not want to say.

Eve, our Tagal Murut interpreter, refused to let him off so easily and peppered him with questions. Eve belonged to one of the many Dyak tribes, similar to the one we thought the old black orchid woman belonged to. Christian missionaries had converted her parents (but not her headhunting uncles) and brought them to Tenom to help spread the good news of the Bible. She worked at one of the half-dozen missions there and came highly recommended as someone who knew half a dozen Dyak languages and dialects. After watching her for a while, I wondered if the person who recommended her to Firash, our fixer, had just wanted to get rid of her. Short and stocky with rich brown skin and long black hair, she was like a terrier with a bone; she just would not let go. She reminded me of T, who I noticed spent a lot of time watching her.

Under Eve's unrelenting questioning, the headman yielded more and more information. A group of Tagal Murut from downriver had arrived not long after the XiZi clearcutting operation ordered by my patron, the sheikh. They were fleeing a mining operation that was polluting the river and killing the fish. They hacked an opening in the forest along the river and managed to get four houses built. Then they started to die. What was unusual was that the first to go were the adults, not the children and the old.

Strong, healthy men and women simply failed to wake up in the morning. What was strange was the look of terror on their dead faces. Their eyes bugged out, but their corpses showed no signs of violence. It was like they were strangled from the inside. The superstitious Dyak of New Village believed a demon had cursed them.

Jimmy and I exchanged glances when we heard that.

Within two weeks, all of the villagers between the ages of 14 and 50 had died. The handful of survivors, the elderly and young children, floated downstream to New Village. The headman sent two of his villagers with them back to their original home to live with neighbors. They were bad luck, and he hurried to be rid of them.

Jimmy and I stayed up a while after the villagers and the others in our party bedded down. We huddled over a dying fire.

"That sounds like the work of your Empaya Iba demon," Jimmy said.

"It does, doesn't it?"

"Did you… ?" He left the question unfinished.

I shrugged.

"Not that I'm aware of," I said. "It doesn't fit the pattern. Whenever I wreak havoc, there is rage or anger involved, even when I don't know whom I'm angry with. I definitely was pissed with the people who ambushed me. I might be responsible in some way for their disappearance, but you told me they had died of diseases the Chinese loggers introduced."

"That's the story we got," Jimmy said.

"Well, whatever. Maybe I was involved somehow with them, but these Tagal Murut who tried to set up another new village, they came after my second trip. I didn't even know they existed, much less that they were building a village."

"It's almost like there's more than one Empaya Iba," Jimmy said. "Or, he has more than one you."

"Is that possible?"

"Theoretically, you're not possible, and yet I never want to get you mad at me, Yank. But how else do you explain it?"

We retired with similar thoughts nagging us: Could there be two Empaya Ibas, or was there someone out there with a tattoo covering half his face, just like mine? Or did Iba use me to kill without my even knowing it?

CHAPTER 20
FOREBODING

THE NEXT MORNING Amanda sat close to me, clutching my arm with both hands while the others broke camp and packed the boats.

"Sebastian," she said, "I have a very bad feeling."

"Are you all right? Have you caught a bug already? Diarrhea? What?" I asked.

She gave me one of her 'You missed the point' looks.

"Physically, I am fine. Well rested. Energized. Not really wild about leftover monkey for breakfast," she said.

"Tastes like chicken," I said.

"Don't joke," she said. "I have a bad feeling about today, about the trip, about dealing with Empaya Iba."

"I'm not wild about it either, but I've got to do something. I don't know what I'm becoming, but I'm not the same person I was a year ago. If there's even a hope of getting rid of this demon, I have to try it. I mean, can you imagine what our lives would be like in five years if I'm still going off willy-nilly killing people who make me mad?"

"You're thinking about us being together in five years?" she asked.

Oh, God, I thought.

"Yes. Aren't you?"

"Yes," she said. "I just wasn't sure about you."

"I'm in. Amanda. I'm in for all time."

"All right," she said. "Me, too."

"Do you want to turn back? We could send you and T back with Adi Putra and one of Mike's people. T's not looking so great."

"I want to go back, but I don't know if I should, or even could. I don't want to leave you."

She questioned me with her eyes.

"Do you think it's possible to feel your own death before it happens?" she asked.

I stared at her.

"I don't know. You hear about men going into combat during wartime and having an intuition that they will die, but I gather a lot of them survive. It's just a feeling, I guess. That doesn't make it happen."

I wasn't certain that was true, but Amanda's question made me uneasy. I wondered if I should insist that she and T go back to Tenom. But what if her feeling of impending death required her to turn back? What if the danger didn't lie ahead, but behind us? The XiZi Chinese were back there and knew about her. Maybe they would ignore my warnings. And even the river was dangerous. To me, given my fear of water, it seemed more dangerous than the Chinese. Couldn't anything be simple anymore?

"You've traveled dangerous places before, including where we're headed today," Amanda said. "Did you ever have that feeling?"

"No, I never did. Not even here. I never felt anything except abject terror, like sitting in an overflowing bath tub."

She laughed. "Every human fear comes down to water for you, doesn't it?"

"Damned right. You escape drowning a couple times, starting at a very young age, and it imprints on you the idea that water is not a good thing."

"Even in a glass?"

"Maybe a very small glass, but gin is always better. Nobody has ever literally drowned in gin," I said.

Lost in our own thoughts, neither Amanda nor I heard Jimmy and Lieutenant Wilson approach.

"Can I interrupt you two?" Jimmy said.

Amanda gave him one of her brilliant smiles.

"What's up?" I said. "Time to go?"

"Not yet. We're going to break out some ration pack components and make some rice. I hope chili and rice will be all right with you," he said, addressing Amanda.

"I will eat whatever everyone else does, although I might share my portion of monkey," she said.

"I'm with you on that. I'm not wild about chicken myself," he said and laughed.

"Amanda has a bad feeling about things," I said.

Jimmy gave her a look.

"Me, too. Never had it like this before, not even when we came looking for you and Johnnie or when we followed you during your suicide mission. It's almost physical. Ujang and Eve mentioned it as well."

"What do we do?" I asked.

"My team is with you. We're not letting you out of our sight."

He nodded to Wilson.

"I suspect he would say the same. We both have the same mission. Other than that, there's nothing to compel me to go farther upriver."

"So, you all think we're going to die?" I said.

"I don't know. Just a bad sense of doom."

"Yes," said Amanda. "That's it. I feel doom."

"Lieutenant?" I said.

"I am not leaving your side, sir. There are no other considerations," Wilson said. "If Mrs. Campion wishes to stay here or return to Tenom, Sergeant Alexander will accompany her."

I looked from one to the other and made a decision.

"How about Adi, the lieutenant, and I continue? The rest of you stay here."

"Adi doesn't speak any of the Dyak languages," Jimmy said.

"Well, then, if we find the woman, we'll bring her back."

"What makes you think she would come?" Jimmy asked.

"Same thing that makes me feel I need to talk to her and think we'll find her—nothing," I said. "It's just what I want to have happen."

Jimmy turned to Amanda.

"You okay with that?"

She didn't say a word, just nodded reluctantly.

"All right. I'll check it out with the boys."

∽

Adi Putra acquiesced reluctantly. T horned in and insisted on coming.

The trip up and back would take two days. Jimmy and I figured we'd wait three days for the old Dyak woman. We spent almost an hour unpacking the boats and rearranging the supplies so we had a five-day allotment of food and clean water.

The four of us who were going to continue upriver wore guns.

Jimmy told me before we left that he and Ujang would break out weapons as well; Sergeant Alexander wore his pistol openly. One of the men would stand guard 24-7.

Adi Putra carried a satellite radio that would supposedly connect with the outside world from anywhere on planet Earth. Jimmy and I knew of at least one place where that was not so—where I first encountered the old Dyak woman, the black orchid, Empaya Iba—but neither of us mentioned it to the others. Satellites had passed over the area trying to map it, but the images never quite showed the detail they were able to capture elsewhere. It was all part of the mystery of Empaya Iba, but I really didn't like what we had heard so far about deaths that left no marks.

Storm clouds were moving in as we shoved off. We all agreed that we should run the Zodiac's motor wide out as far as possible, with the hope of missing at least part of the storm. Our speed and the river, choppy with rapids and brown with mud, made for a pounding ride. Even with a double dose of tranquilizers in me, panic raised bile in my throat. I closed my eyes, tried to think of Amanda, and kept a two-handed death grip on the rope that wrapped around the sides of our boat.

Rivers in Borneo twist and turn, wrapping back on themselves to fit the contours of the mountains. It's possible to go ten miles by boat and progress less than a mile as the crow flies. Even with my eyes closed, I understood that the storm had probably struck upriver already and was sending more water and debris than usual down its dirty brown course.

The boat bucked like a wild animal, and my hands hurt from my grip on the rope. Thunder clapped nearby. I kept my eyes closed tight and tried to think of anything but water. Then the clouds burst open, and in an instant we were drenched. It always rains in Borneo, and I was accustomed to being wet, but this time the wetness came with a ferocity that I had not experienced before. I opened my eyes and immediately wished I hadn't. I knew I was going to drown.

Waves, honest-to-God white-capped waves, slapped the boat and pushed it side to side. Tree limbs green with leaves littered the choppy water. Darkness fell, despite it still being early morning. The water, the sky, the forest on either side of us took on the same shade of black.

The engine roared, but the boat barely moved forward. I turned to look at the others and could only make out rough shapes. Wilson and T were behind me, sitting side by side. One of them—I assumed it was T—was clutching the side of the boat with both hands. In the rear, the form that had to be Adi Putra jerked from side to side, apparently trying to see ahead.

The bow bucked wildly; I suddenly felt dizzy and lost my breakfast all over myself. The rain washed me clean in no time, but left the taste of bile and fear in my mouth.

Ahead, the river veered sharply to the left. I already felt the current pushing against the boat. Off to our right, the entire forest bent to the ground under the force of the wind. Adi Putra angled us toward that side of the river. The engine's roar stopped, sputtered, then resumed. The bow angled farther to the right. The engine stopped again. The bow whipped around, and we raced downstream broadside.

I was going to die. I knew it. Fury rose in me. Iba was getting revenge, taking me down as I had once tried to destroy it. Why? It didn't make sense. If I died, Iba died. Or that was my theory. But maybe Iba was already dead or had my replacement marked and ready to work.

The boat jolted like it had struck something solid and folded in on itself. Something or someone knocked me into the water as it flew over me. I held tight to the rope and rushed downriver with it. I had no idea where the others were. I could see only water. Tree limbs banged into me, and I tried to shrug them off with my shoulders. My hands kept their death grip on the boat.

I tried to remember the path we had taken. Where was the next bend in the river? If I could stay above water, the current might throw me into the bank. But I could see nothing.

Suddenly the boat stopped dead. Water built up around it; it flipped over, loosening my grip and tossing me alone into the dark water.

My life vest kept me afloat, but with every gasp of air, I took in water. I banged into sharp objects, and tentacles of underwater obstructions grabbed at my legs and arms.

That was it, I realized. Amanda and the others had not foreseen their doom; they had anticipated ours.

CHAPTER 21

DROWNING

THE STORM BROKE all the weather rules.

Rains come quickly in Borneo, but typically pass just as quickly. This storm lingered, and the river water tossed me about, dunking me, spitting me up again. I flailed and sank and rose again. I breathed in water with air and puked it out again and again. *Die. Just let me die*, I begged.

Empaya Iba laughed at me. I don't know how I knew it, but I knew it. This was payback. Months ago, I had stepped into this same river farther upstream trying to destroy Iba. I had been so desperate to end its power over me that I was willing to take my own life. I didn't want to die now. I had things—people—to live for. And Empaya Iba laughed and laughed as the rain poured down and the river tossed me back and forth and tree limbs slapped and grabbed at me.

I fought to stay afloat, to breathe, to live one more instant, but exhaustion wore away my panic-induced resolve. My arms reached only so high, my flailing slowed. My waterlogged boots tugged me deeper. The rain beat down, cascading over my eyes. My throat and nose burned from the muddy water and stomach acid that flowed in and out. Water filled my ears, reducing sounds to the dull roar of the storm. I was losing my senses one by one, my connection with the world, my grasp on reality.

I began to relax, my battle slowing to pathetic splashing. I sensed that Empaya Iba had stopped its laughter and was content just to watch my death.

Amid the chill of the rain and river flood, I felt a flow of warmth on my thigh. My bladder released. One step closer to Iba's final revenge, I thought. Who will take my place? I wondered. Had Iba already chosen? Had someone shown a higher loyalty to the demon when he killed off the Tagal Murut villagers?

Empaya Iba, spider spirit, not the demon of this land, but the spirit of the land. Iba the spider, building his web. The web that holds his creation together. Empaya Iba. Not demon spirit. Just spirit. Empaya, guardian, protector of the land.

What was happening? Why was I thinking this? I was sinking, not just into the river, but into the end, whatever that might be.

The Dyak man with the machete. I saw him before me wearing the mark of the spider. He had shot me with the dart and he had killed Johnnie, Chik, and Sammy. I killed him after I had also been given the mark, the spiderweb tattoo. Did he know that Iba had given up on him? I struggled to recall his attack on me. He raised his machete. He was going to kill me. He... no, he wasn't. He was defending himself. He was trying to keep me—and Iba—away from him.

He had failed Iba. Outsiders had come. They had built the new village. They had begun cutting the forest. Johnnie, Chik, and Sammy were hacking a clearing in the forest. Only I had not been attacking it. Only I had survived. Empaya Iba had told machete man to kill the outsiders who cut the forest. I had not carried a machete. I was looking for the black orchid. The orchid that does not exist.

Machete man had failed Empaya Iba. Joe had told me that. Now I understood how he had failed. I understood, but too late.

The job of protecting the land had passed to me. I had accepted the black orchid. I had been given the tattoo.

But I had left the land, and the sheikh had sent in a crew to find the village, looking for the black orchid. The only way to do that was to clear-cut. When the crew reached the village, they found no orchids, no people, just an empty village. But their very presence in the village was enough to spread civilization's diseases, and some of Iba's people had died.

Then the Chinese loggers had died. One by one. Iba was killing them, extracting his revenge for what they had done to the land.

The Tagal Muruts who had built the newer village—they had invaded Iba's land. He had killed the adults responsible.

Empaya had drawn a line. Civilization could come to the new village we had discovered a year ago, but no farther.

That was it. A boundary. And I was trying to cross it.

❧

I threw up again. Mud and acid were all I could taste. I was terribly thirsty. All that water, and I was thirsty. Snot poured out of my nose and down my face, only to be washed away by a wave. Something sharp sawed my face. I knew I was bleeding. My feet were tangled in something. Weeds. Whatever coats the bottoms of rivers in Borneo. So far, at least, the native crocodiles had left me alone; maybe they were struggling against the storm too.

Rain pounded down, but the wind had calmed. Time seemed to have stopped. I had been thinking about... what? The day was lighter somehow. The river surged past me, still wild and angry. Wait. The river surged past me. I was bobbing up and down but not moving downstream. I twisted my head this way and that, trying to get my bearings, but my eyes burned from everything that had washed into them.

I blinked and blinked again. I seemed to be stuck in trees that had toppled over the riverbank. Yes. There was an embankment, perhaps ten feet away. I pedaled my legs to free my feet of the snags. I pulled myself, hand over hand, along a fallen tree trunk until I could stand upright with my feet touching the muddy bottom. A few feet away, just beyond arm's reach, the riverbank lay solid and unyielding, shedding water in streams through tree roots and twisted vegetation.

I surveyed my surroundings. The forest had taken a beating. Trees on both sides of the river bent to the ground. The river raced by, carrying greenery, limbs, and entire trees in its chocolate froth. During two years in mainland Southeast Asia and months here in Borneo, I had never seen anything like this storm. I checked my wristwatch, but it had died, the LED display staring blankly back at me. I had no idea what time it was or where I had finally landed.

I called out, making myself cough from the effort. There was no sign of T, Adi Putra, or Lieutenant Wilson. Given Wilson's military training, I figured he, of all of us, would survive. Adi was local, as it were. He too may have survived. But I worried about T. He came from the high desert of Utah. I didn't even know if he could swim. I was the only one wearing a life vest.

The rain slackened even more, becoming a steady drizzle. How far upriver had we gone before the storm struck? It had taken almost a full day to motor upriver to where Johnnie and I had been ambushed. Had we gone even a quarter of the way there today? And how far downriver had I floated? Not knowing what time it was, I could not even guess my distance from the village where we had left Amanda and the others. It could be just around the next river bend.

I had no radio. No water or food. The Webley was still strapped in its shoulder holster under my life jacket. If it still worked, I would be able to fight off up to six crocs, if it came to that. Now that the storm was passing, I feared it might come to that. I was waterlogged, and I was going to stay that way. I was sure that I had picked up a cargo of leeches already. The humidity settled over everything, adding a layer of wetness to an already sodden world.

If I wanted to survive, I would have to find my way back to the village. I knew from personal experience that the forest was too thick to move in. There was nothing I could do but head downriver, holding onto the bank.

At least I assumed I needed to head downriver. What if I had been swept past the village in the storm? I could be wading to my doom, just as Amanda had felt. My doom, not hers.

I tried to climb up the riverbank onto solid land. When I grabbed the earth, fistfuls of mud came away and I dunked myself, filling my mouth with that horrible brown water again. I seized tree roots, but they slipped from my grasp. Underwater tangles grabbed at my feet. I thrashed, grabbing for a limb of the downed tree that had stopped my journey downriver. Its serrated leaves cut at my palms and the backs of my fingers and hands.

I was so close to land, to relative safety, but the river held me back. I was going to drown, not just in sight of land, but within slippery reach of it. I knew it, and I felt the irony of Empaya Iba's silent laughter.

CHAPTER 22

DEEPER

ONE LAST STAND. I would not let the water—and Empaya Iba—take me without one final effort. I tried to stand but the muddy river bottom sloped away from the bank. I submerged myself up to my chin, took a deep breath and bounced up. Something beat me back down.

A voice.

"Stop fighting. Let go. Trust me."

Hah. Trust Empaya Iba? Never.

The current spun me around, grabbed my shirt, and punched me in the jaw. I tried to swing back, but the life jacket that kept me afloat made me swing wide. I could not connect with the demon. It punched me again. I tasted blood along with the mud and bile. Iba punched me again and again. I couldn't see or hear anything. Iba pounded and pulled me.

It was so strong, and I was so weak, wrung by my battle with the water. Finally, my legs gave out and I slowly slipped deeper into the water.

Amanda, I called out. *I love you. I wanted to live. I wanted to be with you. I'm sorry, sorry for everything.*

My mouth went under and I drank in the terrifying dark water. This was the end. Water in my lungs. *Iba, you win.*

"Help me. Help me, Sebastian. Move your legs."

Iba called to me. Was he taunting me? Was this how my recurring nightmare came to an end? Iba awakening to the reality that it would die if I died?

I swallowed again. Gagged. Choked out water through my nose. This was it.

"Sebastian Arnett. Stop it. Stop dunking your head. You'll drown."

Iba screamed and screamed. Yes, I thought. Now you want me to live. But it's too late.

My head went under again—the proverbial third time. My foot touched mud and thrust me forward. The other foot felt firmness, slipped on mud. River bottom. Coughing, spewing water and blood and phlegm. I churned my legs and opened my eyes. Land. The riverbank.

Move, move, move, I told myself. Work, I willed my legs. Don't let Iba win.

I swung my arms, fighting to keep my balance, the water little more than waist-deep. I might make it. Water streamed off me. I hacked and blew water, gasping for air. The water barely reached my knees. There. On land. A small tree. If could reach it. If I could...

My knees bent, and I lunged forward, my arms reaching out, my fingers grasping the thin trunk. My fingers locked on the tree, and I pulled myself toward solid ground. I held tight as I collapsed, coughing, gasping, retching up water. A horrible weight crushed me from behind, pushing me into the soft rain-sodden earth.

"You fool. You almost killed us both."

❧

Someone rolled me over, half in and half out of the water, and pumped water from me until I thought he would break every rib in my chest. I gagged and coughed up liquid. My throat stung with stomach acid and filthy water.

Finally, the pumping stopped. I lay on my stomach, my face on its side in the mud. Only my tattoo showed, and it burned, as it always did when Empaya Iba was present.

"Sebastian, you almost killed us," said my rescuer, panting.

That voice. Familiar. The tone, the attitude.

"T?" I said, the sound barely audible.

"Yeah," he said.

"You're alive! We're alive."

I tried to turn my head toward his voice, but my strength had abandoned me.

"Barely. No thanks to you."

He was close. T was close. He was alive! I was alive, too.

"The others?"

"Don't know," he said, still gasping for breath. "Mike's guy went under when the boat flipped. Adi. Don't know. I never saw him after the boat rolled."

He stopped for a long while. I didn't know if he had fallen asleep or lost consciousness or died.

The river current tugged at me, but I held tight to the slender tree that had saved me. I could have thought, dreamed, whatever, but I never released the thin trunk.

Beside me T rolled, coughed, and spit. Was he as waterlogged as I felt?

"They told us about people like you in lifesaving class," T said. "The panicky fighters. I never met one like you though."

"I don't like water," I said.

"No shit, Sherlock."

"You were a lifeguard?"

"Some people swim in the desert," T said. "My mom made me learn when she still thought my father would adopt me."

"Oh."

What more could I say?

"Thanks. Thanks, T, more than you can imagine. Amanda will…"

I didn't know what Amanda would do. Be grateful, for sure. But I don't think she could care for him any more if he were her own son.

"You suppose Amanda and the others got hit with that storm?" T asked.

"Don't know, not the way this river goes. I wonder how far we are from the village."

"We can't be that far. We've been floating downstream more than an hour."

"Could we have passed it?" I asked.

"I don't think so. Maybe. Yeah, it's possible. That was a helluva storm. With the rain and dark, I couldn't see much of the banks."

"We have to get back there," I said. "Otherwise we're dead."

CHAPTER 23

DARK

T PRODDED ME AWAKE. He stood over me, dripping water on my face as I lay half in and half out of the river.

"Come on. Can you stand?" he said. "We have to get out of the water. It's getting dark. Something might come along and snag one of us, and that would be the end. Stand up."

T grabbed me under one arm and tried to lift me.

"Ahhhh. Oh, God, that hurts. Don't pull. Don't pull. Let me try to push myself up."

T backed off and plopped back onto the embankment.

I attempted to get a purchase with my feet to shove myself higher up the riverbank but I couldn't make my boots grip.

"Take off the vest," T said. "You're pushing dead weight."

"No!"

I twisted away from him and half stood.

"The vest stays on."

I snarled like a wild animal.

"Okay. Okay. Kept the vest on. Let me help you now. Climb over there, to your left. Pull yourself up that tree. I'll give you a push if you start falling backward."

I wobbled as I tried to stand up straight. Dizziness overcame me. I lunged forward, oblivious to the pain in my chest and everything else.

⚮

Darkness surrounded me when I opened my eyes. So dark I wasn't sure my eyes were opened. I was leaning against something rough and hard. Not completely sitting. More like reclining. My feet were still in water.

I heard the wild river, still bucking and tossing its way downstream toward Amanda and Jimmy, Ujang and Eve, and Lieutenant Wilson. Night birds and monkeys screeched above me. The storm had passed completely. Normalcy was returning. Mosquitoes, spiders, other bugs and snakes would be out and about.

I looked around for T but couldn't see him in the dark.

"T, are you there?"

No answer.

A jagged pain ripped through my throat as I tried to raise my voice.

"T, where are you?"

"I'm here, Sebastian," he said. "Above your head, farther inland. I moved you as far as I could. You're heavy, and I'm feeling a little beat up."

"Are you hurt? I never thought to ask."

"Cuts. Lots of bruises. I think I have a gash above my bad eye. The patch is gone. You?"

"Same. Ribs hurt like hell," I said.

"That's from me trying to pump the water out of you. Maybe I broke some ribs," T said.

"I don't know if I'll be able to move in the morning. Any sign of the other two?"

"No. I haven't heard anything, and it's been too dark to see anything since you blacked out."

We fell silent, exhausted by our brief conversation and lost in our own thoughts.

"You think Iba had anything to do with this?" T asked after a while.

"Why? Do you?"

"I don't know," T said. "It's just why we're here. I was wondering, that's all."

"I think it was just a bad storm. I suspect Borneo gets them pretty often. We just got caught in it," I said, despite a nagging thought that I had forgotten something important.

"I don't suppose you have any supplies hidden away in your vest."

"I have my pistol. What about you?"

"Pocket knife and a wad of soggy Malaysian money," T said.

"Plenty of fresh water pooled in the leaves," I said, "and at least it's warm out."

"What do you suppose it means that I'm feeling a little chilled?" T asked.

"Well, you're wet. And the adrenaline could be winding down. I suppose you could be in shock, but there's nothing we can do about it," I said.

"That's about what I thought.... So, I guess we just chill out until daylight."

"That's pretty much it. T?"

"Yeah?"

"Thanks. I mean really thanks."

He didn't respond.

I loosened the clasps on my life vest; I wanted to take it off, but every time I moved one of my arms, my ribs screamed in agony. I checked the Webley to make sure it came out of the holster. If a croc or one of the local leopards or other big cats came upon us in the night, I would at least be able to get at the gun. Whether I could fire it was another matter altogether.

∽

T was shivering when I awoke. In the tropics, shivering usually means malaria, but I thought it was too early for that, unless he had caught it in Australia.

"Are you okay, T?" I asked.

His teeth chattered.

"You have to try to control the shivering, T. Breathe deep. Focus on your breathing. Can you do that?"

I got no response.

If we were going to get out of here alive, one of us had to move. Neither of us seemed to be able to manage that. T, younger and stronger than me, would eventually have to be the one if the chills didn't completely exhaust him.

I looked around in the growing light, hoping to see something familiar. But any landmark I might have remembered had to have changed beyond description. Left and right, downriver and upriver, everywhere I looked I saw devastation. Every other tree seemed to have been blown down or bent to the ground. The river seemed like a solid mass of slowly moving greenery. For every branch that was thrust ashore at my feet, two more were pulled away from the bank. I had never heard of a tornado in this part of the world, but that's what the landscape reminded me of.

"T, can you hear me?"

I heard his teeth clicking.

"You're alive, I know that. I can hear you. I can't turn around or get up. My ribs hurt too much," I said.

"S-s-sorry," I heard him whisper.

"Not your fault. The water had to go," I said. "Listen. I don't think either of us can move very far. But we have to have help. I'm going to shoot off a round. Maybe I can attract some attention. It's all I've got."

I listened for a yea or a nay, but heard nothing but T's shivering.

I reached under my shoulder to extract the Webley from its holster. The water had shrunk the leather some, and I had to tug at it, which made me wince in pain. The Webley's weight—two and a half pounds of it—felt like a brick in my hand. It was going to be a struggle just to raise it, much less pull the trigger. I cocked it with my thumb and aimed it across the river.

"All right. Here goes," I said.

The pistol kicked back in my weak grip as it exploded with sound. Birds and monkeys, still stunned from yesterday's storm, screamed and screeched and carried on.

"I'm doing another shot," I said.

My arm kicked back from the second blast.

The forest screeching increased to a new pitch.

"One more, T," I said. "Then we'll see."

It was all I could do to cock and fire the Webley one last time. The boom seemed to fill the forest.

Firing just the three shots had exhausted me, with each jerk of my arm as the pistol recoiled sending an ache through my chest. I laid the gun across my groin and let go of the grip. I would rest before trying to reholster the weapon.

I leaned my head back and looked up at the sky. Such a rare sight in the forest. You could often see the blue of the horizon, but dense foliage usually blocked the view overhead. My mind wandered until a thunderclap interrupted it.

"Sounds like more rain, T. Just what we need," I said.

"No." It was a croak that escaped between chattering teeth. "Shot. Fire again."

"You think?" I said, suddenly alert.

The pistol was at hand. I raised it and cocked and fired it.

Another thunderclap answered it.

"Hah-ha!" I was elated. "It's Jimmy, T. They're coming for us."

T made a sucking sound I took for an acknowledgment. He

was in worse shape than I thought. Jimmy's rescue could not come too soon.

We waited and waited. After a while, I started counting off the minutes. When I thought an hour had passed, I cocked, aimed, and fired the Webley again, igniting the forest cacophony.

A harsh boom followed almost immediately. Jimmy was very close now. Working the boat upriver against the flow of debris was taking longer than I expected. But our boats were rubber-walled, and I suspected Jimmy and Ujang were having to pole the fallen trees and branches away from the boat.

Soon a boat came into view downriver, but it wasn't Jimmy's. This was a steel-hulled torpedo-shaped vessel, at least twice as large as our rubber dinghies. It didn't matter. It was going to rescue us.

I raised the Webley one last time and fired into the sky to let them know our position. That produced a commotion on the boat as several rescuers congregated toward our side of the river, pointing.

I swear I was so happy that tears came to my eyes. Then the tears turned bitter as the boat plowed closer and closer. I could make out faces now, and at the bow of the boat stood the young Chinese woman of XiZi Ltd.

EMPAYA IBA SPEAKS

Children of the Black Orchid,
Does our forest
Whisper of my return to you,
Near as I am?
Too long has your father been absent,
Too long have you been left victim to invaders.
Your time of waiting nears its end.
Your father, your Abah, feels our common land.

Pleased am I with the people of the midnight bloom.
Faults with you, I find none.
My pleasure knows its bounds,
And within these lies my servant, who bears my mark.
Strong was he
When he claimed the mark
Of my power
From the one who betrayed us.

His weaknesses and fears, I now perceive
Against one who challenges him,
One young, one strong, one of our land,
One who would claim the mark of the spider.
Fear not if a new servant should come.
So say I, Empaya Iba, spirit of the Black Orchid People,
Guardian of the Mother Soil, giver of the Long Sleep,
Seer of the Many Eyes, mage of the Many Legs.

CHAPTER 24

RESCUE

TANDING AT THE bow of the boat, she approached like a queen on her barge.

Her tan pantsuit and white blouse appeared starched and ironed. Her makeup and boots were spotless, her long black hair pulled back into a ponytail. She looked all grown-up.

"Mr. Arnett, may we assist you?" She called from the bow of the boat.

"No, thanks. We already called a taxi. It'll be along any minute now."

She ignored my retort, then turned to the crew and spoke in Chinese. My college Mandarin was very rusty, but I got her body language and tone. She was telling the thugs to get off the boat and collect T and me.

"I think I should warn you that T is not well. He may have something that's catching," I said.

"Then we will leave him here," she said. "Your taxi will get here eventually."

"I assume you are expecting me to cooperate with whatever you have in mind. No T, no cooperation."

"You seem to think you have some leverage over me, Mr. Arnett."

"Honey, if you piss me off, I can guarantee you will drop dead begging for just one more breath of air."

There it was again, that instant anger. I touched the right side of my face; the tattoo was hot, like a fever. I was much too close to losing it.

Calm down, I told myself. *This is just a negotiation, and you started it.*

Her face may have been ageless, but she still lacked Lee's experience with the poker face. I saw panic in her eyes; so did her hirelings, and they didn't like it.

Before she could respond, I continued.

"I'm hurt. I almost drowned. T had to pump water out of me. I think he broke my ribs. I don't know if I can stand. And traipsing through the forest is just not going to happen," I said.

"We will see," she said.

Again she switched to Chinese for the Gang of Four with her. I recognized three of them from Lee's house. Mr. Eyeglasses, the bombardier, was at the helm of the boat; apparently he handled the technology. Ming, the human wall with a holstered pistol on his hip, used long metal poles to shove debris away from the boat. A fourth man, younger, with muscles bulging out of his wifebeater, scurried back and forth between the girl and Mr. Eyeglasses. I noticed that all four men wore amulets, the kind intended to ward off evil spirits. She did not, at least not outside her blouse.

The human wall, Ming, and Muscles dropped over the side of the boat and into the water. They kept slipping as they tried to gain purchase in the mud and climb the riverbank. T had practically had to throw me up the bank, and I thought these guys would have to resort to that tactic sooner or later.

The young woman spoke sharply, and Muscles grabbed a fallen tree a dozen steps downstream near the stern of the boat. He half climbed, half crawled up the muddy bank. By the time he stood on solid ground, he was as dirty as T and me. Mr. Eyeglasses tossed him a coiled rope. He wrapped it around one of the standing trees and tossed the other end to his waterlogged buddies. They scrambled up the bank, their churning feet dislodging clods of mud.

All three clambered through the blighted forest to T and me. Ming hunched over T, then stood and yelled back at the boat.

"Mr. Arnett, he thinks your friend has malaria. Unless he turns into a mosquito, he is not contagious," the young woman said.

She was a real comedienne.

The human wall extended his hand to me. I lifted mine and winced in pain.

He shook his head and looked at me like I was an idiot. He pointed at my lap.

Ah, the Webley. I had forgotten.

I took it by the barrel and handed it up to him. He puzzled over it for a moment, looking for a safety and a loading gate on the side. My version of the Webley has no safety, and all Webleys load with a top-break mechanism that literally bends the pistol in half. All that was beyond the big guy's comprehension, and he just pushed the gun under his belt. I hoped he would shoot himself.

He offered his hand again; this time I was certain it was for me. I raised my right hand to his, closing my eyes in pain; he grabbed it and yanked me to my feet.

"Gah" was the sound that escaped my mouth as I sank to my knees. Beads of agony-induced sweat popped up on my face.

The woman screeched at the big guy, and he backed away from me. I toppled onto my side, the life vest absorbing some of the fall.

"I can't help you if I'm dead," I said, talking into the muddy ground where my face lay.

Ming said something to the woman. She must have agreed. I couldn't see what was happening on the water, but I could now stare straight at T. He shocked me. Under the layer of mud, he appeared pale. His teeth no longer chattered, but his body trembled with shivers. He seemed only vaguely aware of what was going on around him.

I heard a rope being thrown ashore. The boat's engine revved to a roar. One of the guys scrambled around behind me; I assumed he was tying off the line. The motor eased back but never stopped completely. Chinese voices carried on over me. A board banged against something on the boat.

The big guy and Muscles picked T up and backed out of my view. I did not hear a splash, which I feared, and assumed they were loading T onto the boat, perhaps up a plank.

I struggled with my thoughts. I wanted to get out of the forest, but I desperately did not want to move.

Someone, not the big guy, wiped the slime from my neck. I felt a needle stab me and penetrate far too deeply. They were doping me up, I hoped. With T gone, all I could see was mud, tree stumps, and broken branches. The storm's damage extended at least fifteen to twenty feet away from the water's edge. I marveled at the destruction.

How had T and I ever survived?

Time passed; my thoughts drifted. Voices sounded softly in the background. I had the feeling I was in a hospital, all clean and comfortable.

The big guy broke my reverie. He tapped my shoulder and looked me in the eye. He pointed a meaty finger at me, made lifting motions with his arms and aimed toward the water behind me. I nodded, not really certain of what I had just agreed to.

He stepped out of my line of vision and slowly rolled me onto my back. In one swift motion, he hefted me into the air and turned. My head swirled, and I thought I might throw up. Whatever they had jabbed into me was working. I felt less pain. They had thrust the boat upriver so that the stern was almost abreast of where T and I lay. I couldn't see the plank, but it must have been thick. It held up under our combined weight.

The big guy laid me down on a bench under the metal canopy that covered more than half the boat. Only the bow and stern were exposed to the sky.

"Mr. Arnett, I think you must be crazy," the young woman said, hovering over me. As commotion filled the boat, she sat on a bench opposite, a clean white towel beneath her. I heard the guys haul the plank aboard. We were preparing to get underway.

She leaned forward and continued her thought.

"Three times now you have come to Borneo, and three times you have managed to damage yourself enough to require hospitalization. That could happen to anyone once. I suppose it could happen to an adventurous person a second time, although you are not really the adventurous type—you take pictures of flowers, not wild animals. To have your fear of water and go near it a third time, that seems insane to me. Is that what this spirit has done to you? Turned you into a reckless fool? I intend to inform my superiors that they are dealing with a crazy man."

I grinned like an idiot. She was so right. And such a nice person, I thought. Fascinating really. Logical. I liked her. I liked the big guy. I liked their medicine. I hoped they had given T some medicine, too. I could turn my head back and forth, and nothing hurt. It was wonderful.

Talk to me some more, pretty lady, I thought.

The Chinese voices piped up, so melodic. Why had my college professor described the language as brusque and harsh?

The big guy appeared over me. I smiled. I liked him. He wiped my face with a white cloth that quickly turned brown. Then he lifted my head and fed me clean water from a plastic pouch.

The boat bucked and bounced, and I heard a loud thump. The boat leaned over on the big guy's side; he wobbled, and I blacked out.

CHAPTER 25
CATCHING UP

"SEBASTIAN. SEBASTIAN."

I heard the Chinese girl use my first name. That was interesting. My chest hurt. That was not interesting.

I knew what was happening. The drug was wearing off. The XiZi woman planned to interrogate me. We were probably upstream, perhaps even to the ambush landing. She needed me now to find Empaya Iba. I wondered how she would react if we found it.

"Sebastian."

She called again, and I felt her warm hand gently touching my chest. It grazed down toward my stomach and did something completely inappropriate.

My eyes shot open.

"'Manda?"

My mouth would not form the word as I thought it.

"'Manda. Where?"

"I'm here, Sebastian," Amanda said. "Take your time. Wake up slowly. I'll give you some water."

She lifted my head—it hurt—and water dribbled down the side of my face. It tasted wonderful, no mud smell, just clean, pure, cool liquid.

My eyes took in the hut over Amanda's shoulders. It was much cleaner than the first one I'd awakened in wracked with pain. But hotter than that one as well. This room had a tin roof, which was heating under the sun. Thatch roofs don't do that.

Moving hurt my chest, so I didn't move much. Besides, my right arm was taped across my abdomen. I couldn't move much.

"Amanda, where are we?"

"We're in the village. You're safe," she said.

"What about the Chinese?"

"They're here. They've sent for another boat."

"Another boat? Why? What happened to their boat?"

"It sank. You barely made it back here alive. That evil woman even got dirty, so you know the situation was bad."

"Is everyone… Is T okay? You? Jimmy?"

I tried to inventory the people I cared about.

"Everyone here is fine except you. T is okay. Jimmy thinks he has malaria. He gave him quinine. Now T has to sweat it out," she said. "You're our main concern. Everyone seems to think you have broken ribs. You coughed up some blood in your sleep, and that could mean a punctured lung. We need to get you to a hospital."

"Lieutenant Wilson and Adi Putra made it back then?"

Amanda lowered her eyes and touched my cheek.

"No. They haven't come back."

I rolled my head, a signal that I wanted to lie back. Amanda lay my head flat, but kept her hand on my naked torso.

"What about the Chinese?" I said.

"The woman in charge agrees you have to go to the hospital. She tried to get a helicopter to pick you up, but there just aren't any available. At any price.

"That storm was very bad over the northern half of Borneo. That means we have to wait for a new boat, and I don't know how long that will take. The river is still pretty wild, and it's clogged with debris. You were lucky to make it back here."

I stared at the underside of the tin roof and considered. I felt a bead of sweat roll off my temple, down the side of my cheek, following the track of the spiderweb on my face.

"What happened to the Chinese boat?"

"A stump rammed it while it was trying to turn around after picking you up. It barely made it back here with everyone bailing like crazy."

"Even the woman?"

"Yes, even her."

"What about our other boat? Could you and Jimmy use it to get away?"

"No. She ordered her men to cut it up when they arrived in the village not long after you left."

"Jimmy couldn't stop them?"

"He and Sergeant Alexander tried. Two of the Chinese came in behind them. They killed the sergeant; Jimmy offered to surrender if they promised not to hurt the villagers. That awful woman agreed, then let her men beat him senseless. They chopped up the villagers' boats and threw all of our radios and phones into the river."

"The bastards sound thorough. Is Jimmy all right?"

"Yes. He's cut and bruised, but says he's had worse. They've separated the men and women. If the men try to escape or resist, they said they would kill all the women. We believe them."

"Sounds like they hold all the cards."

"Maybe not all. Jimmy had already spoken with his people about the flood. Someone will be along to rescue us. It's just that helicopters and boats are scarce right now. We're not the only ones in need, and we're actually well off. Better than others."

I yawned.

"What happens now?"

"That's up to her. She calls the shots. I think they're going to take you to the hospital. I don't know about the rest of us," Amanda said.

"Are you okay if you have to stay here?"

"We still have what's left of our supplies. She doesn't seem intent on harming us. She just wants you," Amanda said. "I can't blame her for her good taste."

I loved it when Amanda flirted.

She glanced toward the door and spoke quietly.

"Can Empaya Iba do anything? Her men are terribly superstitious, and they don't like her at all."

"Iba's... I'm not sure what's up with Iba. Did Jimmy fill you in on what happened in Australia?"

"He told me there was a fight, and that you three were all fine. That's all."

Good, I thought. Jimmy is being selective with the truth.

"Iba may have been injured or even killed," I said, "but there's something nagging in the back of my brain about Iba. It's like I saw the solution to the whole Iba thing, and now I've lost it."

"You think there *is* a solution?"

Jimmy's call interrupted us.

"Amanda, she wants you out here with the rest of us. Something's happening."

CHAPTER 26
THREATS

I WANTED TO FOLLOW Amanda out of the hut, but when I tried to get up, pain shot through my chest, and I coughed up a globule of blood. I slumped back to the floor hard, causing stars to appear before my eyes. I kept my head turned to one side and concentrated on taking short shallow breaths to avoid the pain.

I must have dozed. I felt Amanda's warm fingers gently touch my scarred cheek. I smiled and reached up to hold her arm. Warm and soft, it felt thin, too thin. My eyes shot open. It was the Chinese woman. I released her arm like it was on fire.

She looked down on me, puzzlement filling her face.

"We will be going soon," she said.

"You know I'll kill you if you harm Amanda," I said.

"She is safe. I have no intention of hurting her, no need. I have what I want, Mr. Arnett."

I pondered my empty threat.

"Moving you may be painful, but it cannot be helped," the woman said. "I'm sure your friends will be as careful as possible with you."

"So your boat arrived?"

"No. A helicopter is on the way."

"I thought you couldn't get a helicopter."

"XiZi can be very persuasive. We told the authorities that we were on a rescue mission. They were made to understand," she said.

"How many people did you have to bribe?"

"Fewer than you would imagine. Business success is about finding the correct lever, not using the most effort."

She was wise and sly at the same time. I said nothing.

"Your friends will bring you out after the helicopter has landed. It should not be long."

"Send Amanda back in," I said.

"I don't think so, Mr. Arnett. She is safe with the villagers. Don't worry."

"What about T? Are we taking T with us?"

"It's a small helicopter. He brings nothing to the table."

"If you hurt him…"

"Yes, Mr. Arnett. I know. But I wonder if you are not less dangerous than before. Whatever power you possess, I think it must require some of your strength, and unfortunately for you, you do not appear to have much strength right now."

"Don't tempt me," I said between gritted teeth.

"Calm yourself, Mr. Arnett. Everything will be fine. Just so you know, we have one more ampule of painkiller. We can use it and make your ride to the hospital less painful, or not. It's your decision."

She rose to her feet and climbed backward down the log steps outside the hut.

How did I ever get myself into this situation? I had happily led a completely uneventful life for years; now in the span of a year, I had suffered and caused more devastation than a mad pack of mercenaries.

Jimmy and Ujang interrupted my thoughts. They brought bamboo poles and a blanket to make a stretcher. Jimmy looked like I felt. One eye was swollen shut and dark bruises covered his face. The skin was missing from his knuckles.

"I'm sorry about you and Adi Putra, Jimmy," I said.

"Goes with the territory, mate. What do you Yanks say? Payback is hell?"

"Ujang, I'm sorry about Adi Putra," I said.

"Not your fault," he said, but I doubted his sincerity. Ujang had felt the sense of doom, and Adi had gone with me reluctantly.

"Jimmy, is there any hope Adi or Lieutenant Wilson might have survived?" I asked.

"Oh, I suppose there's always hope until there isn't, but I don't think it's likely if the storm we got here is anything like what you experienced. We've already had two miracles, getting you and T back. Hoping for more is pushing the Almighty a bit far," he said. "How are you doing?"

"Good enough for government work," I said without enthusiasm. "Hurts to breathe."

"Are you good enough to remember something?" He had lowered his voice.

"Yes. I hurt like hell, but my brain is working."

"When you get a chance, call the number I'm going to give you. You'll have to memorize it. They'll ask you for a code word. It's Dingo Lingo."

"Amanda said you already got through to your people."

"Perhaps. Perhaps not."

"Dingo Lingo," I repeated. "What does that mean?"

"Australian children's poem. It means something very bad has happened to us and we need help yesterday. Given your history, I'm sure they're just waiting for the call."

"I'm that bad?"

"One more adventure and they'll name a natural disaster after you," he said.

"What do you think of these Chinese? Are you going to be safe?"

"Sergeant Alexander and I made a tactical error; he paid for it. After they got that out of their system, they've left us alone. Plenty of guns, and the woman made clear she'll kill all the women. I suspect when that boat finally gets here, the Chinese will take off. They're very superstitious of you; your tattoo bothers them. And they don't like the girl from XiZi. They didn't want to chase you upriver, but she made them, even after they warned her of the dangers. The river is very bad right now."

"Tell me about it," I said. "What's that?"

"Sounds like your ride," Jimmy said.

Ujang stuck his head out the door.

"I hear it, but I can't see it yet. He's going to have a hard time landing. There's not that much clear space out there."

"What about the rice fields?" I asked.

"Too much mud and debris. Too dangerous," Jimmy said. "The villagers have lost their crop for the year."

"We'll have to help them," I said, feeling a little light-headed.

"Don't worry about them. They're planning to move back downriver. This has not been a good place for a village. You keep showing up."

The Chinese woman stuck her head in the door.

"Get him ready. As soon as the helicopter lands, bring him out," she said.

"I don't think we can do it on our own," Jimmy said.

"The villagers will help. Just do it."

"Pleasant personality," Jimmy said. "I shall miss her... not at all. But I do look forward to our next meeting. Perhaps the circumstances will be different."

"You'll take care of Amanda and T?" I said.

"They'll be fine. Eve is all over T like a mother hen. I think she likes him."

"Just what he needs, another older woman in his life," I said.

"There are worse things."

His words were almost lost in the thup-thup-thupping of the helicopter engine and the flapping of the metal roof in the chopper's downwash.

Three villagers grabbed the foot of the makeshift stretcher and helped drag me out of the hut and down the steps cut into a log. The helicopter was one of those bubble-domed things. There was no way I was going to be able to lie down. There was just no room.

The woman appeared in my vision again.

"All right, Mr. Arnett. Decision time. Are you going to cooperate with me? If so, you get the painkiller and can probably sleep on the way to the hospital. If not, I'm pretty sure you will feel every turn of the blades. What's it to be?"

Having Empaya Iba touch my soul had done horrible things to my sense of morality. I did not hesitate to lie outright.

"Cooperate," I said, "but if anything happens to Amanda, whether you caused it or not, I'll watch you die a horrible death."

"Agreed," she said and jabbed the needle into my neck. The drug acted fast, but not fast enough to prevent the torture of sitting me up, then standing me, folding me into the front seat beside the pilot and strapping me in. I was practically unconscious from pain by the time Jimmy and Ujang finished, and I tasted blood in my mouth. Jimmy patted my knee and closed and latched the door. I couldn't see Amanda or the villagers. I assumed the Chinese held them in one of the huts to ensure everyone's cooperation.

The chopper rose from the ground, its spinning blades clearing the houses and trees with just a few feet to spare on either side. As we rose above the treetops, I could see the devastation the storm had caused up and down the river along both banks. I wondered what Iba thought, and then I wondered why that had come to mind. I wrote it off to the effects of a combination of pain and painkiller and thought no more.

CHAPTER 27
ADMIRAL TERRY

T HE HARDEST, MOST miserable part of working in Southeast Asia is the hot humid air. Sweat trickling down my back and sides, pooling behind my knees, the feeling of grime everywhere, even in the corners of my eyes. But if you're going to photograph orchids, you have to endure those conditions. That's why I always built in plenty of time after my morning photo shoots for a cold shower and a colder drink.

I felt clean and cool now, but couldn't remember having taken a shower. My mouth tasted… I couldn't get a flavor. Certainly not alcohol. It was just dry.

I opened my eyes and looked around. I lay in a bed with side rails, a tube snaking under a crisp white sheet, no doubt connected to my arm. I could wiggle my fingers and toes, but did not feel much. I tried to take a deep breath; a twinge of pain responded. With my free left arm, I reached under the sheet and felt my chest. It seemed bound in layers of tape.

I groped for the call button, but could not find one. I was alone, so often the case. I called out but my voice was little more than a croak, and the effort exhausted me. Sooner or later someone would come. I melted into the clean sheets and wallowed in the cool dry air.

❧

I might have slept, but I was awake enough to see the door silently swing open. A tall athletic man in his fifties entered and closed the door. Everything about him screamed military, from his short haircut to his rigid bearing. Marine, I thought. What's he doing here?

"Water?" he said.

I nodded.

He poured a glass from a pitcher, stuck a straw in it and put it to my mouth.

I sipped. Sipped again and sighed.

"Mike Owens sends his regards," the man said.

"Mike?"

"Don't talk. We don't have a lot of time. My name is Terry Anderson. Can you hear me? Can you understand me?"

"Yes. Vaguely."

"You're in a private hospital in Brunei. You are a captive of a Chinese organization. Your guards are momentarily distracted. We have to leave now. Can you stand?"

"I don't know."

"You have to try or you're staying here, and I don't recommend that."

Anderson whipped the sheet off me and disconnected my IV.

"Here. I'm going to raise you. You have multiple broken ribs and a punctured lung. I don't know how much this will hurt, but probably a lot. Try not to make any noise."

He cranked the head of the bed to a sitting position. At first, I felt nothing, then pressure and finally pain. I had no idea how I would be able to walk.

"Come on," he said, glancing at his watch. "Put your arm around my shoulder. I'll try to take weight off your feet, but you will have to walk."

I slipped down from the bed. When my feet touched the floor, my body kept going.

"Try to stand. Try to stand."

"Uh." I saw stars and my chest exploded in needle-sharp pain. I grasped the bed sheets, and between the two of us, Terry got me standing erect. I was breathing heavily, and every breath hurt.

"This is worse than I thought," Anderson said to himself. "Listen up. We go out the door, turn right, down the hall and out the side door. There should be a car waiting for us."

Should be?

"It's about thirty steps. Let's go. One at a time, but when we leave this room, there's no stopping. Got it?"

I nodded, wanting with all my heart just to lie between the clean sheets again.

"Here we go."

After the first ten steps, I lost the ability to think straight. After twenty, my eyes were closed and drool ran out of my mouth. I don't remember entering the car.

I thought I passed bodies lying on the floor outside my room, but I could have been hallucinating.

Anderson roused me with a powerful whiff of smelling salts.

"Welcome back, Arnett. You did great back there. We're almost at the airport. My plane is waiting to take off. We're operating under diplomatic rules, which means no one will ask your name, but you have to board the plane on your own."

"I don't think I can do that."

I was amazed at his confidence.

"Doesn't matter what you think. You have to do this."

"Hit me with the salts again."

He waved a tube under my nose and my head jerked away from it, sparking more pain.

"That's awful," I said. "Water."

Anderson put a bottle to my lips; I sipped.

"No blood. That's good," I said.

We were riding in a limo. I saw flags flapping from the front of the car, a U.S. flag on the passenger side and a blue flag with two stars on the driver's side.

"Who are you?" I asked.

"Plenty of time for that later. We're almost there. Lean forward. I have to put a jacket on you."

He eased me forward and draped a blue camouflage jacket over my shoulders. It had stars on the shoulder patch.

"I'm a general?" I said.

"Wrong service. You're an admiral for a few minutes. I'm going to stick some papers in your hands. Try to look like you're reading them. Don't say anything, but if you are forced to, act arrogant and impatient."

"Arrogant," I said. "I can do that. I feel better now. I can—"

"Shut up, Arnett. We shot you up with joy juice. You won't feel any pain at all, but you may collapse. Focus on staying awake."

He buttoned one button on the jacket, covering most of my green pajama top. My bottoms were green hospital scrubs. I had light blue booties on my feet.

I knew I could do this. Take away that blasted chest pain, and I could... I don't know, ride a bicycle. This was good stuff, what Terry had given me. Admiral Terry. Terry and the Pirates. Free association. If he was Terry, was I a pirate?

We pulled up to a closed chain-link gate and stopped. A soldier, not an American soldier, stepped out of a white guardhouse with a rifle slung over his shoulder.

"Stop grinning. Look at the papers," Anderson said. He sounded arrogant and impatient. He'd had practice, I thought and stifled a giggle. Oh, right. Admiral Terry and the Pirates.

The driver lowered his window and a wave of humid heat swept in.

"Hurry it up," I heard my voice say.

The guard peered through the open window. Speaking very good English, he asked the driver, "Is he the flag officer? Why isn't he in uniform?"

Before the driver could answer, I spoke.

"Close the damned window."

Terry looked at me. I grinned. Terry punched my leg discretely. I raised the papers, but kept grinning at my performance. I was good.

The guard waved us through. I started humming a tune from my childhood, "Mairzy doats and dozy doats and liddle lamzy divey." Terry grabbed his papers and stuffed them into a briefcase at his feet.

"Let's hope you still feel this good when we get to the plane," he said to no one in particular. "Corporal, as fast as you can without attracting attention. I think he's as good as he's going to get, and the crash is coming."

"Yes, sir."

I felt good. Real good. Well, maybe a slight itching in my chest. I reached up to scratch it, but my arm felt too heavy to move. Odd. Well, it didn't itch that much. But I was certainly getting tired. I yawned and turned to Terry.

"Nap?" I said.

"Corporal, step on it. As soon as we get there, help me get him out and up the stairs. If anyone asks later, tell them he has the flu and had to use the toilet."

"Yes, sir."

Buildings, trucks and planes whizzed by. I yawned again, and my eyelids felt as heavy as my arms.

"Tired. Nap," I said to no one at all. My head nodded.

We jerked to a halt. The driver was out of the car and opening my door in a flash. He and Terry slid me out and stood me up.

A soldier of the Royal Brunei Land Forces, dressed in jungle khakis and a black beret and armed with a submachine gun, stood to attention.

Anderson and the corporal tried to hustle me past him. I stopped, looked the soldier in the eye, and grumbled, "At ease."

He gave a smile, saluted and stood even more rigidly at attention, allowing me to step beyond his line of vision. Anderson and the corporal dragged me up the six steps to the door of the Gulf Stream.

Uniformed hands inside the plane pulled me inside and plopped me on a seat. The door closed, engines whined and the plane began to move. Anderson stood over me.

"Good job, admiral," he said. "Sleep a bit. Then you can tell me why you are so damned important."

EMPAYA IBA SPEAKS

Children of the Black Orchid,
Abah, your father, weeps.
So near was I to you,
And now you are lost to me again.
My servitor, the one who bears my mark,
Who shares the power of the Long Sleep,
He who acts in my stead,
Our land, our sweet home, he has fled.

Your gifts to me touched not his hands.
Oblations he acknowledged not.
The promise of the Black Orchid he denied,
And the sacrifice of blood he abandoned.
He will return us to you,
To take your gifts for me,
Or the blood of his own head
He will surrender.

So say I, Empaya Iba, spirit of the Black Orchid People,
Guardian of the Mother Soil, giver of the Long Sleep,
Seer of the Many Eyes, mage of the Many Legs.

CHAPTER 28
TWO SPIRITS

"JOE!"

I hugged the old Indian medicine man until my ribs hurt.

"Big place you live in," he said, looking around the marble foyer of Amanda's mansion in Denver, a crystal chandelier hanging two stories above him. "Great-grandfather's silver buys a lot."

"I'm thinking of building a shed out back," I said, "someplace where I can touch the walls without needing to pack a lunch."

"Maybe I help you. We bunk together when Amanda gets mad at you."

He looked through the multiple portals.

"Amanda is here?"

"She'll be down for lunch. She figured you and I might want some time to talk."

"Some talk. You and your spirits. You are like stepping barefoot in horse manure. You wash, but some sticks in toes."

"What are you talking about, Joe?"

"Your spirits. I tell you that."

"You mean Empaya Iba, the spider?"

"Him, yes. Other, too."

"What other? Are you saying you see more than one spirit around me?"

"Yes, two. Never do I see more than one spirit with a man. You, you have two. Not right. One, maybe both, got to go. Hope you are still around when that happens."

I shook my head and placed my hand on his bony shoulder.

"Come to the kitchen, old man. I need a drink."

We walked down a long hall that joins the foyer with the rest of the house, rooms on either side, some of my flower photos hanging side by side with original impressionists, including a Monet water garden. I felt flattered every time I headed to the kitchen.

"It's five o'clock somewhere," I said, as I fixed drinks in the pantry off the kitchen. We both preferred gin—Hendricks and a chunk of lime for the old man, Tanqueray classic and diet tonic, 50-50 proportions, with a large wedge of lime for me.

Maria Reina, in command of her restaurant-grade Viking stove in the kitchen, glanced my way several times but said nothing. Joe approached her like stalking a deer. When she turned to reach for something, he stood in her way. At five feet four inches, she could see over the top of the old man's head. He reached up and took her chubby cheeks in his wrinkled hands.

"Maria Reina, our dreams are good," he said.

Tears welled in her eyes.

Her hands covered his.

"Si. Gracias, abuelo. Thank you, grandfather."

They stood, he looking up at her like a child, she soaking him in.

I felt like a peeping Tom and took my drink out to the patio off the kitchen. This was part of Maria's domain, connecting the kitchen and her suite at the back of the house. Her patio overlooked a terrace that flowed to a line of cedars and a high red brick wall that marked the property line and hid a service alley more than fifty yards away. Maria allowed me to use the patio to smoke my daily cigar or two.

I plopped and sipped my gin, wishing I had brought a cigar.

One of Mike Owens's guards eased around the corner of the house, his right hand behind his back. When he saw me, he nodded and backed off. The price of evading Mike's team in Australia had been high. Bodyguards tailed T and me everywhere we went; they drove Amanda in her new armored Tahoe SUV.

With T camping out in several rooms on the second floor, and Owens's people occupying part of the basement, the house felt busy to me, but could easily accommodate the old man, and quite a few more guests, before it could be called crowded, much less full.

Joe appeared, as he did, without a sound. He settled into a padded wrought-iron patio chair.

"I never thought of an Indian sitting in a patio chair," I said.

"These things you say, they describe you, not me."

"You know, you know a lot, but you speak English like a movie Indian. Chief William down on the reservation speaks modern English; so do all of the other Indians I meet," I said, trying to deflect him.

"You don't understand my language?"

"I understand, but I wonder why you can't speak the king's English, that's all."

"You, who can't speak the name my mother and father give me? I speak the way I learned, long time ago. But I think you are like most whites. If I spoke Harvard English, you would still hear pidgin, because you are speaking to a ragged old man with long gray hair. A rez Injun. Am I right Sebastian?"

Wiley old SOB, he turns everything back on me.

"All right, old man, point taken. Speak any way you want. Now you have your booze, and I have mine. What about these spirits, plural, that you were talking about?"

"The spider, very unhappy. Hurt maybe. Afraid maybe. Not like before. This is very dangerous for you, Sebastian. I think I should stay awhile with you."

"Stay as long as you like. Amanda will be delighted to have you protecting me," I said. "But why is it more dangerous than before?"

"If it keeps anger, you cannot survive long," Joe said, draining half the glass of gin and lime.

"What's this other spirit you see?"

"Never seen before. Big. Flies like a bird, but not a bird, I don't think. A killer. Angry, too, like your Empaya Iba. Not right."

Joe drank again, shaking his head.

"How you get two spirits, I just don't know."

CHAPTER 29
FAMILY GATHERS

J OE INSISTED ON hearing every detail of the battle in the Nullarbor and everything we had hoped to accomplish in Borneo but never got to.

"These Chinese people still want you?" the old man asked.

"We haven't heard word one since we all got out of there alive. Mike Owens and Jimmy Beam are convinced they're still out there, still watching, waiting."

A knock on the patio door interrupted us. I looked, expecting Maria to call us to lunch. It was T, holding a bottle of Big Horn Buttface amber ale in his hand. He was drinking early, too. I waved him out to the patio.

"Sorry to interrupt. Maria said you were out here. I wanted to meet the old medicine man before lunch," he said.

"Beer for breakfast?" I said.

"Gin for breakfast," he said back.

"It's an aperitif for me. Sleep problems?"

He studied the patio tiles beneath his bare feet.

"Yeah. Dreams. Montana. Borneo. Everything. Life sucks."

"You came to meet Joe. So, meet him. Joe, this is T, Tom

Kingston, the son of Amanda's former husband. T, Joe. I can't pronounce his real name."

"Nice to meet you," T said, shuffling his feet. "Maria says a lot of good things about you. If you have a free moment, I'd like to get a chance to, maybe talk a little bit about some stuff."

"About your woman," Joe said, not really as a question.

"I don't have a woman," T said. "I did have…"

"Not the one who died. The one who healed you."

T looked stunned; I might have, too. I had not told Joe about Eve, our Dyak interpreter in Borneo.

"She took care of me when I had malaria. That's all," T said.

"Maybe yes, maybe no. I think yes. She will cause you pain before she can give you joy."

T and I stared at the old man.

"Are you turning into a fortune teller now, Joe?" I asked in what I hoped was a playful tone.

"We see. You come, we will talk," he said.

"See you later then," T said, turned and retreated to the sanctuary of Maria and the kitchen.

"You were kind of rough on him," I said.

"After the pain, there *will* be joy for him. I do not say that for you," he said.

"What's that supposed to mean?"

"Your dream," he said. "Tell me again."

"All right. It's pretty simple. I feel tiny, caught in a spiderweb, a bird thing overhead, circling, getting closer."

"Is spider demon there?"

"No. Yes. It's hidden. I can't see it. I feel it. It talks to me. Or at least answers my questions. It says it's better for me to die than it."

"That eagle spirit you fought. Did the old man die, the one who carried it on his chest?"

"No. He was hurt. Put in a hospital, but he walked away the next day. A boy died. The boy who led that old aboriginal around. He got caught in the middle. I mean, right in the middle. T says I died, too. Or stopped breathing for a while. Iba and I talked, but I can't remember what we said. It was important, but I just can't remember."

Joe placed his empty drink on a round glass-topped table and stood. He stepped past me toward the patio door.

Amanda stepped out. She was wearing one of those loose, flowing tunics that she likes to hide her figure. A slash of white soared from one sleeve, crossed her torso and continued to the other sleeve. She looked great, and her face wore a smile that lit up my world.

"You must be the man Sebastian calls Joe. I would like to know your real name so I can use it."

Joe looked up into her eyes and smiled.

"I am Pony That Sees Far, Kahvah Att-un-poon-a-woon-ah."

"Pony That Sees Far, that seems an apt name for you. Welcome to my home and thank you for coming. I know it means a lot to Sebastian to see you. Your visit means a lot to me, too."

"Wait a minute," I said. "You said you wanted to call him by his real name."

"Pony That Sees Far," Amanda said. "That is his real name."

"No. That's cheating," I said. "His real name is Khavah-atta-poon-ah…" I massacred his name again.

He smiled at Amanda.

"I am Pony That Sees Far."

Joe took Amanda's fair, smooth hands into his own wrinkled, bony ones.

"He dreams," Joe said. "You dream, too."

I couldn't make out whether he meant it as a question or a statement. I never thought of Amanda sharing that nightmare, or perhaps worse, having one of her own. I had never asked.

Amanda looked at their joined hands.

"Yes, I dream. A black spider stands over Sebastian. It's so big its legs make a cage that Sebastian can't escape. It has pincers on its face. I never see the eyes, but I imagine the pincers and an open red mouth. The pincers open and close. I don't know if the pincers are to grab me or keep me away or tear Sebastian apart. I just don't know. Not knowing, that's my nightmare."

"I'm sorry, Amanda," I said. "I didn't know you had nightmares, too. You're just always calm when you wake me up."

She released Joe's hands and turned to me. She placed her hands on my cheeks; they tingled at her touch. She stared into my eyes, then turned grim.

"As creepy and scary as it is, I would fight that spider for you."

I was speechless. She kissed me on my scarred cheek.

"Lunch will be ready soon. Come in when you're done here," she said and walked away.

Joe watched her, scratched his chin.

"I'm thinking, Sebastian, those spirits have many ways to cause you pain before you maybe taste joy. You have much to lose."

CHAPTER 30
NEW TRIP

M IKE OWENS DROPPED in on a surprise (to me) visit after lunch and brought his wife, Jan, with him.

Amanda and Jan had been college classmates at Smith years ago; they fell into each other's arms and went off talking a mile a minute.

Mike and I shrugged our greetings.

"How's the voice?" I said, a pang of conscience nagging at me. In the battle against assassins a year earlier in Montana, I had unleashed Empaya Iba. I tried to protect people there who were trying to save me, but too many figures ran through my brain and I could not track them all so I wished them all dead—and they died. I barely held Mike in mind, but Iba strangled him, too, crushing his voice box.

Mike's harsh whisper answered my question. It hurt my ears just hearing it; I hated to think how painful—and frustrating—it must be for Mike to speak. It seemed much worse than when he'd called me to warn about the Chinese. I hoped that was a temporary condition, but I suspected worse.

"Let's go out to the patio," I said.

He growled assent.

The patio, if you can call a brick and stone elevated plaza a patio, wrapped around the public side of the house, offering a killer view of the Rockies. It was as grand as Maria's patio was cozy; that's why I preferred to smoke on Maria's patio.

T ambled out with a tray of glasses and Buttface Amber Ales.

"Mind if I join you old guys?" he said.

He and Mike hugged like veterans of battle who had spent time in the hospital together recuperating from bad wounds. T clicked with Mike as easily as he clashed with me. Maybe it was because Mike had two boys just a few years younger than T.

Mike was the kind of father figure I think Amanda wanted me to be.

"What brings you out to Colorado?" I asked. "Business or pleasure?"

"Both."

His curt response sounded more like 'oath.' To preserve his voice, Mike was speaking as little as possible. He dropped words, shortened thoughts to their essence. It was like having another Joe around. T was the only one who spoke full thoughts, and all he did was ask bothersome questions.

"New boss," Mike said.

"Who's that?" I said.

"Admiral Anderson."

"Ah! How did you get assigned to my white knight, Admiral Terry of the pirates? I thought he was something special in the Pacific."

"Unh." Mike growled in lieu of speaking.

"What does he have to do with me?"

"Feels you owe us."

"Same old, same old. But I don't get how he steps in all of a sudden. His rescue was just a case of being in the right place at the wrong time."

"Maybe. Admiral volunteered to take you. CENTCOM's happy you're gone. Wants to forget you exist."

"He volunteered? I thought he was smarter than that."

"Dumb like a fox." Mike packed a lot of meaning in his short responses.

"Um," Mike said. "Admiral's interested in China. Next U.S. adversary. Figures another star in taking you on."

"So he figures to use me against the Chinese, because of what happened in Borneo?"

"Seems like it. Might be right. New intel says that woman from XiZi may be coming."

"To the U.S.?"

"Here. Denver."

"Why?"

"To get you."

"Shit."

I set my beer down a little too hard on the glass tabletop. Nothing broke, but the bang got everyone's notice.

"She... They didn't learn anything?" I said.

"XiZi is Red Army. A temporary setback," Mike said, then sipped from his glass. "Think how many times they charged the machine guns in Korea."

An uncomfortable silence spoiled the companionable air we'd created.

"Why do they think they can take Sebastian here when they couldn't in Borneo?" T asked.

"Probably figure they'd go around him again, target someone close," Mike said, his voice fading from the conversation.

I thought of what Joe had told me the day he arrived: You have a lot to lose.

"It didn't work last time. This time, I might bear a grudge. I might wipe them out," I said.

"Haven't yet," Mike said. "You had motive. Opportunity. No action yet. They understand action."

◈

T went after another round of Buttface ales. Mike and I chatted, trying hard to ignore the 800-pound gorilla on the patio.

"How are you feeling, Sebastian? Ribs and lung okay?"

"Yeah. I'm good. Bored out of my mind. I need to get out of here, shoot some flowers. Maybe be alone for a while," I said.

"This a good time?"

"In the last fifteen months, when has there been a good time? I'm heading up to Portland next week to shoot an orchid show at Lan Su Chinese Garden. Always comes back to the Chinese, doesn't it? I didn't know your news when I planned it—obviously."

T arrived with a new round. We each took a bottle.

"You consider postponing it?" Mike said.

"Postpone what?" T asked.

"Photo shoot in Oregon. The Garden of Awakening Orchids. Beautiful name, isn't it? I'll be looking for some new species," I said.

"Black?" Mike asked.

"Black orchids don't exist."

"You've had two."

"They don't count."

"Why not?"

"No confirmation from the real orchid experts. I'm just a photographer, not a horticulturalist."

T's head swiveled back and forth like watching a tennis match.

"Amanda okay with this?"

"She knows I need to get out. I've been shut up for three-plus months. She's probably glad to get rid of me for a while."

"Doubt it," Mike said.

"What do you know?"

"Married twenty years. Known Amanda that long."

"Meh."

"T, what you doing?" Mike asked.

"Contract hacking. Living here with these two. This place is so big I can go days without seeing either of them. Maria keeps track of all of us."

"You going on the flower shoot?" Mike asked.

"He hasn't asked me, but I thought I'd tag along, at least as far as Montana. Jenny's parents live there. I thought I owed it to them to visit, tell them how great Jenny was, how she saved my life."

T was learning from Amanda how to handle me. After hearing that, how could I not ask him along?

"Ho, Sebastian."

Joe startled us. One minute he was nowhere in sight, and the next he was breathing in your ear. I was glad he was on my side.

"Sebastian, you serve drinks, don't wake up old man? What do you drink now?"

"Beer, old man. Want one?" I said.

"Bad for you. Make you fart. I drink gin."

"Mike Owens," Joe said, making a simple statement a greeting.

"Pony That Sees Far," Mike said.

"T, make a drink for an old man," Joe said.

"Hendricks coming up," T said.

"I dream, Sebastian. Understand your dream now, too," Joe said.

"Old man, you don't need to justify taking a nap to me," I said, teasing.

"Dragon comes for you now."

"Dragon?" Mike said.

"Joe says I have two demons hanging around me now—Iba and another vague one that flies but isn't a bird. This morning it was just a flying predator; thought for a while it might be an eagle; now apparently it's a dragon," I said.

"Not demons, Sebastian. I do not say demons," Joe said. "Spirits."

"Well, my limited experience with spirits is that they are all bad news, so demons," I said.

"Wait. Two spirits?" Mike said. "Crowded in there?"

He eyed me hard.

"That's what I said, Mike."

"What about the dragon?" Mike asked.

"Joe says he sees it. First I've heard of it, although I guess that could be right. My dream isn't big on details."

"How is Iba with this?"

"Still nervous, if my dreams are any clue."

"Every night?" Mike asked.

"Most nights, yes."

"Plans to stop them?"

"I'm open to suggestions. But essentially, if Joe is correct, I'm just filling time until Iba strangles me in my sleep," I said.

Mike looked at Joe.

"Won't let that happen," Mike said.

"How do you plan to prevent it?" I asked.

"Think of something."

"While you're doing that, think of a way to keep Amanda and T safe," I said.

"On it. Two new security teams with me."

"Replacements? I'm not sure the guys in the basement will like that. They love Maria's cooking, and she loves to see people eat."

"Not replacements. Reinforcements," Mike said. "You won't like the new protocols. But given Borneo, give me a chance."

I shrugged.

"I'm not canceling my trip, and I won't be a prisoner in this house. You'll have to talk to Amanda and T yourself, but I'll support anything extra you can do for them."

"Protection will be for everyone. No exceptions."

Mike's voice was so low it didn't encourage debate.

"We'll see," I said.

"Sebastian. I go to Montana with you," Joe said. "Visit granddaughter."

Interesting. Joe was the first person I'd told about the trip, and he'd expressed no interest. In fact, he was looking forward to hanging out more with Amanda and T.

That was okay. I figured he would be a good man in a tight spot. Yet somehow, I didn't think the Chinese would, or could, touch me.

"Okay, Joe. I'll drop you off in Missoula and pick you up on the return trip."

"What about me? Are you taking the old man and not inviting me?" T said.

He handed out fresh beers and Joe's gin in a tall glass.

"Why not? Plenty of room in the Denali. Mike, you keep your watchers at a distance. And no Chinese-Americans on the watch team. If things get nasty, I don't want to worry about hurting the wrong nationality."

"Right. WASPs, black Americans, Jews, and Muslims. No Chinese-Americans," Mike said. "Pony, why do you put up with him?"

"Sebastian, always interesting," Joe said.

Mike growled. "Chinese curse: May you live in interesting times."

CHAPTER 31
COLD BLOOD

THE PATIO CONVERSATION went on for many more beers and disturbed me more than I let on.

XiZi still on my trail. Empaya Iba AWOL, but probably not out of my life. Admiral Terry playing hardball. Mike, injured by me but playing along with the admiral. My privacy and sense of self invaded by bodyguards and even friends. Amanda, the person I care for most in the world, caught in the middle.

And Joe, the enigmatic old man. I never knew what to make of Joe; still wasn't sure he was even real. After dropping his bombshell about the dragon demon—never mind that he called it a spirit; it was a demon in my book—he had been too quiet, perhaps reserving his thoughts for a private conversation later. More likely, and what I feared, he had had nothing positive to say about Iba or the newly identified dragon demon.

I found it odd that I dreamed of the dragon threat before I even encountered the Chinese. Could Empaya Iba see the future? And make me dream about it? Just how much influence did it have over my life? Was I becoming little more than a puppet?

The thoughts scared me. I'd been down this road before and

tried to kill myself as a way to get rid of the spider demon. Could I even attempt that now, or would Iba stop me?

The trip to Borneo was supposed to answer questions like that, but we hadn't even gotten close to Iba's domain. And despite the distinction Joe tried to make between demons and spirits, I felt only menace.

I'd like to say that all this company—T, Joe, Mike and Jan—filled Amanda's seven-bedroom home, but in fact, she had room for more. Apparently, I was the one who felt cramped as I silently stewed.

Amanda and Jan seemed able to talk without end, sitting on opposite ends of the sofa in her sitting room off the bedroom that Amanda and I shared. They talked on the phone all the time, and I could not imagine what else they could have to say to one another in person. But they did, and Amanda seemed happier for it.

Joe had adopted T, or vice versa—I couldn't tell which—after watching him play sudoku on his cell phone. T then showed him mah-jongg, Chinese checkers, and an updated version of Super Mario, but he hooked him on the technology with a drawing program. Joe discovered that he could paint ancient Ute designs using just his finger on the handheld device. Old Pony That Sees Far saw a lot of potential. T took him out—accompanied by two bodyguards—and bought him a cell phone and top of the line mini-tablet with a data feed, and they disappeared to do geeky things together.

Mike and a big guy whose musculature must have wreaked havoc on his polo shirts walked around and around the house, inside and out, scoping out security vulnerabilities. I didn't see any, but on one of my increasingly rare forays off the property, I noticed the geezers who checked guests in and out of the private development were gone, replaced by off-duty Denver cops carrying sidearms. Two private security guards parked at the entrance to Amanda's six-acre property. They seemed several rungs above your average rent-a-cop, and they carried submachine guns in gym bags.

The difference between a fortress and a prison, I discovered, depended on which side of the wall you were on. It was all too much. After my wife Sarah's death, I had grown accustomed to living alone. Amanda and I were still getting used to one another when T moved in. Now the house seemed filled with strangers, and I flipped out.

For reasons that remain unclear to me to this day, I decided it was time for Empaya Iba to fish or cut bait. While the others were paired off and playing well together, I retreated to my study, a version of Amanda's sitting room on the opposite side of our bedroom.

Rather than seeking solace in my photography, I pounded on Google for hours on end searching for information about XiZi Ltd. and Chinese Red Army business interests worldwide. I hit pay dirt, courtesy of the conspiracy theorists in Congress. An obscure member of the House of Representatives had requested a Congressional Research Service study of businesses owned or influenced by the Red Army. The footnotes in that report took me through a back door of a quasi-public CIA report on the XiZi leadership and links to the People's Liberation Army hierarchy. With a dozen names in hand, I drew a diagram of the XiZi hierarchy.

I probably could have asked Jimmy Beam for the information; I'm sure the Australian Intelligence Service had it, but I didn't want anyone to know what I was doing or what I planned.

After two days of burning my eyes out on the computer screen, I narrowed my list to eight individuals associated with or employed by XiZi who would, or should, have known about the attempt to kidnap T as a way to get to me.

At the top was Chan Ming Su, the XiZi CEO and a former four-star general in the Red Army. His mother had been Korean, and he had apparently been produced during the Chinese intervention in Korea during 1951. His father had been a low-ranking officer in the Red Army, but an honorable man, and he married Su's mother and brought her back to China. That must have really pleased Su's Chinese grandparents.

Next came an executive vice president for international operations, a former vice admiral in the Red Navy named Yi Hsu Huang. Huang's photo reminded me of every banker I had ever met, a man in a dark suit wearing black horn-rimmed glasses.

The head of the Southeast Asian Region came third in line. Li Liang Ma, if I had it right, still held a post in the Red Army in logistics. He had only two stars, but the CIA identified him as a comer. I wondered how that made Mr. Huang feel in that very hierarchical company.

I left Mr. Lee off my list, assuming he was dead or no longer a threat. I figured he must have been at the colonel or one-star general rank, but there were too many Lees with Red Army connections to nail down any details.

Then I got down to the nitty gritty of the three kidnappers, the extra guy on the boat, and, of course, the Chinese woman. I had no names for them, but I remembered their faces perfectly. I wished I could see them now.

Two guys had stayed in the village with the hostages, but I'd never seen them or heard their names. They were complete blanks. Amanda said they had treated everyone well, and on that basis alone, I gave them a pass.

For the next step, I could have borrowed Amanda's yoga mat and sat cross-legged on the floor of my study and chanted or hummed or moaned or whatever people who meditate do. Instead, I waited until Maria had gone off to the market with T and Joe and their three bodyguards.

I took the largest cigar I owned at the time, a 7-inch Partagas Churchill with a 47 ring, and plopped myself out on Maria's deck. I pruned the end of the cigar with my Swiss Army knife, sparked a wooden match against a patio brick, and heated the business end of the cigar. On the first puff, the entire rim smoked and lighted.

My stomach lurched, a result of inhaling the strong smoke or a reaction to what I was about to do. I coughed, paused and considered.

This organization had targeted me. They had kidnapped T and had been prepared to torture or kill him to ensure my cooperation. Mr. Lee intimated he would do the same or worse to Amanda. If Mike and Admiral Anderson's intelligence was correct—and given their track record in Borneo, I believed them—XiZi was preparing a similar operation on my home turf.

I was not a soldier, but I lived in the modern world of unending brushfire wars and terrorist campaigns. I understood that XiZi had declared war. I would now fight back with the one resource I had. I didn't know if it would work, but I felt I could bear the consequences.

I would protect my loved ones.

Cigar smoke swirled around my head as I pictured my resident demons. All I had to go on was my recurring nightmare, so Empaya Iba came to mind as a giant with telephone pole legs; the dragon appeared as the red-tongued, green-winged slithering beast in Gustave Moreau's oil painting of *St. George and the Dragon*.

Normally I never smoke without a drink in hand; it's uncivilized and too hurried. That particular day, I smoked to remember and forget, for bloody business, not relaxation and pleasure. I filled my mouth with smoke, held it and let it leak out of my nostrils. If you stay away from hallucinogenics and focus hard, plain old Cuban tobacco will produce a high.

My eyes watered, and a tear slid from each eye. I puffed and held the smoke, focusing, focusing, focusing. One inch of tobacco turned to ash, then two. The ash dropped onto my lap. Three inches, four, five. I unwrapped the red and yellow Partagas ring band and tucked it into my shirt pocket. I puffed and thought and dreamed my bloody vengeance of strangled headless bodies.

Empaya Iba was with me and was pleased.

Joe shook me hard, his hands on my shoulders and his face in mine.

"What have you done, Sebastian?"

The cigar between my fingers had gone out, a little more than two inches unburned. My hand lay in my lap.

Joe's shaking rattled my head. My dream faded, and Iba disappeared like the Cheshire cat, leaving bloodied heads behind.

Joe prodded me again, and T leaned over behind him with a look that said something was wrong.

"Sebastian, are you all right? Joe seems to think something happened to you."

"What?"

I was groggy.

"Something, not *to* him. What Sebastian did," Joe said.

I tried to remember. It was a different Iba dream. Not so much a nightmare as a triumph. I eyed the cigar. Recollections filled holes in my brain.

"Sebastian, I know you do something bad. What was it?"

I looked straight at him.

"I did what I had to do, Joe. You understand. If Empaya Iba survives with any powers, I have just killed eight human beings in cold blood."

EMPAYA IBA SPEAKS

Take heart, children of the Black Orchid.
My fallen minion, he who bears the mark of my home,
Weak and fearful has he been,
But is no longer.
The servant has returned to his master.
He acknowledges the master's power.
Like a thirst, he craved to join himself to Empaya Iba.
And Abah, your father, has taken him again.

The blood flowed in the home of our land,
Violators of Mother Soil, he fed to Empaya Iba.
And he felt my strength,
And was glad.
I look to the many suns ahead;
And joy it gives to me.
Together we plot our path
As it wanders, without fail, back to you.

So say I, Empaya Iba, spirit of the Black Orchid People,
Guardian of the Mother Soil, giver of the Long Sleep,
Seer of the Many Eyes, mage of the Many Legs.

CHAPTER 32

BAD BUSINESS

J OE WALKED INTO the house, an old man with the wind knocked
out of him.

T stared, his mouth hanging open.

"Did you really? I can't believe. I mean… Your tat looks different. All red? You okay?"

"Yeah, sure. It gets that way."

"Okay. See you later," T said.

Isn't there a law of physics that says for every action, there is an equal and opposite reaction? Watching my friends' reactions, I began to realize what I had done.

I came down to breakfast late the next day and found Mike waiting, his head down, his hands turning a white coffee mug in circles. Maria greeted me with her usual motherly smile.

"Good morning, Sebastian. You are late today."

"Yes. All the reading I've been doing lately caught up with me."

"Would you like breakfast with your coffee today?"

"I don't think so. I'll just join Mike here. Has Amanda gone already?"

"Si. She and senora Jan meet with the lawyers today."

"I forgot that was today. Okay."

"That's special, what she's doing," Mike said, still staring at the table.

Amanda was setting up funds for the families of the six Navy Seals and two Army helicopter pilots whom Empaya Iba—and I—had killed in Montana.

"She's a special lady," I said, "but you know that."

"Yeah. Lousy taste in men though," he said. "Outside?"

"Sure."

Maria freshened our mugs, and we went out to the patio.

"What's on your mind, Mike?"

"Why do you ask?" he said.

"You didn't go with Amanda. And you're not out inspecting security somewhere. And you waited for me. Do I need more?"

"No. Intel from Singapore. Executives of XiZi no-shows for work this morning. Dead. Causes unknown."

"Cut down in the prime of their corrupt lives," I said. "Too bad."

"Know anything?"

I ignored his question.

"Which executives were they?" I asked. "CEO? CFO? Who?"

"You wouldn't recognize names," Mike said.

"How about Su, Huang, and Ma? Any of those among the departed?"

Mike raised an eyebrow.

"You do know something. Huang and Ma. How did you know?"

"Interesting," I said, pondering the implications. I sipped my coffee and thought it tasted better than usual.

"What's going on?" Mike said.

"Have you heard from Jimmy Beam?"

"No. Why?"

"Just curious."

"Did you do this? You and Iba?"

"Mike, Iba's been pretty quiet since that run-in with the old Australian aboriginal. Some of us even wonder if maybe it died or was wounded so badly that it's retired, or whatever spirits do when they're not demonizing."

"Answer my question."

Joe joined us, white coffee mug with black coffee in hand.

"Sebastian, you tell Mike what you do?"

It could have been a statement, but Joe meant it as a question.

"Told me nothing," Mike said, looking at Joe. "Two execs of the company that kidnapped T died last night. He knows their names."

"This is bad, Sebastian. What you do. Very bad," Joe said. "If you use the spider spirit…"

"If I use the demon, Joe, I finally get something out of this business," I said. "It uses me. Why not use it?"

"You make a habit, Sebastian. When you need it, you use it. After a while, you don't know how to live without it. You don't question. You don't fight it. Then, you and spirit are one. Then you are the demon, too."

"That's a long speech, Joe."

"Don't make fun, Sebastian. Now you fight it. Maybe soon, you don't. You tell me this is not what you want."

"Well, what can I do!"

Spittle and coffee flew from my mouth. No one said anything.

"They lied to me," Mike said suddenly. "You can kill long distance."

"Yeah," I said. "They probably lied about a lot of other things, too. Welcome to your military. They can use you as much as they want to use me. I warned you before."

Mike nodded.

"What did you do? When?" he asked.

"Yesterday," I said. "I came out here, had myself a cigar, and smoked eight very deserving people."

"Who else?" Mike said. "We only have the two."

"Check the CEO's health. Unless Iba got sloppy, he should be down, too. The Chinese woman and four of her little helpers. Jimmy could probably track those."

"You just sat here and thought them to death?"

It sounded obscene when he put it like that.

Suddenly I didn't feel like talking. I nodded.

Mike sighed.

"I have to make calls."

After a short silence, Joe spoke.

"What now, Sebastian?"

"I don't know," I said. "I hope maybe XiZi will forget about me. I had to do something. I can't have my family and friends threatened, especially when I have the power to strike back. Besides, I learned something."

"What do you learn, Sebastian?"

"Iba is alive and well."

CHAPTER 33
ON THE ROAD

MIKE BROUGHT A grim face to lunch.

"You a pain in the ass," he said in a low croak.

"What makes you say that?" I said.

Mike huffed.

"Body count rising. Not at eight yet. CEO definitely alive. The woman is missing. You were right. Superiors lied to me: You did kill General Brant; his men had reason to come after you," he said.

"Does that mean you regret coming to rescue me?"

"Regretted that before. Haven't changed my mind. Did no good, and eight good men died. If I had known that you could... that you did, in fact, cause Brant's death, I would have stopped the rescue. You didn't need it. We were just victims, like the snipers."

Mike caught his breath after a long and tortured speech, for his throat and his soul.

"These are the people you want me to trust, Mike," I said. "Never forget that, because I don't. And I like you and value you as a friend, but I never let myself forget who controls you. And if you think Admiral Anderson is any different, you're wrong."

He looked at me in disgust, threw his napkin on his plate, and stalked off.

"I thought he knew I was responsible for Brant's death," I said. "Since the Australians knew, I assumed he had to know."

"Bad business, Sebastian," Joe said.

"You keep saying that, old man. What are we going to do to make it good?"

"Maybe we just go north. Mike figure things out here," Joe said.

"I agree, Sebastian," T said. "Let's load up and go. I'm sure you won't mind an extra day in the gardens. And if Empaya Iba is as good as Mike suggests, security is no longer an issue."

"You know, T, you could grow on a guy. Let's do it," I said.

"You know, Sebastian, you're still a jerk," T said.

I turned to Joe.

"You want to add anything?"

"Bad business, Sebastian. Not over. Bad business."

We made one heck of a sight as we stopped that night in Cody, Wyoming. A runty old Indian, a one-eyed kid with a cut-up face, and me with a spiderweb tattoo engraved into my cheek. (If Mike had people following us, they didn't check in when we did.)

For a moment, I wondered whether the receptionist at the Welcome Inn off I-25 would give us three rooms. Her much older supervisor eyeballed us, noticed that our clothes were clean—T's were even fashionable—and offered us the choice of a volume discount for three rooms or geezer discounts for Joe and me. I chose the volume discount and took a mini-suite for myself and king rooms for Joe and T.

After dinner and several rounds of drinks at a local watering hole, we spread out in my suitelet for a nightcap. My cell phone pinged a sonar tone, announcing that Mike was on the line. I decided to ignore it and laid the device at arm's reach on an end table. T scooped it up and answered.

"You don't like the mobile?" Joe said. He had fallen hard for the technology and sounded a bit offended that I would not respond to its summons. I figured he would learn in time.

"Mobile's okay, at times, but this is Mike calling. I'm sure it's not good news," I said.

Over in the kitchen area, T listened a good ten minutes before hanging up.

Joe and I turned to him as he touched the phone off and set it back on the end table.

"You want to hear what he had to say?" T asked.

"Not really," I said.

"Me, yes," Joe said.

I was outvoted again.

T addressed me.

"Bottom line, you got six and missed two. The CEO and the woman are still alive, apparently with no ill effects. The others died... poorly."

"Whined and carried on, you mean?" I said, more harshly than I intended.

"It took a long time. Slow strangulation, like they were wrung out from the inside. Several of them thrashed so much they broke their necks. Mike said it was almost like they tried to cut their own heads off. Sound familiar?"

I shrugged. What was there to say? I wanted them dead; they died.

"Jimmy's ticked off."

"Of course, he is," I said. "Everybody gets ticked off when I use the spider for my purposes and not theirs."

"Admiral Anderson is very curious about why the girl and the CEO didn't die."

"Six out of eight. That puts me in the demon hall of fame."

"The admiral knows the CEO guy, Su. Apparently, they did some liaison thing earlier in their careers. Anyway, he's going to try to meet with him," T said.

"What for? To ask him if he felt strangled at some point in the recent past?"

I had perhaps had too many drinks over dinner. I could sense my own petulance.

"The most interesting news comes from Jimmy," T said. "His people have been looking into the Chinese woman. Her name is Wan Xiu Lan; it means 'elegant orchid'."

T eyeballed me for a reaction. I shrugged. Orchid connections were becoming pretty routine.

He continued.

"Jimmy figures she might be more of a player than we think. And much older than she looks. She starts to sound a little like Maria."

Joe and I both perked up.

"Amanda's Maria? Not possible. Maria is Earth Mother; the woman—Wan?—is… I don't know what, but not Maria."

"Her mother was an herbalist during the Red Guard days. Actually, a pharmacy student but never graduated and volunteered to go out into the villages and work with the people. Her grandmother was a midwife. Jimmy suspects she may come from a line of medicine women. That's why she's a little like Maria."

"Medicine," Joe said. "She *is* the dragon, Sebastian. In your dreams. She didn't die because Iba couldn't kill the dragon."

CHAPTER 34

SWEET DREAMS

FTER ALL OUR drinking, we slept well that night.

T dreamed of two women: Eve, our Bornean interpreter, and Jenny, the Montana geek who had died protecting his wounded body with her own.

Amanda and I suspected T was pretty sweet on Eve; he had bought her a cell phone and a year of international coverage before we left Borneo. And he made certain his cell number was programmed into her contact list.

I did not envy T his visit with Jenny's parents, and I did not volunteer to accompany him. Joe did.

Joe dreamed of my spirits. The spider seemed revived; the dragon was young and fierce. Joe told us he didn't know what to make of it.

I was pleased to see him confused for once, since I was perplexed pretty much all the time.

I dreamed of Amanda, pleasant dreams I could not remember but which left me feeling very good, the Chinese woman be damned.

On our drive north, we discussed the possible dangers ahead. We had seen no signs of Mike's people and planned to proceed as if we were completely on our own. T had acquired a pistol, a deadly, ugly

Glock, and an ATF license to carry a concealed weapon anywhere in the U.S., courtesy of Mike Owens's influence.

Joe carried in his right cowboy boot a black metal knife with a curved handle made from an elk antler. He used it for everything from cutting apples to whittling sticks, but it was never less than razor sharp.

I kept the Webley in my camera bag, a large padded glorified backpack that goes with me everywhere; I had no permit. I had Iba—and a Ka-Bar in my boot.

We figured Joe would be safest since Wan, the XiZi agent, had never seen him, and it was unlikely that he had shown up in her research. We hoped she did not dream like he and Maria Reina did.

Despite Mike's intervention and her own security measures, we figured Amanda was in the greatest peril. Her manse was like a castle, but any castle can be breached. In addition, she refused to sit still. She had a life to live and was out living it, taking care of those military families, attending board meetings, consulting occasionally on business matters, and, of course, managing her own considerable investments. With the reinforcements from Admiral Anderson, four security personnel were on duty in and around the mansion at any given time.

In the end, unless T, Joe, and I all stayed with her, her safety was up to Mike.

⁂

I dropped the guys off at a discount car rental place in Billings. As we moved their meager gear from my SUV to the rental, I asked T to keep an eye on Joe. Ever since learning what I had done to the Chinese, he had seemed suddenly frail, as well as old. They drove off to see Jenny's parents in some small town east of Great Falls. After that, T expected to take Joe to visit his granddaughter at U. Big Sky in Missoula. I would pick them up there after my photo shoot in three days.

Flying solo for the first time in a long time, I ordered Bluetooth to dial Amanda. She answered immediately.

"Hey, cowboy," she said.

"I miss you," I said.

"That's sweet. I miss you, too. Where are you?"

"I-90, western Montana, heading for Idaho. Where are you?"

"Home. Mike and Jan left this morning. I think he was heading to Hawaii to have it out with that new boss of his, but I don't know for sure. He wouldn't let me take them to the airport. He says it's not safe. He even pulled in a female guard who will live in the house full time. The guys will continue to rotate between the hotel and here."

"I guess it's best to play it safe," I said, not wanting to dwell on danger.

I peered in the rear view mirror, searching for signs of Mike's people. Unless they were driving big rigs, they weren't in sight.

"Did you get the boys to their destinations?" she asked.

"They're in a rental car now on their way to Jenny's parents. I'll meet them in Missoula after my photo shoot."

"How is Pony That Sees Far?"

"As vague as ever. Why?"

"I'm concerned. He's an old man. Suddenly he seems frail."

"Don't worry about him. He'll never die. He can't. He's already pickled in some very expensive booze. I'd like to know what he drank before I started picking up his bar bills."

"He doesn't go to bars."

"That we know of," I said.

"I know he has an apprentice who is working on his own pickling process."

"You think I drink too much?"

"You could cut back a little."

"You're probably right. I was pretty looped last night when Mike called. I didn't even want to talk to him."

"What do you think it means, that those two are still alive?"

"I don't know," I said.

I scanned that beautiful Montana big sky in front of me. All that beauty, and here I was, pushing the Denali to 85 and wallowing in shit.

"Did you and the others talk about what I did?" I said.

"We're together, Sebastian, and people who are together, if they intend to stay that way, shouldn't spend a lot of time judging the other. Your—our—situation is not a typical one. I wish it was different, but it's not. That's what I deal with," she said.

"You've been hanging around Joe too long. You say a lot, and I end up confused."

"I'm not judging you, and I love you. Is that better?" she said.

"Got that. Thank you—for both."

"So, what do you think it means, especially since the woman is still alive. She seems to be the bigger threat."

"The CEO may have been insulated by the people below him, but the girl—that's odd. And coincidental. What are the chances that two people who have demons doing something to them, that they run into one another? Those have to be Power Ball–type odds.

"And if I inherited some deadly power through my demon, what does she have?"

"Doesn't it also depend on whether she knows what she has and has the ability to use it?" Amanda asked. "After all, you're still learning about Empaya Iba."

"There's an awful thought," I said, shaking my head.

"Listen, of course we stay vigilant, but I'm not sure how much danger she represents. Her thugs are gone. Her bosses, the guys who would have known what she and Lee were up to, are out of the picture. Assume the CEO doesn't know. How much latitude does she have? If she is, in fact, on her way to Denver, that takes money. Is she still going to have access to the kind of money she needs? I'm guessing she's going to hunker down some place and see what happens. That translates into no immediate threat, and probably no long-term threat either. I don't see a rational CEO thinking it's a good idea to go prospecting for demons. That's just borrowing trouble."

"And in the meantime, Mike has me smothered in security," Amanda said.

"I know it's bad. I feel lousy for being out here free with you left back in the birdcage."

"I told Mike, and Jan backed me up on this, the arrangement is short-term tolerable. They are all nice, incredibly polite, and devoted to my safety. Maria enjoys cooking for them."

"Is she smothering them in mother bear love?"

"Every chance she gets."

"Well, I don't think there's anything to worry about, but just keep an eye out and be careful."

"I will. You do the same. Remember, Sebastian, I'm just a way to get at you. You're the one they really want."

CHAPTER 35
TAKEN

Amanda's cell phone number popped onto the Denali's dashboard as I drove out of Oregon and into Idaho three days later. I pressed the connect button on the steering wheel, silencing ZZ Top's *Fat Bottom Girls*.

"Sebastian. We're being attacked. They shot Maria."

The call ended almost before it began.

"… fat bottom girls, you make the rockin' world go round."

I swerved to the side of the road and slammed on the brakes. The pickup truck behind me jinked into oncoming traffic to avoid hitting me. Horn-honking and finger-raising ensued. I ignored it.

I shouted at the Bluetooth connection.

"Home. Dial home. Home. Home."

The numbers beeped through their deliberate progression.

The other end buzzed, but Amanda did not pick up.

I punched the disconnect button on the steering wheel.

"Dial Mike emergency."

My hands were shaking, and it was all I could do not to scream into the Bluetooth microphone.

Again, the deliberate dialing. This time, the connection popped after one buzz.

"Sebastian, what's up?"

Mike's damaged vocal cords produced a higher pitched croak.

"Amanda called my cell. She's being attacked. Her phone disconnected before I could say anything. Where the hell are your people?"

"Hold."

I pounded the steering wheel. Passing cars honked. I noticed I still had two wheels in the travel lane of the two-lane highway. I nosed into the shallow drainage ditch, pitching the SUV sideways at a steep angle.

"Sebastian, something is happening." Mike was back on the line. "Police on it. Two minutes away."

"Where are your guys, Mike? Dammit, they're supposed to be taking care of her."

"We have a 'soldier down' signal, but no audio contact." Mike's voice strained with effort. "Who's with you?"

"No one. I left T and Joe in Billings three days ago."

"Go to the nearest law enforcement. Hit the panic button we installed. We can follow you that way."

"Where are your people?"

"Just do what I say, please, Sebastian."

Mike's voice gave out, and he coughed.

"I'm going back to Denver."

"You can't help."

"I'm going back."

"Sebastian…" Mike's voice squeaked out the last word.

"Let me know as soon as you hear from your people or the cops. You get Amanda and you make sure she's safe."

"Sebas—" Mike's voice gave out.

I put on my left-turn signal, checked the rearview mirror, and whipped the Denali out of the ditch, across two lanes of local highway, and through a ditch into a farm field. A semi roared past while I dug up the freshly plowed field. In less than a minute I was tearing down the Oregon highway at 100 miles an hour, closing in on the semi and getting ready to pass.

I shouted at Bluetooth again. "Call Tom."

A subdued T answered his cell.

"Hello."

"It's Sebastian. Someone is attacking the house. I can't reach Amanda. I'm heading back to Denver. Is Joe there? Can he sense what's going on?"

"What!"

T's adrenaline kicked in.

"He's not with me right now," T said. "I'll get him. When did this happen?"

"Minutes ago."

"What happened to the bodyguards? What about Mike's people? They're all over the place."

"I don't know. Mike got a 'man down' signal but he can't reach his team. I don't know what happened to the rent-a-cops."

"Did you talk to Amanda? How do you know?"

I'll give it to T. He's thorough in his questioning, no matter what.

"She spoke maybe five words. Said they were being attacked. Then disconnected. She said Maria was shot. Gotta go. Another call coming in."

I fiddled with the steering wheel, trying to figure how to disconnect from one call to pick up another. I lost both and slowed the Denali to 80. I downshifted to fourth and raced back up to 100. The phone rang again.

"Hello."

"Mr. Arnett, it's Colonel Dale Colder, General Owens's deputy. I have some news and a request from General Owens."

"What news?"

"Bad, I'm afraid. Police have arrived, and we are listening to their live radio traffic. Mrs. Campion's bodyguards and our entire team are down and appear to be dead. The Mexican woman is down, hurt badly. An ambulance is on the way. They're still looking for Mrs. Campion, but the first police unit to arrive saw a helicopter taking off from the rear of the house. Police didn't get any markings. That's all I have. I'm sorry, sir."

"Shit. Shit. Shit. You guys were supposed to prevent this."

"I understand, sir. We're doing all we can right now. General Owens requests that you slow down. We have your beacon and you appear to be speeding."

"What would you do if this were your wife, colonel?"

"I hope I would understand it's a marathon from where you are back to Denver… but I wouldn't slow down."

"Right."

T came on the line almost as quickly as I hung up.

"Two things, Sebastian."

"What?"

"Joe isn't in Montana. He's in Denver."

"Where? What's he doing there? Is he at home?"

"He was, but he's moving pretty quickly away from it."

"How? How do you know?"

"I put a tracker on his phone. I figured he would lose it and we would need to find it for him."

"You're a genius, T. What else?"

"I know you won't like to hear this, but we're talking about Amanda," he said. "Can't Iba do something?"

"I've already thought of that. I was about to try, but one of Mike's people just reported that a helicopter left the house as the cops arrived. I assume they have Amanda. Until I know for sure, I can't do anything. But once I know, I'll be sucking the air out of a 10-mile radius around those assholes."

"Uh, okay, Sebastian. I'm on my way back to Denver. I'll keep trying to reach Joe. I'm afraid he's forgotten how to answer his phone."

"Good luck. Just hope he doesn't throw it away…. Listen, you're going to reach there before I do. Move slowly and don't rely too much on the cops."

"Got it, Sebastian. By the way, slow down. You're really cruising."

"Does everyone on earth know how fast I'm going?"

"No. Just the people who care. You're no good to Amanda if you're dead."

CHAPTER 36
UNTIDY DETAILS

I HAD TO FIGHT myself to keep the Denali at eighty-five; it wanted to cruise at a hundred or more.

Shortly after T hung up, I saw what I had been looking for: a sign for the junction with I-84. I took my foot off the pedal but the Denali raced ahead. In the fast-approaching distance, I spotted flashing lights. A cop with someone pulled over. No, it was several cops and they were blocking the road. I suspected that trucker I almost hit had turned me in.

I hit the brakes, hard. I skidded the last fifteen car lengths but stayed in my lane. Two police cars completely blocked access to the I-84 ramps. A third one sat just off the road pointed in my direction. Three Oregon state police troopers faced my SUV.

Calm, I said to myself. *Calm. Don't mess up. It's a speeding ticket. Take it and then get gone.*

One trooper stayed behind the blocking vehicles while two others cautiously approached the Denali, one on either side. I noticed their hands were on their holsters—standard procedure for approaching a potentially drunk speeder—I kept my hands on the steering wheel in sight.

The trooper on my side of the SUV stopped at the front bumper and eyeballed me through dark glasses. The other guy slowly circled the Denali, staying well away from the SUV. He reached my door and tapped the window with one knuckle. I slowly moved my left hand to the window controls and slid the window open.

He eyed the tattoo. Everybody did the first time they encountered it.

"Are you Mr. Sebastian Arnett?" he said.

"Yes."

"Do you have a photo ID?"

"Yes."

"May I see it? Slowly please?"

With my left hand back on the steering wheel, I leaned forward and wrestled my wallet out of my jeans pocket. I handed it over and placed my right hand back on the steering wheel. The trooper flipped the wallet open; my ID showed through a clear plastic screen. He handed it back to me.

"Follow my car, please, sir."

"Where are we going?" I asked.

"To an airstrip about 30 miles away. There's a charter plane coming to get you."

I think I exhaled for the first time since seeing the flashing lights.

Mike Owens had reached someone and cleared the way. How he managed to get a plane so quickly, I had no idea. Too bad he couldn't keep one woman safe.

I followed the trooper onto the ramp heading west. That route would take me farther from Denver, but I was willing to trust him for 30 miles. He kept his flashers on and quickly hit 90 miles an hour. I rode his bumper, but he either couldn't go any faster or wasn't inclined to.

I called Mike again and spoke as soon as the phone finished its solitary ring.

"Mike, it's Sebastian. Any news?"

Colonel Colder's voice responded.

"Just details. No big-picture changes."

"T says Joe is in Denver but seems to be missing as well. He's not answering his cell phone."

"Joe would be the elderly Indian? He has a cell phone?"

"T bought it," I said.

"And T is Mrs. Campion's son?"

"Close enough. He's on his way back from Billings. He's trying to reach Joe. He's got a tracker on the cell phone and he says Joe is moving around."

"We'll contact T," the colonel said.

"Oregon state cops stopped me getting on the interstate. They said they were taking me to a plane. Is that yours?"

"We arranged it; Mrs. Campion is paying."

"How does that happen?"

"Mrs. Campion told General Owens there might come a time when we would need things that the government would not, or could not in a timely fashion, provide. We have a credit card with a large line of credit attached."

"What are you doing to get her back? And where's Mike?"

"We are coordinating. General Owens has lost his voice."

"Great time to lose his voice. What are you coordinating?"

"There are a lot of balls in the air, and we're making sure that relevant agencies understand the urgency of the situation."

"Have you tracked down the helicopter? They must have a limited range."

"We have. It was abandoned in north Denver. Stolen. We're waiting to see if the local police can find prints."

"You really expect them to?"

"No. Too professional. A neighbor said they wore black. Ski masks, gloves, everything."

"Did the neighbor see Amanda?"

"No."

"Are we sure they have her?"

"She's not in the house or on the grounds. Did she have a safe room?"

"Not that I ever knew. I'm pretty sure not.... How is Maria?"

"In surgery. Not good. Her husband is on the way."

"What about your people and the rent-a-cops?"

"Dead. Looks like sniper wounds, then a shot to the head."

I blew out air. Too professional.

"The guards at the gate?"

"Two shots to the head."

"Video?"

"Disconnected and erased."

"Sebastian."

The voice on the speaker changed. It was Mike, and he sounded awful.

"Can Iba...?"

"I don't know. I don't want to try until I know more about Amanda. And I'm not sure how much juice Iba has left."

CHAPTER 37
KIDNAPPER'S CONTACT

THE DENALI'S BLUETOOTH announced an incoming call as I followed the Oregon trooper off the interstate. I punched the answer button, hoping it was a spammer.

"Hello," I said, as if it were a normal call.

"Mr. Arnett." It was Wan, the XiZi woman. I recognized her cultured accent.

"What have you done with Amanda? If you—"

"We have Mrs. Campion and intend her no harm, if you cooperate."

"You keep saying that, but you keep kidnapping people I care about."

"It is strictly to get your attention."

"Have you ever tried texting?"

She gave a laugh, a very small laugh.

"You know you're going to be a marked woman. You have all kinds of cops on your tail."

"We have a complicated situation. I think you and I should sit down and discuss a way out."

"Why don't we talk about it now? You're on the line; I'm on the line."

"Yes, but I'm sure someone is trying to trace this phone while we speak."

"It ain't me, lady."

"That doesn't matter. I need you to understand that you should not attempt to use your powers again. It would have a very unfortunate impact on Mrs. Campion. You will be contacted."

"Well, that's just—Hello? Hello?"

She was gone.

I dialed Mike. Ahead, I could see the sign for an airfield.

"Colder."

"Where's Mike? It's Sebastian Arnett."

"Not available. How can I help?"

"I got a call from the kidnappers. I assume you track my cell phone. Can you get a trace on it?"

"How long was the call?"

"Not long. Thirty seconds maybe."

"Please hold."

Colonel Colder was gone long enough for the state trooper and me to reach the airport and drive out to a small jet on the tarmac. I clicked my cell on before turning the Denali's powerful engine off. The cell showed that I was still connected to Mike's deputy. I left the keys in the ignition, grabbed my backpack, and jumped down from the SUV.

I waved my thanks to the trooper and ran up the plane's steps, almost colliding with the copilot at the top of the stairs.

"Let's go. Denver."

"Mr. Arnett?"

"Yes. Let's go. Come on."

"Yes, sir."

The plane's engines wound up as the copilot pulled the steps up and closed and locked the door. I kept my eyes glued to the cell phone. Where was Colder? I didn't know if I would have a signal once the plane took off.

I dumped my backpack onto a seat and sat down on a forward-facing lounger opposite it. The jet engines raced and the plane jerked forward.

My cell screen lit up.

"Mr. Arnett, I'm sorry it took so long."

"What have you got? Did you find them?"

"We have it narrowed down to an area in northwest Denver. It's a warehouse district near the rail yards where I-25 and I-70 meet. There are literally hundreds of commercial buildings there with easy access to the highways and the railroad, for that matter."

"Can you narrow it down?" I asked.

"No, sir. Not without an active connection."

"I thought NSA had all kinds of... I don't know. I just thought you guys were in my pocket."

"We are, sir. We know where you are. That doesn't mean we know where your callers are, not without an active connection."

I uttered expletives.

"What went wrong? You guys were supposed to protect her. Get Mike on the phone."

I was yelling loud enough to be heard over the jet's engines. The copilot looked back over his shoulder for an instant.

"We screwed up. We underestimated how far they would go."

"That's just great. You guys claim you want to keep other people from getting to me. Well, guess what? Those Chinese have gotten to me, and if I can get Amanda back safely by working with them, then you guys are just up a creek without a paddle."

"Mr. Arnett, we get it. We are doing everything we can. The Denver police are in charge, but they've asked the FBI for assistance. We have supported that request. We're working on some things of our own."

I was furious and frustrated. I did a mean, vicious, incredibly stupid thing. I envisioned Colder, whom I'd never met, writhing on the floor wherever he was. I heard a gasping, retching sound before the phone disconnected.

Get control of yourself, I thought.

I sensed Joe for an instant. My heart raced, and I noticed my palms were sweating. I felt the tattoo; it was burning.

Breathe, I told myself. *Breathe deep. Breathe slowly. Breathe.*

I closed my eyes and felt a weight pushing me back into the seat. We were taking off.

I opened my eyes to see the ground disappear. My black Denali was moving toward a small office building. Someone had come to clear it off the tarmac.

The pilot seemed to point the jet straight into the sky, banking hard to the left in a dizzying spiral. The engines roared, and I could hardly hear myself think. The phone vibrated in my hand, and I hoped the plane wasn't coming apart under the effort of the steep takeoff.

I glanced down. The phone was ringing. It was Mike's number. I slid my finger across the screen but could hear nothing over the straining engines. I disconnected.

Twice more the cell vibrated and twice I ignored it before the pilot leveled the plane out. When I thought I could hear, I dialed Mike's number.

"Seb… you… doing?"

Mike's voice was a croak, and I caught only every third or fourth word.

"I'm on a plane. It's loud in here. I can't hear you, Mike."

High-pitched croaking filled my ear, but I couldn't make out a single word.

A strange voice spoke.

"Please release Colonel Colder. You're killing him. Release Colonel Colder now or he's going to die. Please, sir. Mr. Arnett."

"Yes," I said.

The strangeness of the unexpected and unfamiliar voice broke the spell. I realized my knuckles had turned white from strangling the phone. I relaxed my grip, and color seeped back into my fingers.

"Mike?"

"Thank you, sir. Colonel Colder is responding."

"Who is this?"

"Captain Jenkins, sir. I'm on General Owens's staff."

"What's happening? Where's Mike?"

"He's tending to Colonel Colder, sir. He—he was having a seizure. General Owens can't speak. His voice has given out," the captain said.

"You guys totally screwed up," I said, working myself up to a fury again.

"You're not helping, sir. We are not the enemy."

"No, you're just a bunch of incompetents. What do I need you for if you can't protect my—my wife?"

I said it, realizing I didn't know how to describe Amanda to someone who didn't know her. "Girlfriend" was not strong enough. Companion was too transitory. Mate, partner… nothing worked except wife.

"We and many other people are working extremely hard on this, sir. We need you to get a grip."

"Well, I wouldn't need a grip if you people had done your job. What use are you?"

"Do you want to get Mrs. Campion back or do you just want to dump on us? Because if you just need a place to vent, I have better things to do."

This smart SOB didn't know who he was talking to. I would show him…. Suddenly, the fight was gone from me. I breathed as hard as if I had just run a 100-meter dash.

Noises came from the other end of the phone, but the captain was quiet.

"What happened?' I said. "How did they get in?"

"They hijacked a trash truck and came in through the service gate. They had silenced weapons and took out Mrs. Campion's security guards in the back of the house. Once inside, they shot all of our people and the Mexican woman.

"Her name is Maria Reina."

"They shot Mrs. Reina. Mrs. Campion must have called you about that time. Then they took out our second person out front. It was as good an operation as you could hope for. It doesn't look like our people got off a single shot. When all of the security was down, a helicopter flew in and evacuated the entire team. A neighbor thinks there were three men and two women. The men and one of the women wore black. The helicopter landed about five minutes away in a city park. Everyone got out of the chopper and into a white van that was parked there. Witnesses didn't get a license number. The call you got from the kidnappers gave us a temporary fix."

The captain finished his report.

"You tell Mike to keep me informed."

I disconnected before he could respond.

I rose from my seat and stepped up to the cockpit.

"How long to Denver?"

The copilot responded.

"Just under two hours, sir."

"Can you go any faster?"

"We can, but it would just mean circling Denver for a landing slot."

"What about one of the smaller fields nearby?"

"We could land in Boulder, but I'm not sure that helps you. What part of Denver is your destination?"

"I'm not sure. See about landing in Boulder. And see if you can arrange for a rental car."

"We were told someone would be picking you up."

"Change of plans."

The flier gave me a look, but nodded.

I returned to my seat to wait out the minutes and formulate a plan. I had no plan. The police. The security company. Mike. None had kept Amanda safe. I had resorted to using Iba again. It reminded me of Joe's warning. Pretty soon, I would not have to make a conscious decision to use Iba—I would be Iba. What kind of human being would that make me? Was it one that Amanda could love? Would I be driving her away by trying to save her?

The cell vibrated again, and for a second, I hoped it would be Mike so I could ream him out again.

I answered without checking the number. It was T.

"I found Joe," he said. "He's found Amanda. And all the other news is bad."

CHAPTER 38
NEW GUY

I LOOKED OUT THE window of the plane at the clouds below and tried to calm my racing heart.

"What's going on, T? Where are Joe and Amanda? Is she okay?"

"Slow down, Sebastian. Joe is in Denver, in the warehouse district off I-25," T said.

"What's he doing there?"

"He took the bus back to Denver yesterday. He said he had a dream, and he just did what the dream said to do. He saw the attack but couldn't stop it."

"Saw it? How?"

"He was in the gardener's shed where you sometimes sneak off to smoke by yourself. That's where he keeps his motor scooter."

"His what?"

"His motor scooter. I bought him a motor scooter," T said. "I thought he should have a way to get out without needing to ask someone for a ride. I couldn't buy him a horse, so I asked him if he would like a scooter. He loved the idea. He even picked it out."

"T, this is an old man. He doesn't know how to ride a motor scooter."

"Actually, Sebastian, he does. The guys at the motorcycle place were amazed by what he could do with it."

"Oh, geez. He's going to kill himself if he doesn't get arrested first."

"It's going to have to be a pretty fast cop that nails him."

I leaned back in my seat.

"T, don't we have enough trouble?"

"No, thanks to Joe we have less trouble. He knows where Amanda is. He's there now, keeping an eye out for her."

"How did he find them?" I asked.

"He didn't. He followed them. He saw the whole thing from the garden shed. Nobody knew he was there. The trash truck came early. That's how he knew something was up. After the helicopter took off, he got on his scooter and followed them to the park. He saw them transfer Amanda to the van. She was fine. She wasn't tied up or blindfolded. He followed the van and now he's hanging out behind a dumpster in one of these warehouse strips. It's right on the railroad tracks, and he thinks they might be planning to move by rail."

I tried to imagine the area, but it wasn't a part of Denver I knew well. Mostly I knew the tracks limited east-west traffic to a handful of streets that cross over them. Otherwise, the streets dead-ended at the tracks, usually lined with small warehouses. Finding Amanda would be like finding the proverbial needle in the haystack.

"There's an old refurbished caboose on a siding right behind the building they are in. Two of the guys who brought Amanda have set themselves up in the caboose," T said.

"How many altogether?"

"The pilot and three shooters, plus the woman."

"All right. Good to know. If you get names or descriptions, let me know. The knowledge may come in handy, you know, in case—"

"Yeah, I got it," T said.

"Listen, I'm on a plane heading to Boulder. Maybe 90 minutes out," I said. "Still figuring out what I'll do when I get there."

"Just find Joe, then hang tight. I'm on I-90 heading south. I'm going to Salt Lake City, pick up a couple friends there, guys who can mix it up pretty well with anyone. But it's going to be another twelve hours before I get to Denver."

"How can you be sure these guys will want to help?" I said.

"Trust me. I know them. When they found out what happened in Montana, they swore they'd tear me apart if I left them out again. This is their kind of gig. And they owe me, big time."

"Hey, I've got a call coming in from Mike. I'll call you back. Good job, T. Thanks. Thanks a million."

"You're not the only one who cares about her," he said.

"I know. Thanks anyway."

᠊ᡭ

I switched over to the incoming call.

"Mike, you better have some explanations." I didn't let him get started.

"Sir, this is Captain Winslow. I'm an aide to Admiral Anderson. General Owens is incapacitated, and I've taken over this operation."

"That's just great. I can see how important you guys think this is. I start out with a general in charge; then a colonel, then a captain, and now a different captain. What's next? An enlisted man? Corporal O'Reilly back in uniform?"

"Just the opposite, Mr. Arnett. Admiral Anderson is now person-ally involved, and I am a Navy captain. That's the equivalent of a full Marine colonel, and while Colonel Colder is an extremely capable officer, he is just a lieutenant colonel. I outrank him by quite a bit."

"Oh." What else could I say?

"What are you guys doing?"

"The FBI has taken control on the ground. They are putting a cordon around the warehouse district where the Chinese woman was located. They may have moved beyond that area, but we think it unlikely."

"They're there. In a building near the tracks," I said.

"How do you know, Mr. Arnett?"

"I have it under surveillance," I said.

"Where is it? We can have a Seal Team there in half an hour."

"No, thanks. You may want to help, but your team screwed up and got us where we are right now. You only get the information I want to give you, period. Are you guys doing anything else, or just hanging around watching the FBI?"

"Admiral Anderson has placed a call to the CEO of XiZi and apprised him of the situation in general terms," Captain Winslow said. "The Chinese woman is freelancing. He's going to contact the woman and arrange an end to this."

"If she goes along with him."

"Look, Mr. Arnett, we're working this. We can do more if you share Mrs. Campion's location with us."

"Not happening, captain. You had your chance."

"You can't go after those people alone," he said.

"Captain Winslow, one thing you will discover about me is that I am never alone."

CHAPTER 39
BAD NEWS

WE LANDED AT Boulder Municipal Airport on the east side of the city. I bounded out of the plane and into the terminal. There was no car rental service, but a taxi was dropping someone off and I hopped in it for a quick trip downtown to the nearest car rental office.

Twenty minutes later, I'd rented a car and was navigating my way through Boulder, trying to find U.S. 36, the fastest way down to Denver.

My cell phone vibrated in my shirt pocket. The rental car had Bluetooth, but I hadn't taken the time to set it up. I fished the device out of the buttoned pocket and almost sideswiped a parked car in the process. I pulled over to answer the call.

It was T.

"Where are you?" he asked.

"Boulder. Looking for 36 South. What's up?"

"Joe called. They are definitely planning to do something with the caboose. They have one guy planted there now. Wan and one guy are still in the warehouse with Amanda. The other two guys took the van out and just came back. Different white van, or at least different plates. Joe noticed that. They brought coolers and boxes of food. They're going on a trip, and they don't plan to go by car."

"Is there any way to know which direction they'll head?"

"This is a rail yard, Sebastian. There are trains coming and going, switching tracks. We might know when they hook up with an engine."

"Can we grab Amanda between the warehouse and the caboose?"

"We? We who? I'm still in Montana. You're lost in Boulder. Joe is by himself, and I don't think he can run them down with his motor scooter."

"The military offered a Seal team," I said.

"How do you feel about that?"

"Not good. I haven't told them where Amanda is. The FBI is putting a cordon around the entire warehouse district."

"Please don't tell them where she is. These guys sound like pros. They probably have half a dozen contingencies, and... oh, man, Sebastian."

"Don't worry, T. I haven't given anything away. That doesn't mean they won't find her on their own. They're probably looking for XiZi connections in Denver. Sooner or later, something will turn up," I said. "Admiral Anderson has taken over from Mike. He called the CEO of XiZi, got him involved."

"Involved how?" T asked.

"More invested than involved," I said.

"What are you talking about?"

"He filled the CEO in on the big picture. Now that he knows about the project, the CEO is connected to Wan. Iba can reach him."

"Oooh," T said. "Yes, he is invested now, isn't he? Do you think he can do anything about Wan?"

"I doubt it. He claims it's a freelance operation that he never approved. I think she's playing her own game. I don't see how she thinks it can end in her favor. She has to know that once I get Amanda back from her, she's dead."

"Unless she thinks she's a match for Iba now. I don't know how, but she didn't die. That suggests some kind of immunity against Iba."

I had no response to that.

"T, where's Joe? I need to meet up with him and see what kind of plan we can come up with."

"I put that info in the lockbox. I don't consider this a secure line."

"Great. I'll stop someplace and get it. Thanks, T. We're going to get her back."

"I know, Sebastian. I know."

T created the lockbox on a file-sharing Web site after Mike let slip that the military was monitoring all of our communications. It allowed the three of us a modicum of privacy. We kept it secure by never logging in from our cell phones, computers, and other personal digital devices.

I came across a public library before I located U.S. 36. I stopped for five minutes, borrowed one of their computers, and logged into the online lockbox. Joe's location was in a note T had written a short time before; it was labeled *Red Rider*. I wondered how Pony That Sees Far would feel about that. Hard to tell; he and T had gotten close.

I set off again, keeping an eye out for the telltale signs of Mike's tails. So far on my trip, they had been strangely absent or exceptionally good. I could not imagine that Mike hired a second plane just for them. And with the electronic tracker still in Oregon in my parked Denali, I ought to be free of them, but I kept checking over my shoulder just to be sure.

Halfway to Denver, my phone summoned me again.

It was Mike's number; this time Mike came on the line.

I could barely make him out. Judging from the sound of his voice, he must have been in pain. I ignored it and laid into him, letting him know how incompetent he and his team had been in allowing Amanda to be snatched so easily, and from her own home at that.

He listened until I wore down. Then he spoke, painfully, haltingly. "Sebastian... Maria's dead."

❧

All the air went out of me.

Amanda would be devastated. She and her family had employed Maria Reina since Amanda was in college. Amanda had kept her on during her ill-fated marriage to Tom Kingston. Maria had her own apartment in the manse. She was way more than a cook and housekeeper. She was scheduler and planner, confidante and friend.

Or she had been. Now she was dead.

"Sebastian," Mike squeaked. "I'm—"

"Okay," I said, interrupting. I hung up and drove south, overwhelmed with both numbness and anger.

One more reason, I thought, to unleash Empaya Iba.

EMPAYA IBA SPEAKS

Sister of my flesh,
To me you brought a new servitor
With promise, you said,
Of betrayal no more.
Sister, attend my words.
Am I returned to our Mother Soil?
Do I see the gifts displayed upon my altar
Given by the children of the Black Orchid?

Sister, no. Sister, I do not.
I abide in an alien land
Far from my people,
And our forests and mounts.
This servitor you chose,
To whom you gave the mark of my home,
Turns his back on Empaya Iba.
Why, sister, why did you choose this weakling?

Gather your needles.
Prepare your ink.
Empaya Iba sees a worthy successor
And gives her understanding.
So say I, Empaya Iba, spirit of the Black Orchid People,
Guardian of the Mother Soil, giver of the Long Sleep,
Seer of the Many Eyes, mage of the Many Legs.

CHAPTER 40
OOLOLOO WHO?

J
UST OUTSIDE DENVER, I pulled the rental car off 36 and parked in a mall lot. I dialed T.

"Hey, Sebastian," he said.

His tone told me he already knew.

"How did you find out?" I asked.

"Joe told me. He's really angry. He's threatening all kinds of things. You need to get to him. Stop him from charging in there alone."

"Okay. I'll call him right now. Listen, it's time to stop using these phones. Do you have a throwaway?"

"No. I can buy one at the next exit. Check the lockbox in an hour or so for the contact info," he said.

"Okay. I've already put mine in. Stay in touch."

⮞

I should have moved on right away, but I couldn't take my mind off Maria… and Amanda. And now Joe was angry. I truly didn't know what that would mean. I was pretty certain that Joe was more than a simple old reservation Indian; I just didn't know what.

One other thing, and I really hated the thought of doing this. Wan needed to know about the cell phones.

She answered Amanda's cell immediately.

"I will make contact. You do not make contact," she said.

"Shut up and listen. I'm dumping my phone. Amanda knows how to contact me. Let me talk to her now. And fast. This is being traced."

She got it, and Amanda came on the line.

"Sebastian?"

"Are you okay?"

"Yes. I'm fine. Have you heard anything about Maria? They shot her, Sebastian."

I couldn't do it, so I lied.

"I know, babe. Last I heard she was in surgery and Emilio was on the way. We're going to get you out."

"I know."

The phone disconnected. I looked down at my cell. The call had taken just over thirty seconds. Was that long enough to trace a call? I didn't know and didn't much care. This would be resolved by the family, not by outsiders.

I pulled the battery from my cell phone and stuck the phone and battery into a pocket of my camera bag.

I turned on the Denver all-news radio station to see what they were reporting about Amanda's kidnapping. The traffic and weather cycled through before the news headlines came on. It was the lead story, Amanda being not only wealthy but a player in western charity circles. They played it as a home invasion and kidnapping for money, the kind of thing people with money worry most about.

Almost as an aside, they reported that the "Mexican maid" had been shot to death along with two private security guards.

The radio made no mention of Mike's casualties. I had to hand it to the military: They knew how to cover things up. I suspected all hell would break loose if the public knew even half of what was going on around me.

I switched the radio off, pulled out into the traffic again, and followed the GPS directions to Joe's stakeout.

Joe! I forgot to call Joe.

I had to reassemble my old cell to find his number. I transferred it to my new throwaway, then disassembled the cell again.

Joe answered faster than I expected.

"Sebastian, you come."

It was an order, not a question.

"On the way. Turn off your phone. Take the battery out or smash it to pieces. We can't let you be traced," I said.

He grunted in agreement.

"I am sorry, Sebastian. I did nothing to stop them."

"Not your job. We'll finish this," I promised. "Keep an eye out for me. I'll try to come in behind you."

"Quick. Things happening."

I was about to question him, but he hung up. I redialed, but got the phone company's recorded message announcing that Joe's number could not be reached at this time.

I saw a sign for a neighborhood library and followed it. I needed to check the lockbox and scout the area where Amanda was held on a device bigger than the palm of my hand.

❧

My research done, I decided to start implementing my plan to get Wan and the kidnappers.

I called the number she had left in the lockbox.

"You do not follow instructions well. I told you that I would make the contact," she said.

"Yeah, yeah. I could die of old age waiting for you to call. Do your new boys know they are going to die? I mean, have you shared that with them?"

"They will do what they are paid to do. My men are all professionals. I think you can tell that from our operation so far."

"I wouldn't brag if I were you. You have the FBI, the Colorado State Police, the Denver Police Department, and who knows how many groups inside the U.S. military chasing after you. Success requires subtlety; I'll bet your guys know that. And I'll bet they're wondering about whether you're up to this."

"And yet I have Mrs. Campion. So perhaps we should have our chat now. Very well. I want your cooperation or I will have to take measures against her. Soon."

"You really are stupid. If you hurt Amanda, you've got nothing I want. I'll just release my demon on you, and you *will* die."

"Mr. Arnett, you are both arrogant and ignorant. Your demon is powerless against me. Didn't you wonder how Lee came to choose me? It's my family. We have lived in Borneo for generations."

Oh, shit, I thought. *She knows more than me.*

"Have you studied the Dyak spirits, what motivates them, what angers them? We didn't have to study them. We lived with them. We know how to work with themand how to defeat them. We have the medicine."

She laughed, and I shivered involuntarily.

"Mr. Arnett, would you still find Mrs. Campion entertaining if she lived, but lived in a deep sleep? Would your demon—*could* your demon—waken her? I think he knows only how to suck the life out of his meals before he eats them. What do you think? You've had experience with him."

"Threats. Always the threats. You want my cooperation, but all you do is threaten."

"Why do you care so much about this demon?" she said. "Do you like having it control you? Are you jealous of someone else having one, too?"

"If you know so much about the Dyaks, why not just go do it yourself? What do you need me for?"

I was both curious and trying to kill time as I closed in on Joe's location. Railroad tracks came at me from my right, from farther northwest than my angle down from Boulder. My library research showed a confluence of rail lines inside a triangle formed by I-76 to the north, I-70 to the south, and I-25 to the east. I hadn't seen signs for any of those highways, so I concluded I still must be some way off.

"So what do you need me for?" I repeated into the phone.

"The location of the village, of course."

"What are you talking about? You have the location. XiZi men did the clear-cutting. You flew in heavy machinery. You created a scar on the land a quarter-mile wide. Did you lose the map?"

"Something like that."

"You can't find a clear-cut path in the Borneo wilderness?" I faked my shock. "There have to be a half-dozen private satellite companies that will draw you a map with a square-foot resolution. That would be far cheaper than chasing after me, kidnapping my friends. And safer for you."

"You truly don't know anything about the spirits. You never learned about the connection between the land and the spirits. That the spirits protect the land, the land provides for the people, and the people pay homage to the spirits. You fool. You don't know that the spirits can hide the land."

I suddenly recalled Johnnie Walker's trouble with the GPS signals and maps. The satellite signals that failed to come in from the outside world.

"Hide the land?" I said.

"Yes. Rain and mists. Floods. Poor harvests. Unexpected diseases. All the things you heard about or encountered at what you call the New Village. Designed, very successfully, to keep outsiders out. You think the logging companies don't want access to forests that are only a day and a half from Tenom by boat?"

I had a sinking feeling that Jimmy Beam might not have told me everything he knew.

"So you need me to show you the way?"

"Yes. We've been open about that all along."

"It seemed such a dumb thing to want."

"Now that you understand, are you prepared to cooperate?"

"Sure," I said. "Why not? But how do I know you won't keep bothering my friends?"

She sighed.

"We won't need to bother them if we have your cooperation. You will take us to the village. I will either find the spirit I seek or not. One way or another, I won't need you anymore."

"Yes. That's what worries me."

"It needn't. You are invulnerable near the spirit of Oololoo."

"Who is Oololoo? Is that the demon's name?"

"He is the father of this spirit. His name is passed down from generation to generation. Whoever the spirit chooses to live with, that person is Oololoo."

"So, does that make me the Oololoo?"

"It could. What happened to the man who had the tattoo before you?"

"I think I may have killed him. But I had the tattoo at the same time he did."

"But not for long."

"I don't think so."

"The spirit chooses one and disposes of the other."

"Wait a minute. What happens if you get the tattoo? Do I die?"

"I would not be the one to kill you."

"But I would be just as dead once you got the tattoo, isn't that right?"

"That is how it has worked in the past."

CHAPTER 41

RED RIDER

I WAS SCREWED.

I drove down U.S. 37, looking for an exit that would take me to Joe and Amanda, knowing I was screwed.

If I went along with Wan, I might be able to save Amanda. But she was absolutely right: Empaya Iba was not going to lift a finger—a spider leg, rather—to help me. That's what the dream was about. I was the stalking horse, the Judas goat, the bait.

"Mr. Arnett, are you still there? Perhaps consulting with your spirit? Trying to figure a way out? Do you still think my operation is so poorly contrived, planned, and executed?"

Forgive me, Lord, but all I could think of at the moment was T. His questions never ended. And that gave me an idea, half-baked but something to work with.

"You may have fleshed out some things I already knew, but I'm curious. You already have a spirit. Why do you need two?"

"One will defeat the other; the survivor will be the strongest spirit on the island. You have no idea what I could do with that power."

"Well, aren't you the greedy one?" I said, hoping to goad her further. "How do you know you will end up with this Oololoo guy?"

"I will be on his home ground. He is all but invincible there. The land, the creation, is the source of his power."

"Yeah, well, I know a bird that can kick the crap out of Oololoo." She hissed.

"The eagle. Where did you find the eagle?"

"It's a long story. Look, if you want cooperation, you got it. Release Amanda, and you and I will arrange to meet in Borneo. I'm not going to have anything to do with getting you out of the country. And I'm pretty sure the feds will be after—"

"I must go," she said. "Do not contact me."

⤴

Well, that was interesting. I get to the point of making a deal, and she hangs up. I hoped Amanda was not doing something stupid, like trying to escape. I was sure Joe would do everything he could to help her, but a 250-cc motor scooter would not take them very far or fast.

I thought of calling Joe and remembered that I had told him to turn his cell off. I tried anyway and did not get through.

Instead, my cell rang. I didn't recognize the number, but the new phone had none of my contacts.

"Hello."

I tried the neutral approach.

"Sebastian, it's T. We've got trouble." T spoke so fast it came out as a single word.

"What's going on?" I asked.

"FBI. They're walking down the tracks, inspecting every rail car that's not attached to a moving train."

"Shit. How far are they from the caboose?"

"Not far. The shooters have bailed out and gone back to the warehouse. One of them, the pilot, I think, took off in the white van."

"How do you know all this?" I asked.

"Joe managed to put his battery back in his phone and called me."

For an old man, Joe was catching on to the technology pretty quick.

"So, the feds could stumble onto the kidnappers and start a shooting war that would leave everybody in the warehouse dead?"

"That's what I'm afraid of," T said.

❧

I scrambled through a tall hedge at the end of a row of one-story rental warehouses, looking for Joe.

"You call that quiet? I hear you come two blocks away."

Joe spoke in a low rumble that came out quieter than a whisper.

"I wasn't trying to be sneaky quiet. I was trying to be nonchalant and look like I belong here."

"How many people walk through woods, climbing fence between buildings?"

I had no answer.

"Where is Amanda?"

I spoke in what I hoped was a quiet enough whisper.

"There," he said, pointing over his shoulder. "Next building. I come to stop you so everyone doesn't shoot."

"You think the kidnappers can hear from inside their warehouse?"

"No. Cops might. Right over there."

Joe pointed to a Denver Police squad car blocking the entrance to the brick warehouses. The car sat just eight units away, a couple hundred feet at most.

"You think they know where Amanda is?"

Between the feds and the local cops, it would be a real messy fight with Amanda in the middle.

"No. He waits for dinner. I hear another ask what he will eat. He wants fried chicken. Sounds good. You bring food?"

"Not fried chicken. Roast beef sandwiches and water."

"Good. I need saddlebags for Red Rider."

"Red Rider?"

"Motorcycle T buys for me. Has no saddlebags. Can't carry anything."

"You named your motor scooter?"

"Motorcycle. Red. I ride it. Red Rider."

I was relying on a 100-year-old Indian medicine man who knew nothing about medicine and was living the life of a preteen growing up in the suburbs. I'm pretty sure I heard generations of Utes spinning in their graves.

Amanda, I thought, *I'm not sure how this is going to work out.*

"Come. We go watch for Amanda. Eat dinner. Plan revenge," he said.

"Okay," I said. "I'm right behind you—all the way."

I hoped he understood what I meant.

We walked along the edge of a ravine at the side of the warehouses. Joe was right. He glided around trees and dodged low-hanging branches without disturbing a leaf. I stumbled twice and dropped our plastic shopping bag of food once.

At the last row of buildings nearest the railroad tracks, Joe stopped. I stopped, too, almost running into him. He peeked around the corner of the building. I peered over him. Ten feet away, a green trash dumpster backed up against the woods. A bright red BMS motor scooter sat beside the trash bin, angled for a quick getaway through the warehouse parking lot.

The dumpster was tall enough so that I did not have to crouch to hide behind it. Joe beamed at his new ride.

"Pretty good, eh, Sebastian. Faster than a horse."

"How fast?"

"80. Then hard to control."

"Says Pony That Sees Far," I said.

"I see plenty far. More trouble comes sooner, maybe later, too."

CHAPTER 42
WATCHING EYES

I didn't need Joe to tell me that our options sucked.

"Which unit is Amanda in, and where's the caboose? Which direction are the feds coming from?"

Joe pointed to the unit one removed from the end of the row nearest us. It had a black garage door, a red steel door for pedestrian traffic, a plate glass window that ran from floor to ceiling, and an address plate, nothing to make it stand out from all the others.

Only one of the eight units stood out: It housed a shop advertising Army surplus goods with a special collection of World War II railroad maps. Two cars were parked in front of the surplus store. Otherwise, the lot was empty. The white van was gone.

People had either left work early or the police cordon was keeping them out.

From our hunting blind, we could look past the row of warehouses, down an embankment and onto a vast railroad marshaling yard. This was Utah Junction, according to the map I'd seen at the library. Some twenty tracks branched off two or three main lines. Collections of boxcars, tankers, and coal carriers sat here and there, waiting to be hooked up to an engine.

I couldn't see the caboose.

Joe read my thoughts and pointed to a worn dirt path around the side of the building. A wooden hut perched atop a raised platform sat at the end of the path. The hut broke the flow of a six-foot-high chain-link fence with barbed wire strands curling around the top.

"Door in hut. New lock. Other side, steps go down to the tracks. Caboose maybe fifty feet that way," he said, nodding away from the warehouses.

"Where are the feds?" I asked.

He nodded in the same direction beyond the caboose.

"How far?"

"Close. Too close."

"Can the kidnappers see the tracks from their building?"

"Small window. Maybe bathroom. Stick your head out, you see everything," Joe said.

"We need to see what's going on with the feds."

"Yah, okay. We go to another shed."

Joe picked up our bag of sandwiches and water and slid down into the ravine and hauled himself up the opposite side. I followed him. We walked from one row of warehouses to another, ambling like we had not a care in the world. About a hundred yards from Joe's hiding place, I saw an asphalt path leading toward the tracks. At the end of the path, a chain-link fence barred the way.

On the fence, a sign warned us to KEEP OUT.

Joe walked up to the gate, lifted the padlock, and motioned me through.

"How did you unlock that?" I said.

He smiled.

We walked over a short wooden bridge to a hut just like the other one. Steps leading down to the tracks faced back toward the warehouse where Amanda was kept. A nondescript brownish-orange Southern Pacific caboose sat alone on a short piece of track. Beyond it, we could see the other hut.

We sat down on the top step like we owned the place, pulled out our sandwiches and started eating.

"Have you seen the inside of the caboose?" I asked.

"Very nice. Benches with pads. You can sit, lie down. Small room in the middle. Bathroom maybe. Table on one end. Cabinets. Bigger than my place," Joe said.

"You have a place? I thought you lived in the mist or something."

"Ho-ho. You funny, Sebastian," he said.

About eight tracks away, halfway between the two access huts, four men in black windbreakers with bright yellow FBI lettering stenciled on the back congregated around three men in orange reflective vests. They stood at the end of a line of fifteen to twenty boxcars.

One of the men in a reflective suit gestured wildly and pointed at his watch. One of the FBI guys shook his head and pointed toward the caboose and beyond, where more clusters of cars littered the rail yard.

"Looks like someone wants to take a break and someone else doesn't want him to," I said.

"Yah," Joe said and took another bite of his sandwich.

We looked around the yard, eating peacefully, occasionally glancing at the human cluster. The discussion had reached the cell phone stage, the two leaders calling for support or encouragement or to break the bad news of a missed dinner. Then the railroad guy shook his head, put his phone in his pocket and led the way toward a row of four empty coal cars and, beyond them, the caboose.

"Uh-oh," I said.

"Yah."

One of the FBI guys glanced our way, stopped, and waved us over.

I waved back.

"Time to go," I said.

"Yah."

The group of men stopped, and everyone looked our way. The first one to notice us waved us toward them again.

I held up my wrist, pointed at it and stood up. Joe was already through the hut and down the bridge to the gate. I gave a friendly wave, grabbed our lunch bag, and followed him, not looking back. At the gate, Joe was crouched outside the fence.

"Are they following?" I asked.

"FBIs want to, but guys in vests pointing toward coal cars. FBIs lose this one, I think."

I closed the gate and put the padlock back on, but I didn't clasp it shut.

"Okay, let's go."

We ambled back through the parking lots. A couple times, Joe stopped and knelt like he had found a coin on the ground. Each time, he checked behind us to make certain we were not followed.

"We have to get rid of those cops before they can get a good look at that caboose," I said. "If they get inside, they'll notice the groceries and put two and two together."

"You call T. He can help."

"How? He's probably in Utah somewhere."

"He has pictures of van. I send him. He can send to government, say van is nearby."

I looked at Joe.

"You know how to send photos from a cell phone?" I said. "You know how to take pictures?"

"Play sudoku, mah-jongg; find art from when I was a boy; draw pictures. You should learn."

"T has created a monster."

"Yah. White man never beat Indians if we have cell phones," Joe said.

I didn't argue. I called T and told him our situation. He promised to point the police to a warehouse on the far side of the tracks.

"We have to see what's going on," I said.

"No. We wait," Joe said. "We see soon enough."

I didn't want to wait. Amanda was less than 100 feet away behind just one door, and I could do nothing but squat behind a dumpster.

Down the way, two men came out of the surplus store, locked the door, climbed into their cars and drove off. Apparently it was quitting time. Soon enough, the sun would go down, and with it the temperature. We were enjoying a lovely early spring, but it would get cold when the sun set.

Shouts drifted up from the tracks, and I thought I heard someone yell, "Go."

In the unit second from the end nearest us, the red door opened and two men clad in black strode purposefully out. They glanced quickly around the parking lot, then headed directly for the path to the railroad tracks. At the gate, one of them pulled a key from his pocket and opened the lock. They entered the shed, and I could see no more.

Out in the rail yard, something was happening. We heard rail cars clattering and banging against one another the way they do when a train is moving slowly.

I looked over at Joe.

"They're picking up the caboose?"

"Yah, I think so, too."

"That means they'll be moving Amanda to the caboose soon, or not at all. What do we do?"

"You run. Get on train. I follow on Red Rider."

CHAPTER 43
TRAIN HOPPING

GET ON TRAIN.

Easy for Joe to say. I didn't know how to climb onto a train. I assumed there would be boxcars, and maybe one would be open, but that seemed a long shot. I couldn't camp out in a coal car, empty or not. And I certainly couldn't just walk up to the caboose and knock on the door.

But before I worried about that, I'd have to get *to* the train before it started moving. But judging from the noise coming from the rail yard on my left, the train was already moving.

I hustled back through the same parking lots I had ambled through less than a half hour earlier. I'd pulled a new throwaway cell phone from my backpack and tossed it to Joe just before setting off on my sprint.

"Call T," I said, heading for the ravine. "Don't lose Amanda."

Fifty steps after setting off, I was gasping for breath and cursing myself for avoiding every kind of exercise. I take pictures of flowers because they don't move; that means I don't have to move very much either. I slowed to a skipping walk.

On my left, I could see the top of a boxcar passing, heading toward the caboose. Okay. At least the train was moving backward. I had some time, just no idea how much. I reached the gate to the shed but had to stop. My chest was heaving, my legs were watery, and I thought I would throw up my sandwich. I needed to regain strength to make the run to the train, but I could hardly think straight.

A loud bang announced the coupling of the caboose to the rest of the train. Time to move again, however reluctant my body was.

I removed the gate padlock, trotted over the wooden bridge, through the shed, and down the stairs without even thinking. One of the guys in an orange reflective suit was doing something between the caboose and the car it was attached to. There were no FBI guys in sight, at least on this side of the train.

The railyard worker didn't see the two guys in black at the top of the shed stairs, but I did. They watched him intently. More black figures joined them at the shed. I thought I saw Amanda's auburn hair, but couldn't afford the time to look. I dashed to the nearest opening between two rail cars; my camera bag slung over my right shoulder slapped me every step of the way.

I ducked down to see if the railway worker had seen me, but he was no longer between the cars. A series of snap-bangs ran the length of the train, and the car I was leaning against jerked forward an inch. I tumbled backward, flailing for something to grab. My right hand caught the smooth top of the coupler and slowed my fall. I knocked my elbow on the ground and sent electricity racing through my arm.

Panic hit me. This train was moving, and I was in the way. I scrambled to my knees and pulled myself up onto a metal ladder. It only had four rungs, but I managed to step onto a narrow iron mesh ledge just above the coupling.

I couldn't ride far on this thing. I would be seen, if I didn't fall off first. I had to get into the car or on top of it, and I had to do it immediately.

Quickly, I discovered that modern boxcars don't have ladders that reach all the way to the top. The ladder on the burnt-orange car I was intending to hitch a ride on had three steps above where I was. After that I would have to pull myself up five horizontal corrugations to reach the top. The corrugations were smooth, slick with grease and grime, and offered no handholds. Once again, I regretted not taking up mountain climbing or bouldering.

Before I could start my climb, I had to get my backpack camera bag onto both shoulders. It was slung loosely over my right shoulder, the way I always carried it. It's easier to set down or grab gear that way. I had to slip my left arm through the shoulder strap and do it quickly, but I was afraid the train would move.

Adding to my concerns, I could not help wondering if some FBI sniper across the rail yard had me in his crosshairs. I hadn't seen the agents during my short dash to the boxcar. Who knew where they were? A helicopter passed nearby, crossing from my side of the rail yard to the far side. Something was getting ready to pop over there. Did the pilot notice the crazy man trying to climb onto a boxcar?

I braced my right side against the boxcar. If it jerked forward, I hoped that would hold me steady. I heard the familiar sound of a series of snap-bangs coming in my direction. I leaned into the car; it jerked away from me, spinning me off the latticed platform, one foot onto the coupling, and threw me onto an identical metal grid landing on the next car, toward the front of the train.

The car had jerked backward a couple of inches.

Make up your mind. Forward or backward.

I was lucky to be alive and highly motivated. I didn't think. I acted.

I jumped onto the coupling, pulled myself up the ladder of the car I intended to climb, and just kept going. If the train jerked back again, I would fall and slam my back onto something very hard no matter where I landed.

My backpack, still hanging from just one shoulder, pulled me to the right, but I kept climbing, my face pressed against the dirty metal of the boxcar wall. My head popped over the top of the car; I could see the cupola of the caboose four cars away. Then I heard it again, the snap-bang chain reaction of one railroad car smashing against another.

My legs pumped up the wall, my left foot slipping on the smooth surface. I slapped the top of the boxcar with both hands, bent over at the waist, my bag pulling me to the right and back.

Bang.

My car jerked forward and kept going. My gut felt like I'd taken a sucker punch, but I didn't fall.

I pushed with my right leg, which seemed to get a better grip. I jerked my shoulder to toss the backpack off my back. My left knee struck the edge of the boxcar roof, sparking stars in my eyes. I slid forward on my stomach, spread-eagled. Safe.

The roof was corrugated, too, and the valleys were filled with oily grime, the kind of dirt you would collect traveling at sixty miles an hour for days, weeks, months on end behind a string of coal cars. My hands and clothes were covered in no time, but I had to hold on.

Through my stomach, I could feel the deep throb of the engines many, many cars away. The train moved at a slow walk, stopped with a jerk, started with a jerk, screeched through open switches, stopped, and started as it wound its way to wherever it was going.

I was now easily a half-mile or more from where the caboose had sat. Up in the sky, two helicopters traced narrow circles across from where Amanda had been held. I didn't know how long I had, but I knew I could not ride far like this. On a curve at fifty or sixty miles an hour I would be thrown off and killed.

As I watched the cupola of the caboose behind me, I realized that was the only safe place to be—on top of the caboose—and that was not without risks. The brownish-orange Southern Pacific caboose carried its cupola toward the rear of the car. I could shelter myself from the wind by lying behind it, and the arms of the ladder on the rear platform would give me something to prop my feet against.

All I had to do was cross four boxcars, jump onto the roof of the caboose without anyone inside hearing me, and not be seen from the cupola windows. And I had to do it before the train picked up too much speed.

CHAPTER 44
MISSTEP

I TRIED HARD, BUT I couldn't remember ever seeing a movie in which someone jumped from one car of a train to another. Crawl across the couplers of a moving train, hang underneath a rail car, cling to the side of a car, kickbox, have a shootout—all that, I remembered. But never jumping.

I wasn't even certain how many feet of empty space separated the rail cars. Six? Eight? Ten? Certainly more feet than I had jumped since I left the high school track and field team to join the less strenuous yearbook staff.

It was irrelevant, I realized. The train wasn't moving, and I had to go.

I stood up, grabbed my camera bag, and held it to my chest. I walked carefully toward the rear of the car, feeling the corrugations and slippery grime with my boots. I reached the end of the car and gazed over at the next car.

I didn't have time to climb down off my boxcar and get back up onto another car. And do it three more times. I would have to jump, and I absolutely had to do it with the camera bag.

The bag held my cell phones, a bottle of water, some energy bars, a windbreaker, the Webley and a box of cartridges as well as my camera gear. I like to travel prepared. I could not toss it onto the next car and reasonably expect that it would stay where it landed. I had to keep it with me, but I couldn't wear it on my back. It weighed twenty pounds and would alter my center of gravity and likely cause me to miss the jump.

If I missed and fell short, I would undoubtedly land awkwardly against the boxcar wall or, worse, the coupling. If I landed and tripped on a corrugation, I envisioned all manner of bad things that could happen, including rolling off the top of the car. Looking off to one side, the ground seemed a very long way down.

I put my arms through the straps of the bag with the bag in front of me. We would go together. I turned and walked back 10 steps, then turned and fixed my eyes on the cupola. Amanda was in that car. I was going to get her.

I took a breath, pulled the camera bag tight against my chest, pumped my legs and flew. I landed well, but the corrugations grabbed at the toes of my boots. I ran almost two-thirds of the length of the boxcar before I could stop.

That was a problem. The caboose was only about two-thirds of the length of the boxcar. If I took that much distance to stop myself, I would have to jump over the cupola—and that wasn't happening—and would still likely run off the end of the car.

I had to shorten the distance, just like a jet landing on an aircraft carrier. Or in my case, more like a lumbering cargo plane. No room for error while attempting the impossible.

I lined up on the cupola again, breathed deep, held my bag, and ran. I jumped cleanly, but my toe caught in one of the valleys of corrugation. I flipped and sprawled on my back, sliding off toward the left. I flung my arms and legs as wide as they would go to keep from rolling. I stopped with my left leg dangling over the edge of the roof. Clamping my hands on the grimy corrugations, I sidled my way back toward the center of the car. I was sweating and had to pee in the worst way. Panic will do that, I guess.

I sat up and looked behind me. I'd used much less room on my landing, but anyone inside the boxcar would have heard my 220 pounds of bone and soft tissue as well as another 20 pounds of padded equipment pound onto the roof.

The train was still stationary, but it wouldn't stay that way forever. There was nothing to do but try again.

Two jumps down, two to go.

I stood up, shook off some of my nerves, and lined up on the cupola. I churned my legs and focused on landing lightly on flat feet. I jumped across what seemed like a vast chasm, slid, tilted backward and slammed onto my back. My head banged down hard, making my teeth chatter and stars pop in my eyes. I lay still, trying to assess damage. My back hurt, but none of my limbs were hanging over the side of the boxcar. Another successful jump. One more to go.

Suddenly, I heard the snap-bang of the train starting to move. I rolled onto my knees and waited for the inevitable jerk. I rocked with it when it came. I got to my feet with my back stiff and sending serious complaints to my brain. The train inched forward. I looked toward the engines; it was moving down a clear line with no more cars to collect. I had to go, and go now!

I hobbled to the rear of the boxcar, peeked over the side at the caboose. The roof was lower and had no corrugations, but it was rounded from the center to the sides, apparently so rain and snow could slide off easily. If I didn't land right, I would slide off easily, too.

Fortunately, no one was looking out the door or the cupola windows. Not that it mattered. I could not stay where I was, and I could not let the train pick up more speed. It was now or never.

I turned and walked toward the front of the boxcar to get running distance. The train gathered speed; moving now at a slow walk. Time to go again.

I pivoted and ran. At my first step, I heard the snap-bang of the train braking behind me. I couldn't stop. I had to jump. My back cramped, my legs slowed, my feet turned to lead. I stumbled on takeoff.

I wasn't going to make it.

CHAPTER 45
DIRECTION UNKNOWN

MY LEFT BOOT clipped the edge of the caboose roof, and the foot slipped. My right shin slammed into the roof edge, scraping pants, skin, and bone from the knee to the top of my cowboy boot.

My torso bounced against the backpack just as the caboose snap-banged to a halt.

I clenched my eyes tight, fighting against the pain in my leg. It hurt so much I was sure it was broken. I rolled onto my back and started slipping toward the edge. Forgetting the pain for an instant, I launched my limbs into a spread eagle. I stopped sliding.

I heard the caboose door squeak open and voices complained below me. I craned my neck to glance at the cupola windows. The kidnappers seemed not to have discovered the joy of riding in a caboose. For that I was grateful, but gratitude did not keep the pain at bay.

The train snap-banged again and moved forward. It reached walking speed, then jogging speed, and the door below me slammed shut.

I was safe on top of the caboose, Amanda somewhere below me. Only the noise of the couplers prevented the kidnappers from hearing my awkward landing.

I lay on my back with my eyes closed, the camera pack weighing on my chest. The train gathered speed, rocking crazily at every switch it passed over.

I had to get settled before the train reached full speed. I had to let T know where I was. I had to figure out where we were heading. But first, I had to test my leg to see if I could stand on it. If I had broken it, all was lost.

I shrugged out of my backpack and scooted back toward the center of the roof, propelling myself with my good leg, dragging the bad leg. Just moving several feet sent sharp pains from my knee through my groin, chest, and head.

I looked down at the leg. It looked straight enough, but my jeans were soaking up blood. I sat up slowly, glanced around quickly and felt the sides of my leg, from the knee to just above the ankle, which was as far as I could reach. I moved my hands up my leg, pressing the bone with my thumbs. It hurt like hell, but I didn't feel anything amiss until just below my kneecap. There I ran into a bump the size of golf ball. I played with it as gently as I could, but still brought tears to my eyes. The bump didn't move. Maybe I was okay, after all.

The train was now traveling faster than some of the rush hour traffic on the roads on either side of us, and the number of tracks was winnowing down to two. I figured we would really pick up speed soon.

I rolled onto my left knee, favoring the right leg, and pushed my bag toward the rear of the car. The closer I got to the cupola, the slower I moved and the lower I sank, until I was crawling on my stomach.

The sides of the cupola were flush with the sides of the caboose. Getting past it required climbing over it. For a moment, I thought of staying where I was, but at some point, someone in the caboose was going to climb up to take in the sights. I could not escape notice.

I thought hard about how to do it. Finally, I decided the safest, quickest way around it was also the craziest, riskiest way. I would have to climb up and crawl across it. I considered leaving the backpack on the front side of the cupola, but someone might see it if it didn't roll off first, and I needed too much of the stuff inside it.

Live by the camera bag, die by the camera bag. That was my thought.

Fortunately, the sun was setting, and I would not cast too dark a shadow through the cupola windows. And the cupola was full of windows, two front and rear as well as on each side. The point of the cupola, of course, was to allow the conductor to see what was going on with the train and its surroundings. Electronic sensing devices had replaced conductors long ago, but this refurbished old caboose still had all its windows.

I tried to imagine where in the caboose everyone would be and what they would be doing. If I were in charge, I would put one thug each at the front and rear by the doors and keep one within reach of Amanda. Everyone else—in this case, Wan and the fourth kidnapper—would be where the most room was, which was toward the front of the caboose.

If I was right, there was only one person below where I wanted to go. All I had to do now was to figure my timing—and wonder if my leg would hold up.

I tried to ignore the latter thought. It would or it wouldn't. There was nothing I could do about it in advance.

The best time to move would be when the train went under or over a bridge or across a switch, offering a distraction. The best bet was when the train was going over a switch.

We were still in Denver, still making our way toward clear track to wherever we were heading; that meant we would be hitting more switches. I could tell in advance when that would occur from the sound of metal wheels at the front of the train scraping against the rails at the switch.

Of course, the cars rocked most violently when going over switches. I would be crossing the highest point on the train, creating an ungainly center of gravity.

I was still pondering what would happen if I tumbled off a moving train when I heard screeches at the front of the train. We were hitting a switch or a curve. Time to go.

I didn't look back. I got on my hands and good knee, shooting fire down my bad leg. I pushed up with the good leg, grabbing the handle of my backpack. I shoved off and slid onto the cupola on my left side. I looked back. A wave of swaying motion was sweeping toward me. Then it hit me. I was stuck on the smooth curved surface with my legs sticking out beyond the edge of the cupola.

The front wheels of the caboose hit the switch, and the car rocked. I lost my balance and started to roll to one side while my camera bag tipped toward the other side. I flung my right arm out to flatten myself, and my fist pounded the roof. I scooted my shoulder blades to the left and flailed for my bag. My fingertips clutched the zipper pull on one of the pockets.

The rear wheels hit the switch, and my body lurched to the right. My fingers slid off the edge of the roof, and I ground my right elbow into the grimy metal. My slide halted with my arm halfway over the edge, the fingers of my left hand dragging my backpack to the curved center of the roof.

The pressure I'd put on my damaged right leg shot daggers of pain through my thigh and into my groin. Drowning in Borneo had been a pleasure in comparison.

I don't know how long I lay there, stars popping in my head and the wind blowing past my ears. I licked my lips and coughed. My brain held one thought: If only I could die.

The train crossed fewer switches, picking up speed and passing the traffic on either side of us faster and faster. I shivered and groaned at the thought of moving again, but as dusk fell, so did the temperature. I needed to finish my journey and nestle out of the wind.

I rose on my left elbow and looked down at my leg. The knee seemed much larger, but the leg appeared straight enough. If I didn't move at all, I could tolerate the pain, but I had to move. I glanced back over my shoulder; at least three good pushes should get me to the back edge of the cupola.

Fine. Do it, I thought.

I pulled back my left leg and shoved. The heel of my boot slipped, and I made no progress. Twice more I tried, with the same lack of results. I was definitely getting cold, and my brain refused to focus on anything but pain.

All right. More than one way to skin a cat. I was in full cliché mode.

I sat up, pulled the camera bag close to me. Straightening both arms at my sides, I lifted my butt and slid backward half a foot.

Rinse and repeat.

It took ten or twelve butt presses before my hands ran out of room at the end of the cupola. I carefully dropped the backpack over the edge, holding one shoulder strap until I was certain it wouldn't slide off the top of the caboose.

Now, the tricky part.

I had to do a 180 without falling off or hurting my leg so much that I lost balance and rolled off. The train's speed created a real wind, and I noticed I was swaying more than the caboose. I tried to think of the best way to do this, but my brain wasn't cooperating so I just let my body do its thing. That was to use the left leg to nudge the right leg around until it dropped off the back edge of the cupola.

My knee bent, and I plopped onto my back in sheer agony. I lay some minutes waiting for the world to stop spinning. Slowly, I eased up onto my elbows and pivoted my left leg over the edge.

There was nothing left to do but do it. I had to slide down the rear end of the cupola. Then all would be well, or at least better. I gripped the edge, pulled myself forward until my butt slid off and I dropped onto the roof of the caboose.

I made it.

Finally, I was where I wanted to be.

But I was cold, exhausted, hurting, and I wondered where we were going and what I would be able to do when we got there.

CHAPTER 46

NAVIGATION

A T THE FRONT of the train, the engineer poured on the speed; utility poles, trees, and buildings raced past. The faster we went, the less the caboose rocked. I was glad for the break. I had a lot to do, and no idea how much time I had to do it in.

I caught another break with the design of the cupola. When the owner refurbished the caboose, he put in matching seats, one facing forward, one facing backward. Each seat blocked one window. The forward-facing seat was on the right, just like the engineer's position on the old steam locomotives.

I stowed my camera bag behind that blocked window and huddled closer to the center of the roof. I hoped that whoever might decide to visit the cupola would be more interested in what lay ahead than what we were leaving behind.

∽

Getting things from my pack proved more difficult than I expected, but I was getting used to things going wrong.

I pulled the windbreaker from the large pocket at the top of the bag and struggled into it. Between the jacket and the shelter of the cupola, I felt less cold, if not exactly comfortable.

My hands, however, had taken a beating in gaining this cover. Black grease covered everything except the cuts and scrapes where blood oozed. Bending my fingers into a fist caused enough pain to momentarily block out the throbbing from my knee. I fumbled with a zippered sleeve of the backpack to extract a new throwaway phone, then almost dropped it as I tried to close the zipper again.

T didn't answer my call, and I wondered where he would be. It was now past six o'clock; T had probably been on the road for at least seven hours, but I had no idea how many times he had stopped to take calls or send photos or answer the call of nature, which was starting to dial my number. I tried not to think about that.

I recalled him saying it would take twelve hours to get to Denver from Montana, but he was going by way of Salt Lake City. Quite frankly I had no idea where he was, or for that matter, where I was, and I was moving pretty quickly as the train reached its cruising speed.

While I waited for T to call back—he would surely have noticed my missed call—I considered next steps. Literally. I mean, I wondered if I would be able to climb down from the caboose roof when we reached our destination.

My leg hurt less when I didn't move it; unfortunately, I had to keep moving it, or putting pressure on it, to keep from falling off the caboose roof. I began to wonder if I shouldn't have stayed with Joe. With the two of us, we might have been able to follow the train. But perhaps not. I was not certain his Red Rider would hold two of us or go very fast with my weight on it.

I was stuck.

Lights blinked on in more and more houses as we left Denver behind. I wondered what the residents were doing. This was a favorite pastime every time I took a train. Oh, how I would kill for one of those narrow butt-crushing Amtrak passenger seats with the clunky footrests.

In my reverie I almost missed T's call. It was noisy on top of the caboose and the ringer volume was low.

"T. Hey."

"Sebastian. What's that noise? You sound like you're in a cement mixer."

"I'm not quite that comfortable. I'm on a train."

"It's awfully noisy. Can you go back inside?"

"Uh, no. I'm literally on a train. On top of a railroad car. The kidnappers have their own train car hooked up to a freight train."

T said nothing. I glanced at the phone. I still had a connection.

"T, are you there?"

"Yeah. Yes, Sebastian. I'm still trying to imagine you on top of a train. What's it like?"

"It's noisy and dirty and cold. What do you think? Where are you? Have you heard from Joe? Can you figure out where this thing might be going?"

"I'm heading into Salt Lake City. I'm going to make a quick stop to pick up my friends—they're anxious to help out. Then we'll head straight for Denver."

"You may want to stop and do some research first on where this train might be going. I would hate to be heading back north into Canada while you're heading to Denver."

I heard screeching on the other end of the connection.

"T, are you all right?"

"Yeah. I made a sudden turn and some guy was tailgating. That was his car you heard, not mine."

"What are you doing?" I asked, trying to imagine what would have inspired the tire squealing I'd heard.

"Research. Hold on."

I held on for long minutes as the caboose rocked and bounced on the uneven rails. If I were in a sleeper, I would be dozing. I thought back to the Indian Pacific. It seemed much smoother, but then I was riding in comfortable seats most of the time then, not on top of one of the cars.

"Okay. Sebastian?"

"What? Speak louder."

"Okay. I have a map of the railway system in Colorado," T said.

The guy was a computer genius. And he was beginning to grow on me.

"It looks like you have five possible routes. You can go due west over the Rockies to central Utah. Do you see mountains?"

"No closer than I do in Denver," I said.

"Okay. If you were heading in that direction, you should probably see more of the mountains. That suggests you're not going that way."

"Good thing, too. It's probably going to be really cold on top of this thing tonight. I'd freeze in the mountains."

"If you're going north, you'd hit Cheyenne. There the rail lines branch off toward Salt Lake City to the west and Nebraska to the east. Have you seen any signs indicating you might be going north?"

"T, I can't see a thing except dark houses with lights in the windows."

"Well, if you're heading east, it should get really flat pretty quickly. There are two lines running east; the northern branch goes into Nebraska and the southern branch into Kansas."

"Hey, T, I think we might be going south. I'm lying on my back; the sun was going down on my left. That would be west."

"Sebastian, it depends on which way your head is pointing," T said.

"It's pointing toward the front of the train, the direction we're traveling. That means west is on my left. We're heading south."

"Mexico. That makes sense," T said. "Immigration or Customs or whoever the cops are on the border these days probably don't check trains leaving the country the way they would if the trains were coming the other way."

"I suppose so. What else is on the way?"

"Colorado Springs. Pueblo. A whole lot of nothing. Albuquerque, then more nothing until the border."

"T, you forgot something."

"What's that?"

"The cabin," I said. "The cabin is south of Denver, almost on the New Mexico border."

"What cabin, Sebastian?"

"Amanda's cabin."

CHAPTER 47
WALSENBURG JUNCTION

T WAS SILENT; MY mind churned.

"You really think she would take Amanda to her own cabin?" T asked, the sounds of Salt Lake City's rush hour traffic playing in the background.

"I think she's improvising. Probably she planned to snatch Amanda and get out of Denver as quickly as possible. No one would ever think of using a train. At least not a freight train. And she was probably heading for Mexico, because that makes sense. But she wasn't expecting the Feds to close in on the rail yard so fast," I said.

"Now she's stuck on the train, and she knows the Feds will eventually check every train leaving the area. When they discover that there's a private caboose attached to one of them, they'll be all over her. She needs a place to hunker down while she makes new arrangements to get out of the country."

I envisioned the landscape around Amanda's ancestral home. Far-off mountains broke the horizon in all directions. Hard-packed dirt and sand sprouted sagebrush, scrub, the odd cactus, and dust devils when the wind blew, which it did often.

"It's flat enough there that a small bush plane could land and take off without a whole lot of work to clear the ground. Just get rid of the sagebrush."

"That's it, Sebastian. That has to be it," T said.

"Wan also has a superstitious thing about the land and the spirits. She might figure taking Amanda back to her roots would have some kind of strange symbolism or something.... Let's assume that's it. What's our next step?"

"You're going to get there a lot quicker than I will," T said. "Do we call in Mike? His people could be waiting there."

I paced in my mind, but my body lay flat, my arms and legs forming a narrow X. With every rock of the train, I lolled from side to side, blinking from the sand and loose dust blowing over the cupola.

"I don't know how much I trust those people," I said. "Besides we wouldn't be working with Mike. He's off the case. The admiral is in charge now," I said.

"That might be good. He already rescued you once before."

"I don't know. Mike would put Amanda at the top of his list of priorities, but this new guy—I'm afraid he'd be happy to get me back and leave Amanda to the FBI. These guys killed when they didn't need to. If they think they're trapped, they're likely to just start shooting. Wan might not have a say in it."

Stars blinked on in the sky above me.

"T, I need more information. There are no train tracks anywhere near the cabin. That means we have to leave this thing at some point. Where is that point and how far away is it? I have to come up with a plan to get off this caboose and be able to follow them."

"Maybe some of Joe's people could meet you."

"I don't know. I don't even know if Joe has any people, other than his daughter and granddaughter," I said.

"Come on, Sebastian. He probably knows everything that moves within a hundred miles of that reservation."

"Have you heard from Joe?"

"Not since he sent me those photos of the van. Pretty neat, huh? He's got real computer skills. I could turn him into a hacker," T said.

"Well, let's get me out of this first."

"I'll check the railroad options and get back to you. You keep an eye out for Colorado Springs. If you don't hit it soon, we've guessed wrong about their destination. After that, I'll give Joe a call."

"Okay. If I don't answer right away, keep trying. It's noisy out here."

"Will do."

The phone clicked off.

∼

As I considered the future, I realized I was probably on my own. T was too far away. Joe would be there at the end, but I didn't see him being there for the messy part before the end.

Mike was out of the picture. He wouldn't lead any Navy Seal team to deal with the kidnappers.

Maybe, I thought, it was time to use Iba. Distance was not an issue; if Iba could kill from thousands of miles away, he could certainly strike through the roof of a caboose.

I tried to envision what that would be like. When I went after the Chinese thugs, I had no idea what their end was like. In my mind, I saw their faces and they died.

But the guys beneath me had Amanda, and they had guns. The people Iba assaulted—I noticed that I blamed Iba now for everything—had not died instantly. They seemed to die of suffocation. If that were true, did they have time to pull a trigger?

The train swayed side to side. We must have been doing seventy. Would we slow at Colorado Springs, or was there a train beltway that would allow us to maintain our speed? I wished I had paid more attention to all the railroad tracks I had ever seen or crossed over. I had no idea how they worked.

Click-clack. The caboose set up a hypnotic rhythm as its wheels rolled over the joints in the rails. Click-clack. In Denver and near switches, where the rail sections where hard and short, the click-clacks came faster; outside Denver on the long straight stretches, despite our speed, the rails were longer and the click-clacks farther apart, but still hypnotic. Click-clack. Click-clack.

Darkness closed around me, and I started to relax as the adrenaline wore off. As I gazed into the sky, something flew across my vision, left to right. I turned to the left, but saw nothing. It happened again. Slower this time. A smudge, it wasn't so much flying as floating. Left to right, it passed out of my sight. I looked to the right and saw only darkness. A third time it moved across my vision, walking this time. I could just make out faint details. It looked like a flying saucer on top. Or a jelly fish with tendrils dangling below it. Off to the right it went.

On the next pass, it took up more of my vision. It was getting closer. It was dark against the night sky, but I could make out a round top. The tendrils stiffened and moved of their own accord. It seemed to look at me, but without any eyes, as it passed out of sight.

There it was again. Closer now, but harder to make out against the dark sky. I felt it close to my face, then it was gone. I swatted with one heavy hand. It instantly reappeared, walking—no, skittering—from the left of my vision right toward my face. Gone again.

I felt I should know it. It touched me, tap danced on my chest. I lost sight of it, but it continued its dance. Tappety-tap. Tappety-tap. Like a spider…

Iba? Empaya Iba?

I woke with a start. My chest… the tap dancing would not stop. I swatted my jacket where the insect should be. My hand struck something hard. It buzzed back at me.

My cell phone. *Where was I?* It was cold and noisy. *Ah, the train.* I fumbled for the phone in my shirt pocket.

"Hello? Hello?"

"Hey, Sebastian. I've been trying to get you for fifteen minutes. I thought I'd lost you."

"T?"

"Yeah. Who else?"

"I must have fallen asleep. Weird dream."

"Have you passed through Colorado Springs yet?"

"I don't know. I don't think so. I don't know how long I slept."

"It's almost eight o'clock."

"Then we must have passed it by now. I don't remember."

I thought a moment, still groggy from my dream.

"Pueblo. Pueblo should be next, right?" I said.

"That would be the next city of any size until Albuquerque."

"Well, if it's almost eight, we should be pulling into Pueblo in about half an hour, maybe less."

"All right, if you don't, you call me ASAP. It will mean we were wrong about which direction you're heading."

"Right. Any thoughts on where these guys might get off this train?"

"Your best bet is a little town called Walsenburg. There is a local road that goes through town over to Cortez and Durango and on to Towaoc. Google Maps says it's about a five-hour trip. Maybe longer in the dark. It doesn't look like a big road."

"All right. Good to know. How far is Walsenburg from Pueblo?"

"Half hour max," T said. "You should expect to get off there. Any idea what you'll do then?"

"Not a one."

CHAPTER 48
THE SCREAM

THE SILENCE ON the other end of the phone felt ominous.

"You don't have any ideas either, right?" I said to T.

"Iba?" he said, parroting our go-to solution.

"I just don't know, but I'm out of ideas and kind of beat up."

"Are you hurt badly?"

"I don't think so, but I might not be able to walk well."

"If you can't walk, how are you going to follow those guys?"

"I wasn't planning to walk. I hoped to be able to get a car or something."

"Where are you going to get a car in a small town at this time of night?"

"If I have to, I'll borrow one," I said, wondering how to hotwire a car.

"Don't you think they'll get a little suspicious if a car follows them for hours from Walsenburg?"

T. So good with the questions. Not so forthcoming with answers, however.

"If they're going where we think they are, I won't have to follow them closely," I said. "It will be more a matter of arriving in the dark so I'm not seen."

"But if you can't walk…"

"Yes, I understand. I'll be up the poopy stream without a paddle."

"Okay, Sebastian. Take care of yourself. Hang in there."

"I will. I have to. Otherwise I roll off this thing."

In fact, if I'd slept through Colorado Springs, I was lucky to still be alive.

❧

As we had hoped, the train reached Pueblo in less than thirty minutes. I hadn't counted on it slowing down, but it did. I wondered what was going on, and so did Amanda's kidnappers.

One of the thugs climbed the ladder to the cupola. Outside I rolled behind the seat as soon as I noticed motion inside the caboose. I didn't think he saw me, but I wasn't taking any chances. I rummaged in my bag and found the Webley. I pulled the pistol out and psyched myself up to use it. I cocked the pistol, swallowed hard, and waited.

Nothing happened.

He sat with his back to me, just inches from my face, and drummed his fingers on the arm of his seat. He was just as curious as I was about why we'd stopped.

❧

The mystery of Pueblo was soon solved. The train eased off onto a siding and snap-banged to a stop. Up ahead, I heard the engines throb as they pulled away. Apparently we were adding or subtracting rail cars for the trip farther south.

About ten minutes later, the engines rumbled back, slamming into the waiting collection of cars. Below me, all seemed quiet. Lights burned in every window on my side of the caboose; as far as I could tell, it was the same on the opposite side.

The Pueblo rail yard was quiet. I could hear the engines idling their deep thrum; as the minutes ticked away and we just sat, I wondered if it was dinnertime for the engineer. I wasn't hungry, but I was really thirsty. The wind of the moving train and the grime all around me turned my mouth into a sand pit. I wanted a drink of water, but I already had to pee so badly that I felt like bursting; I didn't want to take a drink and add to the pressure on my bladder.

I was balancing my needs when the side cupola window slid open. *What did he see? What did he hear?* I gripped the Webley and tried to figure my next step. *I would shoot the man, but then what? What happened to Amanda? I wasn't nimble enough to slide off the car, scurry to the opposite end, and take the car by storm.*

A light flared from the cupola, and soon I smelled smoke. *Cigarette break*, I thought. I eased my grip on the pistol and waited. If the smoker got curious and looked back, he was bound to see me. If I escaped unnoticed… I still didn't have a plan for the Walsenburg junction, where I expected the caboose to end its trip.

In the quiet of the night, I could hear voices down below—a woman's, but not Amanda's, and a man. They seemed to be debating something with some insistence. *Wan must be having personnel problems*, I thought.

Before the guy in the cupola finished his smoke, the engines ahead revved and the train lurched forward with a snap-bang. I rocked uncomfortably close to the edge of the roof. The thug tossed his cigarette, closed the window, and slipped down out of the cupola.

I uncocked the Webley and stuffed it back in the backpack and sidled back up toward the center of the caboose roof. We thrummed into the night, the wind buffeting me as I pondered the odds of a six-shot pistol against multiple automatic weapons.

∽

We slowed again less than half an hour later and eased onto another siding.

Welcome to Walsenburg, I thought. *Now we would find out if I*

*had guessed right. If not, I was screwed. And if I had guessed right, I was
pretty close to screwed anyway because I still had no plan.*

I peered up and over the cupola. The caboose was near the edge
of town, with the rest of the train stretched through the streetlights
and into the dark distance ahead. We slid under a highway overpass
and the train jerked to a halt, then backed slowly over a switch and
onto yet another siding.

We only moved about ten railroad car lengths and stopped again.
I heard footsteps crunching on the gravel as someone approached the
caboose. The steps stopped; I heard mechanical noises and the hiss
of air hoses being disconnected.

This was indeed the end of the line for the caboose and
its passengers.

The door at the front of the car opened and closed. I willed
Amanda not to try to escape. She had spunk and grit and was generally game for anything. She might be desperate to get away, but she
wasn't stupid. There was no chance of escape right now.

"Evening, ma'am," I heard a western accent say. "Here you are,
safe and sound, although why anyone would choose Walsenburg is
beyond me."

A woman's laugh wafted up to me, and I tried to hear her response.

"Have a safe trip to Mexico."

Wan sounded absolutely charming.

"You have a good stay in beautiful downtown Walsenburg,
ma'am."

The steps crunched away; the caboose door opened and closed.

Show time, I thought. *What do I do now?*

Glass shattered, and a woman screamed in pain.

EMPAYA IBA SPEAKS

I am Empaya Iba, spirit of the Black Orchid People,
Guardian of the Mother Soil, giver of the Long Sleep,
Seer of the Many Eyes, mage of the Many Legs.

I sense...
Great danger from above,
Evil below,
Betrayal all around.

I do not fear
For I am wise.
They who would destroy must see me
And what they cannot see... is me.

CHAPTER 49
CHIP AND DALE

BELOW ME, THE lights blinked out. Darkness filled the night. *Oh, God,* I thought, *don't let it be Amanda.*

The only sounds I heard were the fading footsteps of the railway worker who had uncoupled the car. The crunch of the gravel under his feet probably masked the sound of the shattering glass and the pop of a silenced gun.

The shot had come from the right side of the caboose.

I rolled onto my stomach, knocking my bad leg in the process. Fiery pain raced up the right side of my body. I gritted my teeth to remain quiet.

I pulled the Webley from my backpack again and cocked it. The mechanism sounded loud and ominous in the quiet of the night.

Nothing moved, and I peered into the night looking for... anything. I made out a row of trees on the horizon twenty or thirty yards away, but closer to the tracks all I could see were shades of black.

Below me everything was quiet. No moans, no crying, no movement. The scream wasn't necessarily from Amanda, I told myself, and even if it had been, it didn't necessarily mean she was hurt. I itched to go to her, but told myself to be patient. I had to know what new danger we faced outside before I tried to do something inside the caboose.

Suddenly, both doors of the caboose burst open, and I heard crunching on either end as two of Amanda's kidnappers jumped from the caboose and landed on the gravel between the railroad ties. There might have been a pop toward the front of the caboose as their footsteps disappeared into the night. Going for help? Going to flank whoever might be out there? Or just going?

Whatever their intent, I didn't care. They had attacked my home and taken Amanda. I felt no qualms as I imagined them dead.

As my head cleared, as it does after invoking Empaya Iba's powers, I sensed more than saw a presence rising by my side. I turned my head and saw one of the kidnappers slowly rising into the cupola. My muscles clenched. I could barely make out his form in the darkness.

I willed him to look straight ahead, but he turned toward me, and I saw recognition in his eyes. He yelped and twisted to position his gun for a shot at me.

Again, I invoked Iba, and the man clutched his throat and tumbled out of sight. I heard a thump inside the caboose; outside it remained quiet.

Minutes passed. I held the Webley in a death grip; my bladder demanded that I relieve it, and my knee shot messages of pain to my brain every time it brushed the roof of the caboose.

What was the attacker—or attackers—waiting for? Or had he gone? As far as he knew, the kidnappers who had jumped off the train could easily be surrounding him. He couldn't know what I knew.

Behind the tree line two lights swept the darkness and the sound of tires on asphalt broke the silence. There was a road back there, and someone was coming. The vehicle rolled to a stop parallel to the caboose. The driver tapped his horn twice.

This was a rendezvous, but the pickup man obviously didn't know the situation he'd driven into. He waited a moment and honked the horn longer this time and flashed his headlights. Still no response.

After several moments, the vehicle's emergency flashers started blinking on and off. A car door squeaked open and closed, and the driver bulled his way through the trees and brush to the railroad tracks, oblivious to the danger around him.

He disappeared from my line of vision; I expected to see a flash and hear a cry of pain any second.

I heard him march over the gravel and climb the front steps of the caboose and knock on the door.

"Anybody here?" a voice said. "You folks call for a ride to Towaoc?"

Well, I thought, *our supposition was correct.* I knew where the kidnappers were headed, but so did anyone within a hundred feet of the caboose.

The caboose door opened with a muffled command. The driver clomped in and started to say something. I heard the pop of a silenced gun, followed by the sound of a dead weight banging against furniture and hitting the floor. Someone in the caboose did not want witnesses. That did not bode well for Amanda. This had to stop.

The door opened again and it sounded like two people shuffling onto the front platform of the caboose.

"You. Out there."

It was a man's voice. The fourth kidnapper. Where was Wan? Was she still in command?

"If you're wearing night vision goggles, you can see I have Mrs. Campion here. My gun is cocked and the trigger is pulled. My thumb is the only thing between her and death. You hear me?"

Who did he think was out there? The Feds? I was sure Mike and his people didn't know where we were. T couldn't have beaten us down here in his rented car. Joe might have been able to get a pistol, but he never would have taken a shot with such an unreliable weapon, especially with Amanda nearby.

Who was out there shooting?

"You hear me out there?"

A laugh came out of the darkness near my end of the caboose. Even in the stillness of the night, I couldn't make out his position.

"Take your hostage and clear out. I'll see you later. I want the other woman. I know I hit her."

This voice sounded cold.

"Who are you?"

"It doesn't matter. Go away. I'll catch up with you and give you the message I have."

"What message?"

"The same one I have for Wan Xiu Lan: You don't cross XiZi. General Su sends his greetings."

"Su is dead," the kidnapper said.

"General Su is not dead. He is very much in charge."

"You told us Su is dead." The gunman holding Amanda practically hissed.

"A technicality," I heard Wan softly reply. "It does not matter."

"Get out of the way, or I'll kill you now," the cold voice said.

The kidnapper fired. Pop. Amanda screamed. I don't know whether his thumb got tired or whether it was intentional. I started to rise. The kidnapper fired twice more in the direction of the cold voice. Pop. Pop.

A second gun from inside the caboose banged in the night. Wan. This was becoming the O.K. Corral, and Wyatt and the gang would be coming soon to investigate.

The would-be assassin moved in his hiding place, making enough noise to give me a target. I knelt on my one good knee and fired. My bad leg was cramped; it started to give out. My second shot went wild to the right.

Behind the tree line toward to my right, a large engine roared down on us. Tires screeched. Doors opened. At least two, maybe three, people advanced boldly through the dark toward the caboose.

The kidnapper continued to fire as he stepped down off the

caboose and moved toward the street. Pop. Pop. Wan's weapon banged once, twice, and seemed to move away from the caboose.

The area where the assassin was hiding erupted into sound. I aimed again.

"Don't shoot! Don't shoot, Sebastian!"

A violent explosion split the night. The sounds of struggle stopped. On the street, car doors opened.

"Sebastian!"

It was Amanda.

"I'm coming," I shouted.

"Don't shoot! It's me, T, Sebastian. Don't shoot."

Voices mingled in the darkness.

"T?" I said.

The pickup vehicle, its flashers still blinking, screeched off.

"Don't shoot. We got this guy."

"T, are there any more shooters?" I asked.

"I think it was a one-man job."

"I hear people moving."

"Just us. Me. A couple buds. Come on down. I don't think we can stay around here long," he said.

"I don't know if I can. I hurt my leg jumping onto this car," I said. "Maybe you can turn on some lights."

"No dice," a deep voice said. "We got night vision. Don't want to mess with it. You need to hurry. I'm sure someone heard, and this little burg might have a cop. I don't want to meet any police tonight." He pronounced it po-lease.

I plopped onto my butt, grabbed my backpack, and scooted toward the ladder. My bad leg touched it first, and I swore.

"Sounds like that hurt," Deep Voice said.

"It did," I said.

T helped me hop one-legged down the ladder to the rear platform of the caboose. I wasn't going to run anywhere, but I could hobble painfully—very painfully. I put one hand on T's shoulder and followed the deep voice through the trees to the street.

"What about the guy back there?" I said.

"He likes it just where he is," Deep Voice said, pulling off his night vision goggles.

"T, this is getting complicated," I said.

"You think?"

On the road beyond the trees, a darkened 4x4 sat, doors open, engine running. Behind me, a second unfamiliar voice spoke.

"You boys need a ride?"

"Shut up, Dale," Deep Voice said.

"You don't need a ride, Chip, you can walk. No matter to me," Dale said.

"T, who are your friends?"

"Dale is getting in the driver's seat; Chip's got the big gun and deep voice," T said.

I was staring at two large black men who looked like they belonged in the NFL, Chip an offensive tackle, Dale a tall, wiry wide receiver.

"No way," I said.

"No way what?" deep-voiced Chip said.

"No way you guys are Chip and Dale."

"What's the matter? You think our mommas don't watch Walt Disney?" Chip said.

"Yeah, you don't think we be lovable little guys?" Dale laughed behind the wheel.

I looked from one to the other and was glad they were on T's side, and that T was on my side.

"Enough of this touchy-feely," Chip said. "We need to separate ourselves from these premises."

"Good idea," I said, leaning on T as I tried to maneuver backward into the vehicle.

"Ho, Sebastian. Ho, T."

I stopped. Chip whipped a huge black semiautomatic pistol toward the sound of Joe's distinctive voice.

T shouted. "Don't shoot!"

"Who's that?" Dale said, whipping his head back and forth, looking for danger.

Chip crouched beside the 4x4, his arm extended, ready to fire. "Who's there?"

I sighed.

"That would be Joe," I said. "And he either appeared out of thin air, or there's a little red motor scooter hidden around here somewhere."

CHAPTER 50
LOCAL LAW

"Where's your ride, old man?"

Chip lowered his pistol, but looked very dangerous in the dim light of the 4x4's running lights.

"Over where you park. Noisy, you black men. Just like Sebastian," Joe said.

"Who is this guy?" Dale asked.

"Never mind for now. Everybody in. Dale, get back to where we parked. Turn out the lights," Chip said.

Chip practically tossed me into the back seat after Joe. I gasped in pain at the sudden movement. T climbed in behind Dale. Dale whipped the 4x4 into a U-turn, drove off 100 yards back toward a gas station closed for the night. He parked at the end of a line of cars awaiting service, not far from a dumpster. Pale light from a streetlight farther up the way created thin shadows.

"T, explain," Chip said. "You never said anything about an Indian."

"It's okay," T said. "Guys, this is Joe. Joe, that's Dale behind the wheel, Chip riding shotgun."

The Indian said nothing. Dale put on a cowboy accent.

"Howdy, Tonto. What you mean about us being noisy? We the quietest dudes in the 'hood."

"Shut up, Dale. Old man, where's your ride?" Chip in charge, but nervous. I suspected that was a dangerous combination.

"Behind dumpster."

"Not possible. We parked by that dumpster. We didn't see or hear nothing."

"You look," Joe said.

"Dale, check."

"Man, you don't have to order me around like that. How about you just ask?" Dale said.

"How about you just move? Cop comes, we spend the night explaining things we don't got explanations for," Chip said.

Dale got out and walked over behind the dumpster.

"T, I agree with your friend here," Chip said. "Things getting complicated."

"Actually, Big C, you haven't seen anything yet," T said. "Sebastian, any sign of Iba?"

"Yeah, Iba's around."

I was in that post-Iba letdown phase. Empaya Iba had killed three men, perhaps evil men or misguided men doing evil things, but I was an accomplice. Maybe more than an accomplice, maybe the ringleader. And I was no closer to rescuing Amanda than I had been in Oregon—What? Was that just earlier today?

Dale returned, pushing a red motor scooter.

"The engine's still hot, man. How did he get back there?"

"Don't worry about it, guys. He's okay," I said. "We need to get moving."

"What's the hurry? We know where they're going," Chip said.

"The hurry is that two dangerous people have my friend, and I'm afraid they're going to harm her. That's what the hurry is."

Chip gave me a dirty look and started to say something.

"We got trouble," Dale said. "Cops."

A patrol car slowly cruised up the street toward the caboose. It was a football field away, but headed in our direction.

"Everybody down."

We all huddled below window level. Dale hid behind the 4x4 with Joe's scooter.

The cop cruised all the way up to the gas station and did a U-turn through the pumps, his headlights sweeping across the 4x4. He ignored the parked cars and drove back toward the caboose, turning his spotlight onto the rail siding through the trees. His light flashed against the caboose, and he pulled to a stop. His radio crackled in the night, but I couldn't make out any words. He played his light back and forth along the length of the caboose.

I couldn't imagine he could see anything through the trees with his spotlight casting dark shadows on the solitary railroad car. He noticed something that drew his attention. The light fixed on one spot. His radio crackled again. This time I thought I heard him ask for backup.

With his spotlight focused on the caboose, he hit the flashers on top of the patrol car, and red and blue lights flared in the darkness. He popped his trunk and got out. At the rear of his car, he pulled out a rifle of some sort. I could tell it was a shotgun when he started pumping shells into it.

With his car door still open, he headed through the trees straight for the caboose.

"Police. Anybody there?"

His bellow carried, and we could hear him all the way to the gas station. We waited with him for an answer to his summons.

"Is anyone in the caboose? This is the Huerfano County Sheriff's Department. If anyone is in the caboose, come out slowly."

"Is that dude serious? He's going in there alone."

Dale expressed the amazement we all shared. This guy had more cojones than sense.

The cop—a deputy, I guess—approached the caboose, staying out of the light from his spotlight. We lost sight of him.

"Let's go while he's down there," Dale said.

"No," Chip said. "That would just make us the prime suspects."

"At some point, we'll have to move. When they find those bodies, this place will be crawling with police," I said.

"We know. Not there yet. We wait," Chip said.

My knee hurt, I was worried about Amanda, and the inevitable guilt of having used Iba weighed on me. The deputy would find two bodies inside the caboose when he entered it. One would have bullet wounds, the other would not. I was responsible for the latter.

My worries soon grew.

Another patrol car, its lights flashing red and blue, pulled up to the parked cruiser, nose to nose. A radio blared. These guys were not sneaking up on anybody. Maybe that was the point.

The driver stepped out and unbuttoned his holster and drew his pistol.

"Carl. You out there?" The new arrival sounded young and nervous.

"Yeah. Other side of the caboose on the siding. There's a window shot out where my light is shining. I got no movement."

"I'm coming down," the second deputy said.

"Head for the front of the caboose but don't cross my light," the more experienced man said.

"All right."

The other deputy moved into the trees, crouched low and holding his pistol out in front of him.

"I think we may need to go before more police arrive," I said.

"You may be right this time," Chip said.

"Yeah, but which way?" Dale said. "Anybody know where to find the road we need to take?" Dale asked.

"Right past those guys," I said. "The road we want is just on the other side of the tracks."

"Is there another way?" I asked T.

"I assume so, but we would have to go through all these neighborhoods. Between the shots and those police radios, everyone in town is probably looking out their windows wondering what's happening," T said.

"All right, so we got to do it," Dale said, grabbing the driver's side door handle. "Let's do it. We'll lose 'em on the way."

"You wait," Joe said. He crawled over T and out the door. "Sebastian, I see you later."

"Joe, what are you doing?" I said.

He took the scooter's handlebars from Dale, climbed on, and started the machine. The lights came on immediately, and we all ducked. The scooter jerked ahead, and Joe let out a blood-curdling scream.

I would like to say he sped past the cops, but the scooter took a while picking up momentum. Joe leaned over the handlebars and raced the engine. It sounded pathetic.

The young cop burst through the tree line as Joe putted past.

"Stop. Hey, you, stop."

He raised his pistol. Joe wasn't going fast enough.

"Don't!" The older deputy shouted to his partner. "Go through the neighborhood. Cut him off before he gets to Walsen."

The experienced deputy slammed his car door, hit his siren and pulled around the patrol car blocking his way. The younger deputy roared toward us but screeched through the first left turn he could make, his siren warbling.

"Let's go. Let's go. Let's go."

Dale didn't need Chip's orders. He hopped into our 4x4, backed out of the gas station, and pulled ahead at a legal 25 miles an hour. Just past the caboose, he turned on his lights.

Beside me, T played his phone like a computer game, pulling up his GPS and calling out directions.

At the intersection with Walsen Avenue, off to our right, we saw the deputies take a sharp right. On our left, another lit-up cop car sped toward us.

"How many cops this town got?" Dale said.

After the third cruiser roared past us, Dale turned left and drove over the railroad tracks. A block later, at the junction with Route 160, we saw a sign directing us to the Sheriff's Department a block away. Our drama had played out almost in sight of the local police.

Dale sped through town and west into the darkness toward Amanda's cabin five hours away.

"You think they caught that old man?" Dale asked.

"Not a chance," T said. "He was faking it on the speed to make sure they followed him and didn't get lost. He's on a motorbike. He can go places they can't. I'd be willing to bet he beats us to Amanda's place."

"Speaking of which, what's the plan?" Chip was all business all the time, but like T, he asked good questions.

I wished I were as good with answers. Amanda's life depended on it.

CHAPTER 51

CHASE

FTER LEAVING THE western outskirts of Walsenburg behind, Dale pushed his speed up to five or ten miles per hour above the posted speed limit. With no other traffic around this late at night, only the most conscientious cop would give chase to a high-end 4x4.

Still, I worried about that third sheriff's deputy who had sped past us at the stop sign. Once they lost Joe—and I was certain they would—all three deputies would return to the scene of the crime to compare notes. Any vehicle seen coming from that area would warrant attention and close follow-up. When that happened, I hoped they assumed our very noticeable 4x4 had hit I-25 for points north or south.

Meanwhile, Wan, wounded, paranoid and no doubt pissed off, was speeding west suspecting she might be followed. Would she improvise again? Kill Amanda and come after me another day?

She was a marked woman now, and she knew better than I how determined XiZi's leadership would be about exacting vengeance. Even if she managed to get out of the United States, she could hardly just return to Borneo.

Empaya Iba was still around, still able to deal death when I asked.

And I had demonstrated again that I would call on the demon to serve my own needs.

Yes, things were getting complicated.

∾

"They had a fifteen-minute head start. Assuming they have enough gas and don't stop, they get there before we do," I said, thinking out loud.

"Fifteen minutes. That don't mean nothin'," Dale said. "And this thing has almost a full tank."

"Where did you get it? How did you get here so fast?" I needed a briefing while I considered our options. As usual, I had no plan.

"Flew," T said. "We got a ride with a friend of Dale's. He dropped us at a little airport north of town."

"This place has an airport with a car rental shop?"

"Not exactly," Dale said.

"Okay. Never mind," I said. Some things I did not need to know. How they got the car was high on the list.

"Are you sure this monster has enough gas? T, is there any place along the way where we could gas up? I know a little about the area around Amanda's cabin, and there is no gas, and if there was, it wouldn't be open at night," I said.

"I'll check," he said, tapping instructions on his cell. I leaned back against the seat and tried to think.

∾

"Sebastian? Sebastian?"

T shook my shoulder.

"Hey, Sebastian. We need to talk."

"Okay. Sorry. I must have dozed off," I said.

"Dozed. Man, you snored," Dale said. "I thought sure you would wake everybody up when we got gas."

"Great. You found an open gas station," I said.

"Not exactly," Dale said.

I let it go.

Outside, it was pitch black. We wove through wooded canyons with not a sign of life.

"Where are we?"

"I think we're about an hour away," T said. "We need to know what your plan is."

Oh, yes. My plan. That's what I was working on when I fell asleep.

"What time is it?" I asked.

"After three o'clock."

"Have you heard from Joe? He probably knows a dozen ways to sneak into the area. Can we call him?"

"He's up ahead, following Amanda. We can get in touch," T said.

"What about an ambush?" Chip said, his first words that I was aware of since leaving Walsenburg.

"I don't see how we set it up. Besides it's too dangerous for Amanda," I said.

"I don't mean us ambushing them; I mean them ambushing us," Chip said in clipped tones.

"I doubt it. There are only two of them; Wan is wounded. One of them would have to watch Amanda."

I thought aloud.

"They want to get to where they're going. If I were the woman, I'd be setting up an air pickup for first light, which will be in a few hours."

"And if you're wrong?"

"It's been known to happen," I said. I was tuning Chip out.

I knew what I would do.

CHAPTER 52
AMANDA'S CABIN

"DID ANYONE SEE how badly Wan was hit?"

I needed to know what shape she was in. Probably better than me. My leg throbbed, and despite my nap, I felt too exhausted to move.

"It can't be that bad," T said. "She came out of the caboose shooting."

"Yeah, well, I was shooting too, and I'm not feeling great," I said.

"She's younger and in better shape."

"Thanks."

"What difference does it make?" Chip said. "We get close enough; we take care of business. Right, T?"

"No offense, Chip," I said. "She has, ah, different traits than your usual... person."

I turned to T's shadow next to me seeking confirmation, but got none.

"I think this is going to require some subtlety, and I would like to know how focused she can be.... T, can you get in touch with Joe? He and I need to talk."

A mile down the road, our headlights washed across Joe sitting on his scooter on the side of the road.

Dale pulled up beside him.

"Hey, Joe. Nice ride you got there," I said.

"You make fun, Sebastian; me, my ride, we save your ass yet. You buy me saddlebags later, say thank you, be polite."

"Amanda can buy them after you and I save her."

"Yah. Okay."

He grinned. I explained my plan. Chip didn't like the plan.

"Look, you guys," I said. "You've done great. You saved Amanda back there, and I'm grateful. But you don't know what you're up against with that woman. I'm not quite sure I know what we're up against.

"Joe will take me in. By the time we get to the cabin, it should be getting light out. They need to see me alone. I'll take out the gunman, then deal with the woman whatever way is necessary. If I can't, and she gets a plane in there, I'll go with her. You'll take care of Amanda."

"Whoa, whoa," Chip said. "You gonna do this alone? How? You can't even walk straight. T, come on, tell him, man. We're with you. Let us help."

"I'll have Iba. I just need to get close enough for them to see me, and see I'm not armed," I said.

"Iba? What's an Iba?"

"Not what. Who. T can tell you later," I said.

Chip faced T.

"You sure, T?" he asked.

"Leave it to Sebastian," he said. I sensed reluctance in his voice, but appreciated his backup. "It's complicated, and more than a little unbelievable."

"What do we do then?" Chip asked.

"Wait," I said. "Come get Amanda when it's over, no matter how it turns out."

∽

Five miles outside of Towaoc, Joe turned off the road. I wasn't sure there was a turnoff, but we left the road anyway.

I rode behind Joe, my right leg tied to two tree-branch splints. The little scooter used every one of its 260 CCs to haul our combined weight. Now that we were off the road, I worried about blowing a tire. It had become obvious I couldn't walk.

The bike's engine strained as we bounced through the scrub, just a little faster than walking speed. It was absolutely quiet around us, except for the whine of the motor scooter. Sound traveled long distances out here; I was certain they would hear us coming. I wanted them to hear; I did not want any surprises.

I'd planned to walk the last quarter mile, but I couldn't bend my leg. And it hurt, a lot. I rode with it stretched out at the side as straight as the improvised splints could keep it. Every bump sent stabbing pains to my brain. The desert night was cold, but I was sweating.

Ahead, we finally made out the cabin with its flickering lantern light. We were approaching from the rear. I couldn't see their van; I assumed they'd parked it out front, right by the porch, all set for a fast getaway if needed.

I felt certain they wouldn't be staying long. The cabin had no food, and neither did they, unless the van driver had stocked up for them. The nearest store was on the Ute reservation, and they would not be welcomed there.

The XiZi sniper had disrupted their plans, but I was willing to bet that Wan had adjusted, assuming she had not bled to death already.

A few hundred yards from the cabin, Joe flashed his light a half dozen times and revved his engine. We wanted them to know we were coming.

About 50 yards from the cabin, Joe repeated his performance. The light in the cabin dimmed.

Joe shoved off, and we putted closer still to the cabin. He killed the engine and flashed the light. I swung my bad leg over the back of the scooter. My head swam a little as I tried to stand. I hobbled to the front of the bike and stood in the light.

"Amanda. It's Sebastian," I called out. "Joe is with me. We've come to take you home. Are you okay?"

The gunman shouted back.

"She's okay, but you're not. I've got you in my sights."

I couldn't see him, but I could picture where he had to be crouching to be able to see out the window and still have the protection of the stone fireplace.

"I don't know who you are, but this doesn't involve you. It's between me and your boss. Drive away now, and I won't care, as long as Amanda is all right."

A flash exploded in the window, followed by a loud pop. Off to my left, dirt flew. If my leg hadn't been killing me, I'd have hit the ground. So I stood there, looking braver than I felt.

"Talk to me, lady," I said, "and explain the facts of life to that guy."

"Hello, Mr. Arnett. You got lucky coming here," Wan said. "What would you have done if we had not come?"

"No luck to it," I said. "We've been following you since you shot Maria and took Amanda. I rode on top of the caboose with you. We've known where you were every step."

She was silent for a moment.

"Are we going to do this, or not? I'm going to need a doctor sooner rather than later, and I know the XiZi shooter hit you, too."

"You can come in, but the old man stays where he is," she said.

"Not possible," I said. "I think I've broken my leg at the knee; I can't move without him."

"All right. Come together, but slowly. If you try anything, my friend here will shoot the Indian first, then Mrs. Campion."

"I got it. You know I'm no threat to you," I said.

I hoped she understood my meaning, and that the gunman didn't.

Joe fired up the scooter, and I swung my leg carefully over the rear seat. I grabbed Joe's wiry sides and leaned my head against his back. Faintness played hit and run with me.

Joe whispered.

"Lot of spirits here, Sebastian. Not happy. Not safe. Not for you, me... anyone."

EMPAYA IBA SPEAKS

I am Empaya Iba, spirit of the Black Orchid People,
Guardian of the Mother Soil, giver of the Long Sleep,
Seer of the Many Eyes, mage of the Many Legs.

Come, all who would destroy me.
Attack with claw and teeth
Overwhelm my size,
But beware my eyes.
Outsize creatures, you frighten me not.
Huge, lumbering, clumsy beasts.
Rip limbs, foliage, and forest,
And find me, if you can.

You alien spirits.
Tarry not here in this waste.
Come to my lush paradise
Where the Black Orchid dwells.
See, then, what you can do.
Here, there is nothing.
Nothing for any to win.
Everything for all to lose.

If it must be, let us do battle where my spirit dwells.
To the victor, the precious Mother Soil.
The Children of the Black Orchid.
The power of the Long Sleep.
Come. So say I. Empaya Iba.

CHAPTER 53
SHOWDOWN

THE SCOOTER GROANED under my weight, but it moved forward. I clung to Joe.

"I'm not feeling very well, Joe. What are we going to do?"

"You faint, I think I die. You don't faint."

I took a deep breath, inhaling the scent of the old man's sweat and herbs I could not identify. Around us, the night began to lighten. Dawn was not far off.

"Joe, is Iba there—with the spirits?"

"Yah. Your spider. Dragon spirit. Eagle spirit. Never this many strong spirits in one place. Too many."

"I think I know what you mean," I said, and took another breath. "It feels like Iba's itching to start a fight; I've never felt that before," I said.

Joe inched the motorbike forward.

"You faint yet?"

"Not yet. What's your hurry?"

"No hurry. Can't go slow much longer. Almost at cabin."

I raised my head from his shoulder, and the world did an

award-winning pirouette. I clutched Joe's shoulders and breathed deeply again.

"What's happening?"

"Iba dances. Others watch. Just watch."

"So, they're waiting for the show to start."

"No. Like waiting for a meal."

For a man who did not believe in ghosts a mere year ago, I was now surrounded by more ghosts and goblins than Joe had ever seen in one place. I felt deeply uneasy and tried to focus on freeing Amanda.

"You think the eagle spirit is the one from Australia?" I asked.

"Don't know that one. This one from here. It don't like others being here."

"Well, I'm not wild about it either, but here we are. So, you think Empaya Iba will come down on our side?"

"No. He's for his side."

He shivered. My ageless, wise Indian friend shivered; that scared the bejeezus out of me.

"Maybe the guy with the gun ends it all, and the spirits don't matter," I said.

"Not him," Joe said. "He is a dead man waiting for his grave to close over him."

About ten paces from the cabin, for just an instant, I thought I saw a red firefly appear above the window where the gunman with the itchy trigger finger watched us.

I looked around, but saw no other fireflies. Joe and I had drunk through the night at the cabin on more than one occasion, and I could not recall ever seeing a lightning bug. Certainly not a red one. An uneasy feeling that we were not alone took hold of me.

"Close enough," the man in the cabin said. "Both of you, off the scooter."

Joe held the scooter steady, and I lifted my injured leg over the back of the bike. When my bad leg touched the ground, pain shot through me, and my eyes went blank. I swayed a bit.

Behind us, the sky was starting to lighten.

"Let me talk to Amanda," I said.

"You don't give the orders."

"Let me talk to Amanda. I'm no threat. I want to make sure she's all right."

"I'm all right, Sebastian. Tired, but all right," Amanda called.

I conjured up an image of the layout of the one-room cabin. She was likely on the other side of the fireplace, maybe sitting or lying on the ancient bed. What was important is that she should be out of the line of fire, if things went south.

"Did they hurt you?"

"No. I'm fine. Have you heard anything more about Maria?"

"Yeah, Amanda. We have. She didn't make it."

"Oh, God, no," she said, and I heard her take a sobbing breath. "Oh, Maria."

"All right, Wan," I said. "You've got me. Let Amanda go. Joe can take her home. I'll do what I said I would."

"Not so fast. You deal with me," the gunman said.

He clearly did not understand his position. I ignored him.

"Come on, Wan. Let Amanda go. How do you and I get out of here?"

"A plane will land as soon as it's light enough. We will tie Mrs. Campion up on the bed. She will be comfortable enough. When we are safely on the airplane, the Indian can come in and get her."

"Works for me. I'm glad we are all being civilized about this," I said, not believing for a moment that the massacre back at the house and Amanda's kidnapping was civilized at all, or that it would stay that way. "How long 'til the plane lands? I need a doctor. I seriously screwed up my leg."

"We will get your leg taken care of. You will have to put up with it for a day or so," she said.

"Maybe you can get me some aspirin for it. And remember, I can't go tromping through the jungle with a bum leg."

"You would not have this problem if you had waited for my call."

"Someone kidnaps someone I love, I don't wait. You apparently didn't learn anything from your buddy, Lee," I said. "Hey, quick draw, did she tell you what happened to the last guy who helped her? Ask her what happened to his knee."

"You talk big for a guy with a bad leg himself. Oh, and who has the gun on his girlfriend?"

Good, I thought. *I have him thinking. He should have shot me in my good leg.*

"Wan, what happens to your gunman? You leave him like you did Lee?" I said.

"He comes with us, of course."

"I don't think he has it in him. He's not a XiZi guy."

"Shut up." The gunman did not like being talked about as though he wasn't there. "Sit down on the ground away from the bike."

"Not a good idea. The leg won't take it. If I sit down, I'll never get back up again."

"Sit or I'll shoot your other leg. Then you'll be lying down."

Okay. He's not so dumb.

"I'm telling you…"

I never got to finish my sentence. All hell broke loose.

CHAPTER 54
SHRIEK

I SAW A FLASH from the house. Something hit the motor scooter between Joe and me and knocked it off its kickstand.

The fool had shot at us!

"Hey! Stop shooting at us, you idiot," I shouted.

A red firefly appeared against the cabin window, and the glass exploded. Someone had fired at the cabin.

A commanding voice bellowed: "You in the cabin. Federal agents. Throw out your weapons immediately or you will be shot."

I shouted. "Amanda, get down."

Federal agents? Like an FBI SWAT team? How would they get involved? Whatever, someone had planted them here before Amanda and the kidnappers arrived. They must have a spotter nearby or a drone watching over us.

I flopped to my belly, smacking my forehead and injured leg against the hard ground. That kicked up all kinds of pain and made stars spin before my eyes. Joe was already on the ground beside me.

"In the cabin, throw out your weapons. This is the last warning."

Some warning, I thought. The firefly was a laser, and whoever was using it intended to do more than just break the window.

Silence settled, and the sky took on color behind us.

"Joe, are you okay?"

"Yah. Don't like getting between white men in a fight."

"I'm not wild about it either."

"What we do?"

"Let's try to crawl over to the right and get out of the line of fire," I said.

"Very good plan. I go first."

"I'm right behind you."

Joe crawled on his belly like he walked. There one minute, and gone the next.

I dug in with my good left leg and pushed off at an angle. My leg felt like it was getting a gravel massage. I stopped and rolled to lie on my left side. Now I was trapped. I couldn't move with the good leg underneath me, and I couldn't tolerate the pain of dragging my bad leg.

A hand tapped my head. I looked up and saw Joe lying on his back, his arm extended toward me. *He's a game old man*, I thought as I reached out to him.

Suddenly, a wail that Yoko Ono might produce on a bad hair day started in the cabin and crept toward us. It was both shrill and eerie at the same time.

That has to be Wan, I thought. Joe tugged me toward him.

Behind us, I heard someone jogging heavily toward the cabin.

"Be careful," I called out. "There's a hostage inside."

A sack of potatoes landed just behind us, to our left.

"Roger that," it grunted.

Elsewhere I heard other feet pounding the hard pack around the cabin. It sounded like two more people, although I couldn't be sure because of the screeching coming from the cabin.

Wan wailed on and on, seemingly without taking a breath. My head felt like it was collecting flies, and I shook it, trying to clear the penetrating cry from my brain.

Was this how she summoned her dragon spirit? I poked at my ears, grateful that Empaya Iba at least worked silently.

The wail deepened and thrummed like a swarm of bees. The federal agents made no further demands and stayed put. I took a quick look behind me. The sniper who'd taken the shot at the cabin lay on his side, his limbs twitching like he was having a seizure.

What was going on? Where was his rifle? Why wasn't he aiming at the cabin? This was all wrong. He should be rushing the cabin. They all should.

It was almost like Iba was attacking them, but that was impossible. Wasn't it? I hadn't wished harm on anyone since leaving the caboose. Maybe Iba was acting independently of me.

I was doing it again, I thought, *destroying the very people sent to save me.*

At my side, Joe was jerking around, his hands covering his ears. The wail changed pitch again, no longer buzzing, but rising back toward a screech.

My eyes suddenly hurt, like something sharp was poking at them from the inside, trying to get out.

The SWAT team assault had either halted or was moving forward in absolute silence. I detected no motion from the agents. This was not how they did it in the movies.

Just like that, the shrieking stopped; I could hear again. Somewhere in the distance, I sensed the sound of an airplane.

Then the shriek started over again. How was she doing this? There was no letup, no relief. On and on, she wailed. My hearing turned stereophonic, one set of sounds going in one ear and another set—the sound of a small plane approaching—in the other ear.

The piercing shrill bored into my body. My nose dripped, and I wiped my hand across my face. It was blood. I was bleeding from the nose.

Beside me Joe stopped twitching. His hands fell from his face.

In the growing light of dawn, I saw blood on his face and ears. What was happening?

The light from an explosion zapped past me before the blast roared by. It flashed against the cabin, and I looked back over my shoulder. Small fires, apparently burning pieces of the plane, fell from the sky.

Whose plane was it? Wan's? Or the federal agents'?

Someone's plans had just gone up in smoke.

After the explosion, the night sounds were so peaceful. In our drinking bouts, Joe and I had always enjoyed the sounds of dawn. The last chirps of the night insects, the first tentative bird calls.

If only the noise in my head would stop. I put my hands over my ears and rolled my head, trying to shake the noise out. I rolled over to Joe. He lay still, but his eyes showed something I had never seen there before or since—pain and fear.

CHAPTER 55

FLAMING DRAGON

"Joe. Joe. Talk to me. I can't hear you."

My head throbbed from the screech pounding against me. It was no longer just sound, it was physical, like a fist banging on me.

I kicked out at the ground with my good leg, trying to get closer to Joe's bleeding face. The pain ripped through my knee, and my body doubled over. My head bounced off his arm. I looked up again and saw his bloodstained lips mouth words I could not make out.

The wail changed pitch again, higher, thinner, like needles stabbing my ears.

"Joe, talk to me."

His eyes were rolling back into his head. Was he really hurt that badly? Could he be dying? If he was in that shape, what was Amanda like? She was closer to Wan. She must be out of her mind. I had to do something.

I tried to rise, but that meant taking my hands from my ears. I couldn't do it. Something warm trickled to my lips; I tasted blood.

I started writhing the way Joe and the federal agent had. The noise was too much. It was an ax splitting my head open and pushing barbed wire inside. My eyes twitched. I saw streaks of black light in my eyes. Moving, stretching, dancing.

Not light. Sticks. Walking sticks. No. Something like that. Legs. Yes, black legs. Spider legs. Tappety-tap dancing on my eyeballs, spinning in circles, twisting in odd shapes, playing a frantic game of Twister all by itself. More and more frantic.

The wail kept on and on.

This is unnatural, I thought. No one can *make a sound so long without taking a breath.*

It was a nightmare in real time. Worse than my Iba dream. That had been quiet. In that dream, I heard only the sound of my own voice speaking to Iba. This nightmare was a shapeless wall of sound enveloping me, building a cocoon around me, squeezing me so tightly I couldn't move.

Still those black stick legs flashed and danced. Yes, that was it. The dancing legs were Iba's. But they had changed somehow, moved, turned over, as if Iba had flipped on its back now. Legs flailing and twitching, but slower now.

Iba felt the sound, too. I knew it. That sound. That suffocating sound.

I coughed. I needed air, but the sound was taking all the air. I couldn't breathe. It was… It was like drowning. No air. Just water.

Oh, God. I'm drowning. I'm dying.

Iba, are you killing me? Is this how we separate? Is this how I become free? I die, squashed like a bug?

Squashed like a bug. Through the wail, something about that seemed important. Squashed. I was being squashed. Not strangled. Iba takes breath away. This was different. My whole body was being squeezed as if by giant claws. The sound was wringing me out from the inside.

Iba was being attacked, and so was I. Iba and I together. Wan's wall of sound was compressing us, and Iba was not fighting back. Iba was a demon spirit. It should be able to fight back. The Chinese woman from Borneo, even with her medicine, was only a mortal like me. She… She… I couldn't think.

Squeezed like a nut in a vise, my brain wouldn't work. This was the dragon spirit, crushing me in giant claws. How to kill a dragon?

I wheezed and gasped. My head pounded. My chest was being crushed under the weight of sound. How did St. George slay the dragon? On a horse. With a spear. I had no horse. I had no spear. This was the worst nightmare ever.

If only I could have the old nightmare back. It was quiet. It was peaceful. Iba hid. I stood like a decoy waiting for the flying creature to grab me. Grab me and leave Empaya Iba safely hidden.

It grabs me and—what? What happens after it grabs me? It takes me away. Away to devour me? To—what? Maybe. Maybe it just takes me away. Away from Empaya Iba. Away from here. Away from the grinding, crushing weight of sound. Away.

Just away.

Something sparked in my brain. My Iba nightmare. It had taken months, but I finally understood. My nightmare wasn't from Iba. It was a prophecy, and now it was coming true. The flying creature was an eagle. Not the dragon. The eagle spirit, protecting its land. From Iba. From the dragon. From Wan and from me. Just like Australia. I—Iba—had invaded Bunjil's territory, and the eagle rose to confront us.

The eagle whose screech preceded the capture. It had come to end the dream. It had come for Iba, and that meant me.

Would that be my last coherent thought? I wondered. I was moving beyond thought, beyond the power of my senses. I could not see the rising sun or hear the unending wail or taste the blood running from my nose onto my lips. I only felt—and understood.

I felt the wailing screech of the eagle. There. I felt the claws swoop toward me. This was real. This was finally happening. No longer a dream. I lay flat, unmoving. The eagle's cry held me fast to the ground.

Iba twitched on its back, its legs bent like claws, grasping, clutching me, lifting me, holding me above itself, hiding from the eagle, offering me as a decoy, a sacrifice.

This is how it ends, I felt.

I was torn from Iba. No longer his slave. I felt calm and quiet. I felt the silence, cradling me. I felt... me again.

Up and up, I rose, higher and higher into the sky. Below me, the sun crept over the eastern horizon, turning the desert orange. *Insects—beetles of some kind*, I thought— *lay unmoving around the cabin. Five of them. Three all brown and crushed looking. The other two entangled in some kind of machine. One of them terribly familiar but growing distant.*

Higher and higher the eagle flew, its wings pulsing in time with my heartbeat, heaving us farther and farther from the ground with each breath I took. Was this what death felt like? To be quiet. At peace. To have no fear. Or thoughts. Or memories.

Memories of pain. Memories of loss. Memories of despair. Of Sarah when she died. Of Amanda when she pushed me away. Of Iba. Wicked Iba. Evil Iba. Empaya Iba. Spider demon. Black Orchid spider demon.

But I did have memories. I did have thoughts. I remembered the wailing, that awful sound the eagle made.

That can't be right. The eagle has me in its clutches. It must be... what? What must the eagle be? What must it be doing?

Memories. I had memories. The wailing. It hurt like needles piercing my brain. Joe, too. I remembered Joe. He said, "Help."

Help!

The eagle was carrying me away. Joe. Amanda. Stop. No more. No higher. Let me go. Let me down.

Iba. Where was Iba? I was the decoy. Iba, you are still alive?

The wailing. The wailing stopped. It wasn't the eagle. It was the Dragon Princess. She thinks I'm dead. Joe's eagle spirit carried me away, and the Dragon Princess thought it had Iba as well.

But Iba, you are still there, still alive, still able. You can kill the dragon. You must if you want to survive. And I know how you can do it.

I felt Iba stir. I had never felt Iba before. But I did now.

Iba, listen to me. Iba, I command you. Iba, kill for me.

And Empaya Iba spoke to me, for the very first time.

Kill who? Kill what?

Kill, Iba. Kill. I command you to kill.

Kill how? You are not here. You have gone with another spirit. I cannot follow.

Kill, Iba, or we die. You and I and Amanda and Joe. We all die. The dragon will kill us all.

You have gone from me. You serve me no longer.

Give your powers to someone else. Give them to Joe. He's there beside me.

I cannot share with the seer. I cannot share with another spirit.

Use one of the agents, one of the SWAT team.

They are gone from this earth and will never return.

Who then? If you can't kill the dragon, we will all die. You will perish, just like me.

I had no more words. Below me, I saw no humans, no bugs, no creatures.

Where does this flight end? I wondered. *How high does the eagle climb? Do I continue to outer space? Am I dead already? How will I know?*

My thoughts slowed. My heart no longer pounded. My heartbeat became a soft thump now and again. This, now, is better than drowning. No mud or messy water in my mouth and ears and eyes. No churning in my gut. Peace. Yes, this is peace. The peace we will all share. Joe. And T. And Amanda.

Amanda!

I jerked one last time in the eagle's clutches.

Iba, give your powers to Amanda. Show Amanda what to do. Iba, do it now. I command you, Empaya Iba!

I saw—not felt—I saw what happened.

A flash in the cabin, like a small explosion.

Dragon fire.

Amanda. I ached for her.

Through the broken window, I saw flames flickering.

Inside the cabin, the flames danced about, passing in front of the shattered window and away again.

Suddenly the eagle was gone. I was in free fall. The wail resumed, wavered, faltered—Wan took a breath—and a human scream of agony emerged.

Helicopters—where had they come from?—appeared out of the sun, hugging the earth, kicking up storms of dust as they shot toward the cabin.

A burning torch rounded the corner of the cabin, heading straight for me. The Dragon Princess. Her head flamed and her mouth made a black O as she staggered toward me.

St. George, how did you slay the dragon? With your spear and shield.

I had no spear to kill, no shield to keep the flames from me.

Joe, my shield, lay unmoving by my side. All I had was my Webley, stuck in the bag over my shoulder, the bag I had bought in Borneo. I could feel the heat of the human torch that Wan had become, five steps from me, four, three. Another step and she would just collapse onto me, setting me aflame with her.

I reached for the Webley, incredibly heavy in my hand, cocking it as I moved. My arm swung over my head as I tilted back, Wan melting above me.

The Webley roared and spun out of my hand, striking my temple. Wan's scream stopped abruptly, and the new day turned to night.

CHAPTER 56

SADDLEBAGS

"Yo, Sebastian. Wake up."

I tried to open my eyes, but they were glued shut.

"You wake up. I know you are there. I see your spirit."

"Water." That's all I could say. That's all I wanted.

Wetness splashed over my face. My eyes flew open.

I thrashed, causing pain throughout my body.

"Drowning. Help."

"Yo, Sebastian. You don't move. You hurt yourself again."

The voice was familiar, but I couldn't make out the face. My eyes
were filled with water.

"No more water."

"Sebastian, you make up your mind."

"Joe?"

Was it Joe? It sounded like Joe.

"Yah. You wake up. We need to go from here. Now."

"Where are we? What's going on? Is Wan…?" I didn't know what
had happened to the Chinese woman from XiZi Ltd.

"She is dead. Gone. Your cowboy gun, it don't leave much to
look at. Dragon spirit gone. You wake up. We go."

"Go? Go where?" I asked. "Joe, where am I? What happened?"

"Leave here. Nurse comes again; gives me shot. You and me, we go now."

"I can't move. Something's on my leg. It's caught on something."

"Tied up. I will cut rope. We will go. Before nurse comes again."

"No, don't. Don't cut the rope."

Too late. My leg flopped onto the bed. I felt it through the painkiller. If there were nurses about, I must be in a hospital. Why Joe was here, I had no idea.

The door swung open. Joe left my side. I turned to see his naked bottom hanging out of a hospital gown as he climbed into an adjoining bed.

"Mr. Pony That Sees Far, have you been out of bed again?" A vision of green scrubs made a beeline for Joe's bed.

"Sebastian. He calls for water."

It sounded lame to me.

"You should just have used the call button. I showed you how to use that. Mr. Arnett, if you're awake, I'll be with you in a jiffy. I just have to give your friend an injection."

"No. You stab too deep."

"Oh, now, Mr. Pony That Sees Far—I do love your name, sir—that wasn't deep. You just be brave."

The nurse spoke with the bonhomie that only health care providers can manage.

"You're awake, are you, Mr. Arnett? Right on schedule." She turned her attention to me. I hoped I didn't need an injection, too.

"What happened to your leg?"

"Um," I said, "I think I broke it."

"Silly, I know you broke it. You almost tore it clean off," she said. "I mean, why is it out of traction? What happened to the cord? It looks like it's been cut. Mr. Pony That Sees Far, did you do this? I have to get a doctor and put this back…"

She kept talking as she walked out of the room.

Between the drenching and the leg dropping, I was well awake.

"Joe, quick, before she comes back, fill me in. Is Amanda okay?"

"Yah, she is fine. You cannot kill that one. You marry her, have kids."

"What? I'm too old; she's too old. What are you talking about?"

"Strong woman. Make a good mother."

"Well, not while I'm around. What happened? Try to make sense. Or I'll tell that nurse you asked for another shot."

"You fight dirty. Always, white men fight dirty."

"What happened, Joe?"

"That screeching, we all sleep. Amanda, she wakes up, hits woman with lantern. Kerosene burns hair and face. She stops singing dragon song. Runs out of cabin. Tries to kill you. Dragon wants to burn you. You shoot cowboy gun. Woman dead. Lucky shot, you.

"Amanda, she saves everyone. You. Me. Those SWATs. We are bleeding, all of us. Nose. Ears. Eyes. That song, squeezes blood everywhere. Amanda stops the dragon song. You, me, Amanda, all live."

"Where is she now?" I asked.

"She talks to doctors. Arranges things. We all go home when you wake up."

"She's okay?"

"I tell you, yes. You do not listen. She is a strong woman. You cannot kill her," Joe said.

"I'll take your word for it. What happened to you? Why are you here?"

"Crazy man shoots at us. Hits my bike. Piece breaks off, hits my arm." Joe held up his left arm for me to see. "Doctors say metal is dirty. Needs shots. New bike all shot up. T says it cannot be fixed. Amanda says she will buy new one. Red. Just like T. Saddlebags, too. Leather. Daughter says she will sew beads on, shape of the eagle."

"Why an eagle? I'm not sure I like eagles."

"Eagle saves you, too. Just like Amanda."

"I dreamed of an eagle, Joe. It snatched me out of Iba's legs. We flew into the sky. Wan's noise stopped. I was the decoy, Joe. I was Iba's decoy. The eagle took me instead of Iba."

"Yah. Dragon can't fight two spirits. Dragon song is not so strong then."

"I told Iba to give my powers to Amanda. Does she know?"

"She wakes up. Bloody face just like all of us. Sees lantern and hits woman. That's all. She is still angry at that Chinese, coming after you, killing Maria."

"Is T all right, Joe?"

"Him, he's sick. In love. Wants to see that girl again. Amanda says she will miss him. He says he will come back, visit, bring babies."

"Bring babies? He just met the girl," I said.

"Maybe I see too far," Joe said.

⌁

Joe and I were released from the hospital that day, thanks to Amanda's power of persuasion.

He, Amanda, and T attended Maria's funeral together and sat behind Emilio, Maria's sorrowing husband, and her adult children. I was still laid up in traction and was not allowed to attend. T provided a live feed via his cell phone. The church was packed, as it should have been.

After the service, Amanda spoke to Consuela Reina, Emilio's cousin's wife, about coming to work for her part time to cook and keep house. She plans to convert Maria's bedroom into a playroom for Connie's five kids.

That will add some life to a house that is far too quiet now that T is gone, back to Borneo to live with Eve. Jimmy Beam offered him a computer job; I don't want to know anything about that.

One more thing I don't want to know anything about, the gift from Chip and Dale, sent via T. He's a German shepherd, a dropout from the DEA drug detection school. I don't want to know how they acquired him. They named him Walter, after Mr. Disney. I've never had a dog. Never wanted one. But I like Walt; he never leaves my side.

Before T left, he took Joe out and bought another motor scooter. Amanda commissioned one of the artisans on the Ute reservation to custom fit a pair of leather saddlebags for it. Joe left for the reservation right after the purchase was made. One of the visiting nurses who comes daily to help me asked him how his arm was doing. That was all the inspiration he needed to head back to the reservation.

I don't know where Joe lived before, but he will move into Amanda's ancestral cabin as soon as it is rebuilt. She deeded it to him and is putting in electricity and, more importantly, Internet access so he can keep in touch with those of us who are not as sensitive to his dreams.

I tried to persuade Amanda to let me install a renovated caboose out back along the tree line as a little getaway for me. She killed that idea cold. Too many memories. She did say I could take over the storage shed for smoking cigars this winter and generally getting away.

Amanda gave over the entire basement to a new, larger security team. They are very discreet, but I have to be careful about where we are when I pat Amanda's backside.

They also maintain regular contact with a team Admiral Anderson put in place nearby. It was a nonnegotiable demand from him for cutting me a little slack. The U.S. government will not allow me to roam freely.

Mike invited me out to North Carolina where he and Jan have retired early, with him on 100 percent disability. He's learning sign language and offered to teach me as well. I will probably take him up on that.

All of my jumping around on the tops of railroad cars hammered my broken leg bones into the bottom of my knee cap. I will lose the entire flower season this year, and I'm not sure I'll ever be able to kneel again on that knee for close-up shots.

I no longer dream of Iba every night, although I do pay close attention to my dreams, as Joe taught me.

I decided not to go back to Borneo, at least not anytime soon. I have very mixed feelings about Empaya Iba and the power he has given me, but at least I learned one thing: Iba obeys my commands now.

EMPAYA IBA SPEAKS

Children of the Black Orchid,
Abah, your father, speaks.
All is in readiness.
The veil covers his eyes.

Together, my children,
My servitor,
Who bears my mark,
And I will rejoin you.

So say I, Empaya Iba, spirit of the Black Orchid People,
Guardian of the Mother Soil, giver of the Long Sleep,
Seer of the Many Eyes, mage of the Many Legs.

ACKNOWLEDGMENTS

No author writes a book completely alone. And I am no exception. My son, Richard D. Haase, a sci-fi savant and discerning reader, kept me honest about what worked and what didn't from one version of the story after another after another. This book is dedicated to him.

Donna Verdier, my editor, kept the story and the language on track.

Ken Lawrence, my writing buddy, was always ready with a quick retort and sound advice.

Ken and the other members of the *Royal Writers Secret Society* reviewed chapters during our monthly critiques and taught me to hate prologues and dream sequences. They include Dara Carr, Bill Grigg, Sarah Hollister, Patrick Hyde, G.M. "Gin" Malliet, Adam Meyer, Tom Milani, and Rick Pullen.

Beta readers Tracy Blount, David Jacobs, Eric Legg, and Cheri Udy took the completed manuscript for a test drive and pronounced it not quite fit for the road. As a result, I eliminated many stereotypes and fixed at least a dozen major inconsistencies and a bunch of other stuff no one needs to know about.

My wife Elizabeth and daughter Xannie stayed with me every step of the way.

Their feedback was priceless; any errors are entirely my own.

AFTERWORD

Psst.

You.

Yes, you.

I hope you enjoyed the book. If you got this far, I suspect you did, and that makes me happy.

May I ask a favor?

Would you please write a short review of **Beware the Spider**?

Reviews are critical for writers. Readers like to know that people like them enjoyed a book. And, believe it or not, some advertisers won't sell an ad to an author unless a book has a minimum number of reviews.

Your review doesn't have to be long or take a long time to write. Just say how you honestly felt about the book.

And thanks for reading. I appreciate it.

DLH

Also by
David L. Haase

HOTEL CONSTELLATION: Notes from America's Secret War in Laos

It's 1970. War rages in Viet-Nam, while intense, sometimes violent protests against it rage at home. Impelled to test his courage against that of his WWII hero father, college student David L. Haase arranges to study at the Buddhist University in Saigon. Detained on arrival and quickly deported from Viet-Nam, he searches for a way to get back in.

Instead, he stumbles into the secret CIA war next door in Laos. For the next two years, he witnesses the unraveling of the American politico-military strategy, the decimation of a primitive hill tribe people, and the destruction of a tiny jungle kingdom, all of which he laboriously transcribes in limp, lined school notebooks each day. Those handwritten notes became this memoir of a young innocent abroad growing older and cynical.

Memoir

Made in the USA
Lexington, KY
13 December 2019